NO MORE,
MY *Love*

Sara Powter

Bible Quotes from King James Version

ISBN:9780645441536
Paperback Edition

Pacific Wanderland Publications
ABN 99 768 734 831

Kincumber NSW 2251

saragpowter@gmail.com
www.sarapowter.com.au

1st edition 2023 printed by Kindle, an Amazon Company.

Graphic Acknowledgements

Cover by Beckon Creative
beck@beckoncreative.biz

All graphics used with permission from

Cover Creation
by Beckon Creative
beck@beckoncreative.biz

All graphics used with permission from
Background painting - Joseph Lycett - colonial artist.
https://find.slv.vic.gov.au/discovery/fulldisplay?
docid=alma9916721083607636&context=L&vid=61SLV_INST:SLV&lang=en&search_scope=slv_loc
al&adaptor=Local%20Search%20Engine&tab=searchProfile&query=any,contains,Lycett%20Joseph,
%20newcastle&offset=0

Jess, front cover & inset
Rosamond Hester Elizabeth Pennell Croker,
later, Lady Barrow (1809-1906)
was painted by **Lawrence** in 1826.
The painting is in Public Domain
https://garystockbridge617.getarchive.net/amp/media/lady-barrow00-e2d984

Marcus sketch - final chapter
Théodore Géricault by Alexandre Colin 1816
The drawing is in Public Domain
https://commons.wikimedia.org/wiki/
File:Théodore_Géricault_by_Alexandre_Colin_1816.jpg
& https://www.metmuseum.org/art/collection/search/771363

Acknowledgement of Country:
In the spirit of reconciliation, I acknowledge the Traditional Custodians of
country throughout Australia and their connections to land, sea and
community. We pay our respect to their Elders, past and present and extend
that respect to all Aboriginal and Torres Strait Islander peoples today.

The Convict Stain Collection
Australian Historical Novels

Unlikely Convict Ladies Trilogy
Dancing to her Own Tune
(co-authored by Sheila Hunter & Sara Powter)
Amelia's Tears
A Lady in Irons

Stand Alone Novels
No More, My Love
The Vine Weaver
Waiting at the Sliprails
Scotch at The Rocks (Sequel to The Vine Weaver)
Convict Shadows of the Past
In Defence of Her Honour
Gentle Annie Soames
I Can't Stop Tomorrow
Madeline's Boy
Tuppence to Pass
When Upon Life's Billows

Lockleys of Parramatta
Hands Upon the Anvil
Out Where the Brolgas Dance
Diamonds in the Dirt
The Earl's Shadow
Once a Jolly Swagman
Jonty's Journey

Shelia Hunter's Trilogy
Mattie
Ricky *{Jonty's Journey is a sequel}*
The Heather to the Hawkesbury

<u>In England</u>
When the mechanisation of the woollen machines started happening,
there were riots from the workers, fearful of losing their livelihoods.
This sadly occurred too many times.
The rioters were called the 'Luddites' named after the ring leader.
<u>In Australia</u>
The industrialisation of the woollen mills
helped the growth of the Australian wool industry,
so I have tied the two stories together.
Many convict women were sent out for petty crimes.
For the theft of a shilling's worth of something,
transportation was arranged at the pleasure of the crown.

Marcus and Jess in this story are completely fictitious.

However, they represent those who wanted to help the poor in the best way
they can. They put their faith and beliefs into action.
Not everyone lined their own pockets at the expense of the poor.

Thanks to my husband,
Steve, for all his support in my writing.

To Roby Aiken
for your patience in correcting my punctuation
and
to my Beta readers
Noreen Robertson and Linda Upcroft,
for doing the final read-throughs
and to
Rebekah Robinson for my new cover.

Table of Contents

*The grammar and language in this book are
Australian English spelling*

Chapter 1   Death Comes Knocking

*T*he dark curly hair was not clean; she had not had time to see to her personal ablutions since her family became ill. She was too tired to care. Her heart was already broken. Judith, their only child, was not yet laid in her grave, and her father may yet join her.

Jessica rested her forehead on her hands as she sat in vigil at her beloved husband's side. Lucien, her childhood sweetheart, did not even realise their daughter was gone. She had not had the heart to say anything to him. Hopefully, there would be time for them to grieve together when he was well. He couldn't die; she could not imagine life without him.

Lucien roused, and she felt his hand reach for her. Instantly alert, she took his hand and kissed it. His eyes tried to fix on hers, and he mouthed, "Thirsty." Jess turned to the jug on the stand and poured him some barley water. She carefully raised his head and helped him sip the liquid. As she lowered him, he whispered in a croaky voice, "Sorry, love, so sorry." His eyes were almost dazed, he was desperately trying to focus on her face, but the effort was too much. "Love you so much," he said before falling asleep again before she sat down. She took his hand and again took her place beside his bed; she sat gazing at his beloved face. He'd been sick for so long that there were now hollows under his eyes. He looked gaunt and grey.

Jess had only moved from his side when Judith was awake.

Mrs Matthews had sat with her.

When Judith woke, Jess would hurry to her side and stay with her until she slept again. Mrs Matthews or Jaques LeBeau, Lucien's valet, would take her place beside her husband. With Judith now gone, Jess did not leave his side for more than five minutes at a time. Exhausted, she again put her head on her hands to doze.

She had no idea how long she had slept, but she knew he had gone when she woke. His hand was cold. "No, oh no, Lucien, my love," she sobbed. Realising she was now alone, she stood and stepped back from his bed. The chair she had been sitting on tumbled over, and she stumbled from the room. Tears overwhelmed her, and she could no longer see by the time she reached the door.

Her housekeeper had been within earshot, as had Jaques. Both hastened to her side, realising what had occurred.

Jess fell into Mrs Matthews's comforting arms. "He's gone, Felicity. We're all alone now." Felicity Matthews had been with Lucien since before he married. She had taken to Jessica as soon as she met her when she was just seventeen, and the bond had strengthened over the eight years since their wedding.

Lucien had inherited the house in London while he was serving in France. Then he later purchased their other properties when his business became highly successful after a business competitor sold him the exclusive rights to import Oolong tea.

While in France, during the war, Lucien had come across Jaques. The young boy had been injured when the French army destroyed his farmhouse near Waterloo. The lad's parents had been killed, and he had nowhere to go. Surprisingly, he spoke English well, so at twelve and with a broken arm, Jaques entered Lucien's service and was told to stay silent unless spoken to. Jaques adored his rescuer and obeyed this rule. He realised it was for his safety. Now Lucien was gone, and knowing that Judith was also dead, Jaques had no idea what he would now do. He had just turned twenty. He knew he would stay close to his mistress for as long as she needed him.

Mrs Matthews knew that her future was secure as she was the housekeeper and had been for over ten years. She had been recommended for this position of housekeeper even though very young. Sir Lucien Elkin hated the stuffiness of a strike household, and all his staff was only a few years older than he was. With him now gone, she presumed the new family, whoever they were, would keep her on as Sir Lucien had. In the meantime, she would care for the grieving widow. She felt so sorry for Lady Jess. Losing both husband and daughter was far more than a double hit; it was life-shattering. Judith would have inherited it from her father, but with them both dead, their house would be now inherited by a man who was distant family. Little Judith had been the last in the direct bloodline. Sadly, Jess had never fallen with child after Judith was born. She had wondered if it had something to do with Sir Lucien's illness when Jess was expecting. His face and other body parts had swollen badly, and he had been very ill for a long time. Felicity Matthews looked down at the grieving young woman in her arms. No words of comfort would help, so she just hugged her and let her weep.

Without words, she motioned for Jaques to get Rex Harris, their butler. Jaques nodded, and soon Rex was sent to get both Doctor Marable and Reverend Brooks.

Jess was numb. By the time both the doctor and minister had come and gone, Judith's and Lucien's bodies had been laid out, and they would be buried together late that afternoon. Jess sat watching over her silent loved ones, still not believing that a picnic out-picking field mushrooms could end their lives.

Felicity found Jess's mourning gown from her mother's death three years before. Somehow, she managed to have Jess presentable when the minister and doctor arrived.

Jess didn't care what she wore or anything else for that matter. The food turned her stomach, but she did drink a couple of cups of tea. The two men saw to their mournful duties and left without making a fuss.

At two o'clock, Rex answered the door to four black-clad gentlemen. Outside their house stood a Black Mariah. He saw the two coffins waiting to be brought inside and swallowed his own tears. Life wasn't fair.

Felicity escorted Jess upstairs to get her hat, shawl and reticule. While Jess was downstairs, Felicity had completely stripped their bed, changed the mattresses and sheets then fixed up the room. She had already done the same to Miss Judith's room. She had laid out the required items on their bed and helped to lay out both Sir Lucien and Miss Judith. Even just thinking of those two words made her shiver.

By the time they returned downstairs, the table where the bodies had lain was empty. Holding her mistress close, Felicity escorted Jess out the door. Jaques was the only other staff member to travel with her to the graveside. He would make sure she got home safely.

~

The next hour was the most horrific experience in Jessica Elkin's life. Since her marriage, she had already lost both parents. She was now alone; she also knew that the new owners of her house could appear at any time from tomorrow. She had asked Felicity to pack her bags and get her mother's jewellery from the safe. She would have to be ready to leave as soon as they arrived. She would go without a fight; fighting the inevitable was no use. But where to go?

She somehow made it through the double funeral. Jaques held her arm as she bent to take a hand full of dirt and throw it on the coffins. The small coffin on top of the large one finally undid her strong resolve not to weep. She soon fainted from sobbing so hard, and with no food in her stomach for over twenty-four hours, she was light-headed.

By the time she roused, she was under the tree in the cemetery. Jaques had left to get the doctor for her. The last time she saw that man, he pronounced her husband dead, and she could not face him again. Shrugging off various offers from the minister and his wife, who had stayed by her side, she decided to walk home. She left the cemetery gate and glanced at the new grave. Two gravediggers were already throwing in shovels full of dirt. She could hear the thud of the soil landing on the coffins. The sound and sight made her gasp, and the tears followed once more. She needed to leave and fast. Jessica stumbled towards the church and out the cemetery gate, pulling it closed behind her. She made it past the church and out of the church grounds. Then she crossed the first dirt road and headed down the street, totally oblivious to everything around her. She knew she had to cross another street to get home; she rested in the shade of a large tree. With her eyes still filled with tears, she listened and could not hear anything coming; she walked in the elongated shade of the tree onto the road. She had stepped off the grassy verge and was halfway across the street when the sounds of a speeding phaeton turned the corner way too fast, and it collected the edge of her gown. Jess was thrown to the ground, hitting her head as she fell. Jess felt herself falling and wished the wheels had collected her. Her heart was already broken.

~

Marcus was running late, and although he was a skilled whip, he knew he should not have been driving so fast through the town. He had not seen the woman until it was too late. Swathed in a black gown, she emerged from the shadows as he rounded the corner. There was no way to avoid her. As he felt a bump, he pulled up as fast as he could. Marcus flicked the reins to his tiger and jumped down to help the prostrated lady.

Giles Green hopped down from the high carriage and went to the horses' heads. The young boy was a street waif whom Marcus Ryan had found sitting in the gutter crying when his mother had died years ago. Now fifteen, Giles owed much too Marcus.

Marcus gasped as he pulled back the lady's dark veil. He had to check that she was not badly wounded. He could see no blood, and other than a bump to her head, she seemed uninjured. He had never seen a woman so stunningly beautiful. "Oh my!" He checked her throat for a pulse; it was strong and steady. He carefully hoisted her into his arms and took her to his vehicle.

Giles watched as his saviour gathered up the lady and placed her carefully on the phaeton's floor. There was nowhere else to put her. He didn't see any blood, so she mustn't be hurt too much. Marcus motioned for him to pass the reins and hop on the back. In a lithe movement, the young lad made a quick jump and landed on his rear perch.

Marcus noticed she had been crying as her eyes were puffy and a little reddened. She was in mourning garb, so that was expected. He knew the cemetery was not far away. He presumed that she had come from there.

Within minutes of the accident, he was on the way home. He had no idea where this woman lived or who she was, so he decided he would take her to his home. It was only a mile or so further on; then, he would call for his personal physician to attend to her. She was obviously a lady of some note if her clothing was anything to go by. He may have to call his mother home to chaperone her. His housekeeper would suffice in the meantime.

With Giles keeping watch over the unconscious lady, Marcus drove carefully over the dusty roads. He slowed down and turned into the mews at the back of his house. The cobblestones of the mews made the light carriage bounce. It was so rough that Marcus told Giles to drive the phaeton to his stable. Giles hopped into the driver's seat and held the reins while Marcus carefully gathered his precious load into his arms. Marcus carried her the remainder of the way to his house. Her warm breath was regular against his neck. He glanced down at the beautiful lady and gave a sigh of relief that she was still alive.

As he appeared in the courtyard, various staff arrived from all areas. One raced inside to let the maids know; others offered to take Marcus's load. Marcus shook them all off. He would not release his burden until she was safe on a bed. She was almost feather-light, and her skin was so white that he had initially thought her dead. She was obviously in mourning, and she was married as she wore rings on her left hand. She must have family somewhere. He hoped she would rouse soon so he could return her to her husband. Marcus carried his precious cargo upstairs to his mother's room. She was staying with his sister as she was expecting a child, she would not need her room for some time. Marcus's housekeeper had preceded him into the room and folded back the bed.

Two maids bustled around, preparing for the lady to take her place in the bed. One had pulled out a night rail belonging to his mother. Reluctantly Marcus relinquished his precious cargo to the ministrations of his staff. He paused at the door, and Mrs Busselton shooed him away. "You leave the poor unfortunate woman to me, Mr Marcus. I'll call you when we get her comfortable. You go and get yourself changed, sir." Mrs Busselton closed the door in his face.

Marcus had little recourse but to go and do what his housekeeper advised; this was actually the last thing he wished to do. Releasing a great sigh, he walked into his own room across the hallway.

Marcus changed and stood in his dressing room with the door open, awaiting the all-clear to return to the mysterious lady's bedside. He had never felt so utterly helpless. His own recklessness had caused this incident, and he accepted full responsibility. Hopefully, his doctor would soon arrive; in the meantime, he intended to sit with her until she roused.

It took over half an hour before Mrs Busselton called for him to return. He felt he had nearly worn a track on the luxurious carpet. "Is she awake yet, Mrs Busselton?"

"No, sir, she's as silent as to when you brought her in." Mrs Busselton saw the concern on his face. "I'm sure she'll be all right, sir." She saw a micro frown cross his face.

"I think I hit her with a glancing blow, but didn't run over her. It was just a bump," he explained guiltily. "Honest Mrs Busselton, I didn't see her. She was in the shadows and dressed in black. I just didn't see her." Marcus ran his hand through his immaculately groomed curly hair. Something that Mrs Busselton had never seen him do before.

"I'm sure it's not your fault, sir; truly, I am." She placed a caring hand on his arm as she ushered him into the room.

Marcus went to the woman's side. She lay on her back with her inky black hair spread out like a fan on the pillow. Her hands lay still on the bedclothes. He very gently picked up her right hand and clasped it in his. Gazing at her face, he said, "Who are you? Where do you come from? I know you are married, and I'm worried your husband will be fretting. I certainly would be if I lost you." He did not get a response, but he didn't really expect one. As he waited for the doctor, he kept talking to her. He had once heard that an unresponsive person could hear people talking around them. He was determined to stay with her until she regained consciousness. "I will stay with you at least until the doctor comes." He felt a flicker of her fingers in his. He kept his eyes on her face, but there was no movement. At least unresponsive, he could gaze on the stunning beauty who lay in the bed beside him. He knew he should not be here, but he would not leave. However, he made sure a maid or his housekeeper was in the room at all times.

Marcus didn't have long to wait until he had to relinquish his position at her bedside. Reluctantly he released her hand as he heard the footsteps draw near. When the doctor entered, Marcus was standing at a respectful distance from the lady. He left after he explained what had occurred.

Doctor Wayne had known Marcus since he was young. The physician had delivered his younger sister and still cared for the family. He happened to be in London as Marcus's sister Gemma was about to deliver her first child, and their mother, Elizabeth, was with her. Marcus had asked for Doctor Wayne to attend to his patient. It was a busman's holiday, working while away. The Doctor's wife was permitted to accompany him, and both were residing with Miles and her husband only three blocks away.

Doctor Wayne listened intently to Marcus's explanations and then sent him away. Mrs Busselton and the doctor walked to the patient's bed, and he proceeded to investigate the wound thoroughly.

He hummed and hawed while he poked and prodded the lady's head before calling Marcus back in. "I think she will be fine, Marc. She hit her head when she fell, but she has no other injuries. You did not hit her at all; there are no wheel marks or bruising on her person at all. Her fall is the cause of her present condition." His discerning eye saw the worried frown on Marcus's brow. "Truly, Marc, she will be fine." The doctor had known Marcus since he was in short pants. "The only thing you will need to do is make sure she drinks, and for this, she will need to sit up."

Marcus's eyes were fixed on the lovely lady in the bed on the other side of the room.

Doctor Wayne watched him, intrigued. Marcus had never shown any interest in any woman before. He was kind and generous and certainly not a man to play around or sow his oats. There had been no breath of scandal about him, and he had a firm faith that he willingly shared. "Marc, I'll come back tomorrow, but call me if she stirs. We'll be at the opera tonight, so I would love an excuse to leave early." He chuckled at Marcus's smirk.

"I would too, doctor. I avoid it like the plague. Thankfully, Mother doesn't like it either." Marcus had not moved his gaze from the prostrated lady. Instead, he took a step towards the bed and reluctantly dragged his eyes from the beauty in his mother's bed; he turned to the doctor. "Doctor Wayne, I will do anything for this poor lady. I don't care what it costs."

"We'll see what tomorrow brings, Marc. I'm sure she'll stir soon enough." He placed a caring hand on Marcus's shoulder, and the doctor took his leave.

Marcus waited until the door closed and took his seat at the lady's side, and waited. Once again, he picked up her very elegant hand.

Chapter 2   The Lady Stirs

When Marcus arrived home with his unconscious cargo, all else had fled from his mind. Marcus had forgotten all about the meeting he was supposed to have attended. His secretary, however, had sent a note to the chairman of the board with his master's apology. Marcus was informed that the meeting had been cancelled when he had been waiting for the doctor. He had merely nodded thanks to Jeffrey.

As Marcus waited in the bedroom, he spoke to the prostrated, unresponsive lady. He told her of his farm in West Sussex, of his odd house that he adored, and the neighbour's immense property. Living next door to one of the largest stately homes in England made their late Elizabethan Manor House look minute.

Occasionally, Marcus would get up and walk around the room. If he had to leave for some reason, a maid took his place. His mystery lady was not to be left alone for a second. Some words kept flowing through his mind, *No more, my love, will you be alone,* but he dared not voice them. He certainly would not allow himself to be alone in her room. One of the female staff always in attendance when he was with her.

After some six hours, Marcus knew that she would need some fluid. The doctor had told him to sit her up and hold a glass to her lips. Hopefully, she would drink automatically. He had just had something to eat himself, and when he returned, he saw his staff had brought a fresh jug of lemon barley water for her. He sat on the bed beside her and gently eased back the sheets. The night rail was fine lawn and almost gossamer thin. Realising he was staring at her exquisite form that was visible through it, he quickly pulled up the sheet and covered her. He drew her into his arms with extreme gentleness and cradled her against him.

Mrs Busselton hovered close by and handed him a glass of barley water.

Marcus held the glass to her lips; amazingly, she sipped and then drank deeply. After drinking half the glass, she murmured, "Lucien, Jude, all gone, all lost." With that, she wept again, this time turning to him for comfort. She had not realised who he was or that she was not in her own room. She cried on his shoulder for some time until she fell asleep again. Marcus gently lay her down and let her sleep. He stayed nearby in case she stirred again; however, she was as still as she was before. Occasionally she would jerk in her sleep, but her breathing was even. Marcus sat her up every few hours and gave her more to drink. Mostly she would only sip, but each time she would weep before sleeping again. Marcus began to live for these moments. He had never had a beautiful female in his arms needing him so desperately. He knew she had no idea he was there, but his desire for this beautiful woman grew each time he did something for her.

Finally, he was so tired that he knew he must sleep. He stood at her door gazing at her sleeping form. Before he left, he murmured, "No more, my love! I will care for you; I will ease your burdens any way I can." He had wondered if Lucien was her husband, and if so, then who was Jude? Quietly pulling the door closed, he retired to his own room and dreamt about her all night. He could almost feel the softness of her cheeks in his dreams. The black curl that kept falling onto her brow, he reached out to move, only to wake and realise he was again dreaming. A few hours later, the singing of the larks stirred him, and he finally gave up trying to sleep and rose. He pulled on his brocade dressing gown and went to see if his patient had awoken. He knew the name of Lucien. He had come across a man with such a name when he sold his tea-importing business. Marcus padded across the hallway in bare feet and saw the door was ajar. He pushed it back quietly and saw Mrs Busselton still sitting in her chair knitting. He saw her look up and beckon him into the room.

The housekeeper whispered her report to Marcus. "She's not

awoken yet, sir. However, she is restless. She keeps saying Maria, Luke and Jude. At least, I think that's what she's saying."

Marcus nodded. "Has she had anything to drink this morning?" He hoped not, as he wished to hold her and move that errant curl.

"No, sir, I let her sleep." Mrs Busselton stole a glance at her employer. She could see that he was not only concerned but was beginning to feel something for this unknown lady. "I'll get some barley water, sir." As she went for the glass, Marcus walked to the bedside. In the dawn light, she was even more beautiful than he remembered. Before he did anything, he let his dreams play out. He ran the back of his finger over her downy cheek, and then he gently moved the curl. As he did so, she moved. He pulled his hand back as though burnt. "Had she felt me?" he thought to himself. He hoped not. He stood watching her, and she didn't stir again.

He was totally oblivious to Mrs Busselton standing waiting for him. She saw the smile hovering on his face as he stood watching the sleeping lady. Eventually, he stood erect and turned to her. "Thank you, Mrs Busselton; let us give our dark angel a drink." He sat himself down beside her and eased her once again into his arms. Now leaning against him, she stirred again. As he spoke, his voice was soft and soothing, "You have to drink. Are you ready?" Marcus held the glass to her lips, and she again drank greedily. Her eyes had not yet opened, but she seemed to be a little more aware each time she had a drink than the last time.

She opened her eyes and looked directly at Marcus as she finished the glass. Her dark brown eyes were misty with sleep. She looked around her and shrank closer to the comforting arms holding her, not realising where she was. Lucien would keep her safe. He always had. Then it hit, Lucien was gone, and Judith was gone. She turned to the person holding her, and her gaze met a stranger's face. He was still in night attire. Had he abused her as she slept?

He was speaking to her. "Oh, ma'am, you are awake; that is good." He turned to look across the room. As did she, and she saw an older lady there. "Mrs Busselton, can you please call the doctor?" She watched as the lady walked to the door. As she left, a maid entered and took her seat.

Jess's mind was swirling; who were these people? Why was the man holding her? Her gaze returned to him. She frowned.

"Can you sit up by yourself?" He bent down, picked up some

pillows, and then helped her sit up in bed.

She murmured a reply of "Yes, thank you."

Once done, he moved further away and sat in a chair next to the foot of the large four-post bed. Marcus's heart was pounding. She was even more beautiful now awake. He saw her pull up the sheet to cover the almost transparent night rail that she wore. He was pleased she was modest. "Are you ready to hear what happened?" he asked hopefully. He knew soon he would have to leave her room.

"Yes, please, sir," she replied in a soft but musical voice.

The way her lips moved when she spoke mesmerised him; he could hardly tear his eyes from them. Marcus recapped how she had come to be in bed at his place. He explained that she was uninjured, other than a bump on the head.

She looked around the room and saw her black gown hanging on the wardrobe door. Her hand flew to her mouth, and two tears rolled down her cheeks. "They are gone." She melted. Her tears were now flowing unchecked. "They are really gone. I was returning from their funeral." Her gaze had not left her gown.

"Who, madam? Who has gone?" Marcus saw her frown, and one of his own flashed on his face.

"My husband and daughter, sir. Both are dead!" She gave a delicate sniff, then continued with her head bent. "Because I was coming from their funeral, I was so deep in grief I did not hear your approach." Her dark eyes flicked to his. "I presume your carriage hit me, sir?"

Marcus nodded. "I was late and was driving far too fast. I take full responsibility, and it's why you are here in my home now. You had no identification on you, and we did not know who you were or where to take you," he said apologetically. "Let me know whom I can contact, and I will send someone directly to them."

The lady wept afresh. "They are both dead, sir, as are both parents." Her weeping this time was uncontrollable.

Marcus wished to sweep her into his arms to bring her comfort and was about to do that when he heard footsteps. Doctor Wayne had arrived, knowing he would be banished from the room. "We will talk later, madam. What is your name, by the way?"

The lady looked at him and uttered, "Um, Jess, no, it is Jessica." With that, she turned to her pillow and sobbed.

Wishing he could comfort her, he knew he couldn't. He bowed and left her. Jessica, oh, how it suited her. Frustrated at the interruption, he shut the door and let the doctor do his work. Marcus went to get changed. His valet, Colin Morrison, had his clothing laid out for him, and he dressed in record time, not wanting to waste a minute if he could be beside her. He waved away the breakfast tray and gave instructions to set up a table in the lady's room, and they would eat together. Once dressed, Marcus opened the door so he could hear when the doctor was ready to talk to him. He was not usually an impatient person, but he had never experienced time dragging before. At every sound, creak, or door opening, he jumped. Finally, after about twenty minutes, Doctor Wayne emerged from her room.

He noticed Marcus's concern and saw him hovering, anxious for news about Jessica. "She's going to be fine, Marc. She's not dizzy, but she is not coping with her loss. Did she tell you she has just lost both her husband and daughter?"

Marcus nodded.

The doctor continued. "Did she tell you how? It's tragic."

Marcus shook his head, this time, anticipating that it was from some deadly disease.

Doctor Wayne looked grieved. "She spilled the entire story to me, Marc. The family, Mrs Jess, her husband, and her six-year-old daughter, Judith, went on a picnic picking field mushrooms. They had had a glorious day and went home to cook them. They had not collected many as most were still in the button stage, so they left those to open. Anyway, they decided to cook them up for the daughter's supper. Mrs Jessica was called away as one of their servants, their cook, had become ill. Her husband and daughter had their mushrooms on toast, and then he put the child to bed and read her a bedtime story when both started vomiting as the cook had done. The little girl died the next day, and her husband the day later. Their cook had tasted the mushrooms and eaten just one small spoonful of the food. She survived, but the other two died. I have known others to pass in this way." Doctor Wayne shook his head. "Such a tragic loss for your lady. I'm guessing they mixed some death caps with the field mushrooms. Easy to do, but so sad. Did I say the girl was only six? She stood no chance of survival. Therefore, I believe your lady is now alone as her parents died some years ago. Her husband has some distant cousins who will now inherit the home, but she has not met them. Poor woman!" The doctor looked anxiously towards the stairs. "I must go, Marc, as your sister's time is close. Her pains had just started when I left. I should not need to return here, so the lady is free to get up when she wishes." With that, he took his leave.

Marcus watched until he was out of sight, then quickly went to the open door of his mother's room. He knocked and was invited in. Jessica was now clad in his mother's dressing gown; Mrs Busselton was changing the sheets with one of the maids. His brown-eyed angel was sitting in the chair he had used earlier. "Good morning, madam; I wondered if you would like to break your fast with me?"

Jessica nodded. "Tea and toast are all I need, sir." She didn't even want that but knew that she must return home and see to the house and estate. She needed to get Felicity to pack her things, Lucien's Bible, which they read nightly, and get her mother's jewellery from the safe. She had no idea when the new owners would turn up, but as she had now been missing for two days, she was eager to return home. She knew that she must thank this man for his care of her, so she gave him a wan smile and accepted his arm to walk to a small table set out on the other side of a dressing room-cum-sitting room.

He usually ate a light breakfast, and when he saw what awaited them, he hastily had the maid remove the dish of mushrooms. Sadly, she had seen it already and stumbled against him. Moments later, she was in his arms, weeping. Mushrooms, he hated them anyway; why serve them today of all days?

He embraced her until her weeping subsided. He had no wish to release her, but she pulled away from him. Reluctantly, he set her free.

"I'm so sorry, sir. I'm not usually a wet-mop, sir. I am overwrought with everything. Did the doctor tell you my story? I presume he must have done, or you would not have removed that dish." Jessica's eyes were still swimming in tears, but the effect added to her beauty.

"He did, ma'am; I need no further explanations. Let us eat before the toast gets cold." He held the chair out for her and joined her at the small table. They ate the toast and marmalade, followed by two cups of tea. As much as he wished to pump her for her story, he steered clear of questioning her at all.

She gave little information about herself, as every time she did, it triggered more tears. After some time, he could see she was feeling somewhat uncomfortable. Marcus escorted her back to the bedroom, and after assuring her she could stay as long as she wished, he explained that he had business to attend too and would return to see her later. He bowed over her hand, kissing it briefly. He wished to hug her and take away all her pain, but he knew no hug could or would do that. He wanted her to know that she always had a place with him if she wished, but he left the words unvoiced. It was far too soon, and he knew it would not be appropriate for her to reside at his bachelor's house unless his mother were present.

Marcus left her in Mrs Busselton's care and took his leave. He took a final glance at her before he closed the door. She was so beautiful, even in her distraught state.

Downstairs his secretary was awaiting him in his office. He had two days of correspondence to attend to. He also had to deal with the issues arising from the meeting that he had postponed on the day of the accident. With a deep sigh, Marcus slowly descended the stairs. Work could no longer wait; Jeffrey Anthony had rearranged this meeting with the chairman of the board for his wool importation business. He knew what he wanted, and with Jessica now, hopefully, in his life, he would refuse his request. He had no intention of travelling to New South Wales and being gone for a year or more to buy a farm and grow his own wool. Someone else could go. He knew as much about wool as anyone, but his mills were interested in the new fine merino fleece he heard was now being produced in the colony. He walked towards the office door with this thought in mind, ready for the chairman's requests and arguments. He would tell the chairman that he would let him know, but Marcus had no intention of leaving. The meeting proceeded much as he expected.

Jeffrey saw Marcus frequently glance toward the door as though he wished to leave. A frown flickered across Jeffrey's face. Typically, Marcus gave his full attention to these meetings to the point of obsession. Something was diverting him, probably the lady upstairs. He smiled to himself; his master never usually was distracted by females; he was business through and through and was driven to succeed. Jeffrey was surprised that Marcus had given no answer to the plea by the chairman. Usually, Marcus would accept his chairman's suggestions as the business would prosper.

After two hours, Marcus was relieved that his chairman had taken his leave. Marcus had managed to delay his decision and promised that he would let him know as soon as he could work things out. He had made sure he was not tied to time for his reply and would consider his chairman's proposal seriously. He knew a trip to the colony was inevitable, but the timing could not be worse. He wanted to be there for Jessica if she needed him. He would take care of her, and if she were forced out of her home, he would arrange that she could live with his sister and her family. With this in mind, as soon as he heard the front door close, he left the office and took the steps upstairs two at a time. He arrived at her door almost breathless. Pausing to regain some decorum, he paused to pray, then knocked.

Mrs Busselton opened the door to him. "She's gone for a breath of fresh air, sir. I don't think she'll be too long, sir." She was watching the maids do their work. "I didn't think she'd be this long. Maybe you could go and sit with her outdoors."

Marcus nodded and arrived at the front door in record time. He asked his butler, "Has Mrs Jessica returned, Phillip?"

Phillip Clarke looked surprised. "Sir? She has not left through this door." He saw a look of astonishment cross his master's face. "Sir, mayhap she left by the mews," the butler said hopefully.

Marcus didn't reply but walked to ask his groom if they had seen her.

The groom had not, but his tiger had seen her leave. Giles had seen her quietly open and close the back door and slip into the courtyard. She then opened the back gate, quietly closing it behind her. Giles only noticed as he was taking a smoke break and was sitting out of sight of the other staff. He relayed what he had seen to Marcus. "Sir, I would have followed, but you gave no instructions for me to do so. I did see that she turned south, but then she was gone from sight."

Marcus walked to the small side gate, opened it and saw the deserted mews. There was no one in sight. She had gone, and he didn't even know her name or directions. Damn that meeting!

Chapter 3   Cast Aside

*J*essica had not intended to sneak outside, but she saw a man arriving at the front door and hid in the hallway; as the voices approached, she moved towards the rear of the house; there, she saw a door and found it opened into the stable yard. She could see it had a gate opening into the mews from the elevated steps. The house layout was similar to her own home but in reverse. She had no idea where she was, only that it must be the same town as her place. As she and Lucien lived most of their time in his country home near Crawley, they had not spent much time in town. It was why she had wished to have a picnic. She and Judith had craved open space. Lucien had relented, and the picnic had been the result. The thought of their demise had once again brought tears to her eyes. She could not afford to delay her return home, so she angrily swiped away the wetness on her cheeks. Once she oriented herself, she realised her home was a few blocks away. Being careful not to be seen leaving from the mews of a gentleman's house, she quickly walked away. She arrived home mid-morning after the mile-long walk. Her boots pinched, and she wished she had not worn these, but they were black. She knocked, and Rex opened the door.

The look of relief showed on his face. "Oh, my lady, we did not know where you were. We sent for the constabulary, but they could not find you either. Ma'am, Sir Lucien's cousin has arrived and taken over your rooms already." Rex was looking very anxious.

"Ma'am, they have laid off Jaques and brought in some of their own staff. Mrs Felicity has been given notice, and I have been told I'm to move to the Crawley as James has been retired." He was speaking softly while assisting her to remove her coat.

Jess was not surprised. Lucien told her that his cousin was a dandy at best, and it was why he did not wish to have contact with them. Egbert Elkin was a popinjay according to Lucien. He called him a tulip of fashion, and Jess had once seen some of those mincing through town. Egbert's wife was apparently even worse. They had not sought them out when they stayed in the house in London, let alone chase them while in Brighton, and Jess realised that although she was pleased about this back then, she was going to be punished for that now.

She was still in the hallway when she heard unfamiliar footsteps approaching. "Cousin Jessica, welcome to *my* humble abode. I am grieved for your double loss, but as you can see, we have arrived and will now take Cousin Lucien's affairs from your hands. I'm surprised that you weren't here to greet us, but your staff said you were staying with friends after your double loss." Egbert gave her a minute bow that barely acknowledged her status as a titled lady.

Lucien had earned his Knighthood, and Egbert could not use it; however, she was still Lady Elkin and would remain so unless she remarried. Jess was not prepared to fight him; she just wished to leave with her things. She wanted Judith's toy bear, Lucien's Bible that they read together daily, her mother's jewellery box and her clothes. "If I may gather my personal possessions, I shall leave you to *your* humble abode, Egbert." She refused to claim any relationship with the mincing tulip. Lucien's description of him was vastly understated.

She went to walk past him, but he blocked her path. "I have not given you permission to enter *my* home yet, cousin. I shall get *your* housekeeper to pack your things and bring them to you in there." Egbert sneered, then pointed her into the sitting room.

As she entered, Jess gasped; they had completely rearranged the furniture during their short time in residence. She shivered; no wonder Lucien disliked the fellow. Felicity appeared a few minutes later. She had obviously been crying. Her eyes were red, and she was not the usually bubbly woman Jess knew and loved. Something was seriously amiss.

Egbert didn't leave them alone. He stood just inside the door while Jess gave Felicity instructions on what to pack.

Felicity was quick to do her bidding, knowing that she had much of it already prepared. Felicity had met him before and knew what to expect when he arrived and took over. Jess presumed that she would have to return to her uncle, now living in her father's ancestral manor house. She had no desire to live in the dilapidated Dower House near Egbert in Crawley as there she would be at his beck and call. She sat and waited for Felicity to return. She was not offered tea, refreshment, or any other comfort. Jess also knew Egbert would be on guard just outside the door, so she sat still in her widows' weeds, as Lucien used to call them, and she waited.

It only took Felicity half an hour to collect the items she required. They were hers and had nothing to do with the inheritance. She knew she had £100 in her reticule from her monthly allowance from Lucien. There was also over £1000 in her wallet, unspent from her allowance over the years. She doubted she would be allowed to keep her money from the safe, it was sitting in her jewellery box with her grandmother's and mother's jewellery, but she refused to go without that box. Felicity returned with Rex carrying a carpetbag filled to the brim with her clothing. Judith's bear was sitting on top, and Felicity gave her a big smile and a wink, so Jess knew she had also managed to get Lucien's Bible. Felicity drew her into a hug as she handed over the bag. Felicity whispered, "Meet me in the park in half an hour and don't mention your mother's box."

Jess understood. Somehow, she had managed to get the box for her, or at least she soon would. Knowing that she had a wardrobe full of gowns upstairs and many more left in the country house, she knew her uncle would not appreciate her arriving with virtually nothing. However, there was little she could do. She was still numb and in shock at her double loss; the cruelty of Lucien's cousins added to her distress and discomfort. She would go to the park and wait. Hopefully, Felicity would not be long.

Without argument, Jess took her leave. The bag was heavy; obviously, Felicity had put in everything she could. Jess's entire life possessions were now in this bag. She would sit guard over it. By the time she reached the park in the next block, Jess was exhausted. She took a perch on a bench seat and waited. She wished she'd been able to use the facilities at home at least, but she dared not ask. She supposed she would have to stay in a coaching house tonight as she dared not return to the nice man's house. She had found from the doctor that his name was Marcus Ryan; what a nice-sounding name.

She felt terrible that she didn't say thank you or farewell. She would write when settled at her uncle's place. She worked out his address as she walked home. She realised she knew his street, as Lucien had taken it as a shortcut to their home. It had not taken much for the learned doctor to talk about the kind man. Now she felt sorry for him as he would not know what had happened to her. Guilt swept through her once more.

Jessica saw Felicity and Rex enter the park; both made a beeline directly to her side. Felicity had an oversized reticule with her.

"Oh, ma'am, I am so sorry," Rex said. "Mr Egbert said I could take Felicity for a walk. He thinks we are courting, so he allowed us to leave. Ma'am, we have been out looking for you every day. We were frantic when you didn't come home from the funeral on Monday." Rex released Felicity's arm, and she hoisted up her bag and dug into it. In her hand was the jewellery box Jess never thought she would see again.

Jess was astonished. "Felicity, how did you manage to get this out of the safe?"

"Rexy got it for me, ma'am; he knew what is in there is yours and had nothing to do with Mr Egbert. He couldn't get the wallet, though, ma'am. Sorry!" Felicity started to rearrange the contents of the carpetbag. "If you take out the money from in there and put it down your corset and maybe even wear some of the gems, you will be less likely to lose them."

Within minutes, Felicity had Jess's bag repacked with the small jewellery box safely at the bottom.

Rex told Jess that they would accompany her to the ticket office so she could purchase a seat on the coach to Oxford. They all knew that Lionel Bates would not be pleased to see his niece, but she had no other option.

"I would come if you wished me to, but I have to wait until I am dismissed as I have little money, ma'am. I'm hoping that he may give me a position at Crawley with Rex, even if it's a senior maid's role." Felicity was weepy and sad to see her young mistress in such a state. "Ma'am, may I ask where you have been for the last two days?" She was hesitant to ask, but she wanted to know.

"Felicity, Rex, I will tell you both, but it's to go no further. I collapsed at the funeral, and Jaques took the carriage to get the doctor. I recovered before he returned and set about walking home. I was nearly there when a speeding carriage bowled me over. The driver was a single man, and I have been at his house for the past two days. I was unresponsive, and we were never left alone, but I would not like this information spread around." Jess looked at her two faithful servants, waiting for their assurance not to tell anyone else. "I know nothing about him, but his name is Marcus Ryan's, and he lives in Queensbury Mews. He and his household nursed me and assured me I would be safe if I needed to stay. If I didn't have Uncle Lionel to go to, I may well have stayed. I would have had no other option. His mother normally resides with him, but she was away, and I was in her room." As it was now hours since she left, he must be wondering what had happened to her. She felt sad but assured herself that she would send a thank-you note to him when she could.

None noticed that another group had entered the park. It was a place many families let their children run and play. She had often brought Judith here when in town. As the group drew close, Jess realised it was Egbert and two constables. The snivelling voice she had heard not so long ago said, "There they are, constables, there are the thieves." Egbert was pointing to the group of three. "Look, she's even flaunting her jewels."

The blue topaz necklace Jess wore had been her grandmother's. Her hand flew to the lovely necklace; she usually wore this but had taken it off for the funerals. "This was my grandmother's necklace; you may ask my Uncle Lionel. He has had my jewellery box in store for years. He only gave it to me on my marriage." Surely her day could get no worse.

Within minutes Rex, Felicity, and Jess had all been arrested. Egbert stood watching, snickering behind his hand. Jess glanced at him and thought, "What a horrible man." If she could get Rex and Felicity freed, they could hopefully go to Mr Ryan and beg his assistance again. He had no reason to want to help her, but she had absolutely no one else to turn to. One constable took the arms of both ladies, and the other took Rex and the carpetbag. Egbert was about to take the jewellery from Jess's neck when the constable told him it was evidence. "Sorry, sir, that stays in situ. As does everything in the bag. We shall take it with us and get to the bottom of the case. The magistrate will make a judgement."

Lucien had a business meeting with over a dozen of the local businessmen only the Wednesday before. Jess could hear Egbert cursing and smiling. She knew three of the local magistrates, and hopefully, one of them would be whom she was called in front of.

The next three hours saw Jessica begging to speak to Magistrates Riley, McKinney, or Kennedy. Sadly, the man she was taken before was someone she did not know. Magistrate McArthur was a man she'd never met before. She had a feeling that he had taken a pet against her as she was not in tears and begging for mercy. As she had done nothing wrong, she didn't feel she had to beg for anything. Without a murmur of protest, she had left most of her worldly possessions in the hands of the new owners. Egbert had no reason to be so spiteful other than the reason they had snubbed him while Lucien was alive. Jess called for permission to call character witnesses; all her pleas were dismissed. Jess was placed in custody.

The magistrate did accept that the staff had done nothing beyond following her demands to them. They were not blamed for anything and had been released. Jess had told the court that they had met by chance in the park while they were out walking. They had brought her nothing. She met Felicity's shocked face and gave her head a subtle shake. Jess needed them out of gaol. One or both had to let her uncle know, and maybe Mr Ryan too.

She heard the Magistrate announce her sentence. "Guilty of theft of a valuable leather bound Bible that is not yours. I shall allow that the jewellery is from your family. You shall be transported for seven and serve them in the Antipodes."

Jess gasped! Transported, for taking Lucien's Bible? With those words, her world once again went black as she collapsed.

Felicity saw her mistress faint but was prevented from going to her aide. Rex, thankfully was at hand and caught her before she hit the floor. He lay her down carefully before being tugged away from Jess. The court was adjourned, and soon only one constable, Rex, Felicity and Jess, remained in the room.

The constable bent and unclasped the topaz necklace and handed it to Felicity. "Take this; it will get stolen in prison. Go through her bag and leave nothing valuable in there. Could you keep it safe for her? I'll give you five minutes. So be quick, If we are caught, say you are carrying it for me. Rex, I remember you from dinner last week. I was on guard duty outside your house."

Felicity saw to Jess while Rex ransacked her bag, removing the jewellery box, Judith's bear, and the nearly empty purse. Thankfully Rex had taken none of the family jewels; these gems truly were all hers. Rex made Felicity stuff the treasures down her bodice, and he carried the empty and now intentionally broken box under his arm. He had carefully pulled the tiny nails out of the hinges. If they were stopped and asked to see inside, he would open the damaged box showing it contained nothing.

All too soon, Jess roused, and Felicity assisted her to stand. The friendly constable let them say their farewells in relative privacy before escorting Jess out of the room. Jess had managed to say, "Felicity, tell Uncle Lionel in Oxford, and Rex, if you can find Mr Ryan, please thank him and tell him I'm sorry I left without saying farewell. If you can find nowhere else, leave my box and the contents with him. Ask him to keep them safe for me." With that, Jess was dragged from their sight.

Rex had spent a night or two in the cells downstairs in his misspent youth. The cells were not conducive to comfort. Hopefully, Jess would manage to keep most of her luggage, but she was in the Lord's hands whatever happened now. Rex escorted Felicity out of the building as quickly as possible. Both of them had things to do. He had to find a man by the name of Ryan in Queensbury Mews.

The first thing Felicity needed to do was send a message to Jess's uncle. She had no idea how long she had until Jess was transported; hopefully, it would be months. However, both knew they had to act fast. Once out of the building, Rex stopped Felicity, "We have to work out how to help her, Flick. Let us tell Mr Ryan and see what he can do."

Felicity loved his nickname for her. "Rex, I think we should send a message to her uncle first. It's a one-hundred-mile trip each way, and he'll need to come as soon as possible. We can't lose a minute." In the end, that's what they decided. The message was sent express, using one of the £10 notes Jess had passed to Felicity while Rex was checking the luggage under the watchfulness of the constable. By the time they returned to their other quarry, they had found he had left for London.

Rex left a written message with Mr Ryan's housekeeper, and it also contained Jess's note of thanks and an apology. They left their direction and the jewellery box, once again stuffed with all Jessica's gems and Judith's bear sitting on the top.

By the time Marcus returned five days later to his Queensbury Mews house, he was sheet white with anxiety. He had gone to London because he had a report of a widow seen entering the mail coach. It wasn't Jessica, but he had only found that out after searching for her for two days. He had stayed and searched everywhere before returning disappointed to Brighton. If only he had been able to have that long talk with her. He had no sooner entered his office before Mrs Busselton sought him out. "Sir, the day you left, you had two visitors. They were staff from Sir Lucien Elkin's household. They came to tell you that Jessica, Lady Elkin, has been arrested for theft and will be transported."

The groan that Marcus emitted shocked Mrs Busselton to the core. "Oh, what have I done? Why did I follow on a blooming wild goose chase? I had no idea she was Sir Lucien's wife, sorry, I mean, widow. I had heard of his passing, but I had no idea there was any correlation between the two deaths." Marcus stood looking at his housekeeper; she obviously had more to say. "Go on!" he said.

Mrs Busselton continued to unfold the story. "The two who came were her butler and housekeeper. They carried a letter and a box. Lady Elkin asked if you would care for it for her." She passed over the box, and it had a letter and a bear sitting on it.

"They brought a note. Really?" He put the box down and picked up the letter. He flicked open the seal and turned to read the missive. It was short but filled in some information for him. She hadn't run away; she'd been arrested. He released a long sigh of relief. He smiled to himself; all was not lost; she had turned to him when she needed help. He would not let her down now. Marcus couldn't believe she was to be transported, but if she were, then he would follow her, as his chairman wished him out there anyway. He would not desert her now. Not when she needed him. His first port of call was to Sir Lucien's house. From there, he would see what occurred next. Rex Harris had given him lots to work with.

Chapter 4   *Chasing His Tail*

*M*arcus set out for Sir Lucien Elkin's house just a few streets over from his house. He took the carriage as he did not want the new owner to know he lived so close. From Rex's note, he knew that Egbert Elkin had inherited the property and that from what Mrs Busselton had said, they referred to him as a proper popinjay. Marcus called at the house and tapped his brass-topped cane on the door. A liveried footman opened the door and bowed.

Marcus nodded his head to acknowledge the greeting, then introduced himself as he handed his card to the butler. "Marcus Ryan, Gentleman." He then waited; there was no sign of recognition of his name; this obviously wasn't Rex. Was he at the right house? Yes, twenty-six was the number on the door. The puce clad butler asked him in, and he was shown into the sitting room, but the furniture was in the wrong placement for his taste. He could see Jessica sitting in the window reading. But there was no settee for her to do that. All the furniture faced inwards and was to highlight the occupants. Yes, it was just wrong. He felt uncomfortable.

Marcus waited impatiently. Soon, he heard mincing footsteps heading his way. Mincing wasn't wrong! The apparition that appeared in the doorway was astounding. Marcus had always considered himself well-dressed.

The new occupant of the house was beyond comprehension. A dark peach-coloured vest accompanied the man's daffodil-yellow jacket, and dazzling red polka dot hose were visible under the too-short striped gold trousers. His shoes were mirror-image, shiny black that came to a minute point. But it was the shock of bright red curly hair, brushed, not into a windswept style that was currently popular, but into a high beehive of a macaroni of yesteryear. The man was not just a popinjay but an absolute mimic of the effeminate macaroni of a hundred years before. Marcus found it hard not to laugh at the entire ensemble, let alone the man himself. He bit his cheeks in an attempt to control his mirth. Instead of laughing, he smiled and returned the man's rude gaze with a deep bow. Marcus's bow was far lower than needed, but Marcus realised this man needed to be pandered to.

"I come to visit my friend Sir Lucien Elkin and find him from home, sir. Could you furnish me with a possible return date?" Marcus gave him a beaming smile.

Egbert was unaware of this man and thought he had better tread carefully. He minced further into the room and suggested that Marcus take a seat.

Marcus flipped up the tails of his jacket and perched leisurely on a comfortable chair.

The popinjay spoke. "I have some sad news to relate to you, sir. My esteemed cousin, Lucien, and his young daughter met with tragedy last month. They are both dead. I am now the owner of this establishment."

Marcus noticed the absence of any mention of Jessica. "And Lady Elkin, is she still in residence? I'm sure she would not have left without direction." Marcus asked, putting the fop in his place.

The macaroni smirked. "An unfortunate incident occurred, and she has been arrested. I believe she is in London awaiting transportation. I attended court myself to see what I could do; however, the magistrate would not listen to my case." What he said was true. He wished her to be charged with jewellery theft, which would have seen her gone for life. Instead, she received a mere seven years for stealing Lucien's stupid Bible. He couldn't work out why she would want that anyway. He waved his hand nonchalantly, showing his lack of interest in her welfare.

"May I ask which courthouse is she in?" Marcus was now not laughing but was nearly ready to knock his lights out. He was livid but plastered a false smile back on his lips.

Egbert looked surprised at this man's interest. "I have no idea, my good man. What interest is it of yours? She is a criminal and will be treated as such."

Marcus again controlled his temper and politely said, "I happen to be heading that way for work. Lucien and I worked together before, and I have to make a trip to the Antipodes soon. I shall take her clothing as she will need more than what they allocate. Please see that her clothing is packed up and sent to my address as soon as possible. I will be departing as soon as I can arrange a passage. Also, I will take her personal staff with me. Mrs Matthews, Mr Le Beau, and the previous butler, Mr Rex Harris, can bring over the luggage. Mrs Matthews will know what she needs; I also would like my Bible back, please. I lent it too Lucien until they found a new one. It was from my family, and I loaned it to him to read." Marcus hoped that this fop would have no interest in Lucien's Bible or that it wasn't a family book. He realised that it was for stealing this particular book the Jessica had been arrested. It was like rubbing salt into the popinjay's feelings, if he had any. Marcus drew his breath and waited for an explosion. Thankfully Rex had left detailed instructions for the staff and had efficiently outlined the situation. If Jessica wanted her husband's Bible, then he'd make sure she got it. Marcus was determined to let the man know that he had met his match.

Egbert knew his wife didn't fit most of the remaining gowns as Jess was so much more delicate. Also, they were not frilly enough for his liking. His gapped, toothy smile belied his attitude. He, too, knew that he had no choice but to comply. "I have your card, and I will send around the luggage, but I have dismissed the three staff you mentioned. The butler was supposed to go to Crawley, to my country home, but he was insolent, so I dismissed him." Again, his foppish hand waved in the air as if the man was of no consequence.

Marcus was nearly seething by this stage, "I believe he was an old retainer, as was Mrs Matthews. Have they been given cottages somewhere?" Marcus asked. He was desperate to find the three of them. He would hire them, even if they sat and twiddled their thumbs, but if Jessica were in Sydney, he would ask them if they wished to accompany him and join her there. He knew the system as he had been there before. If she went free, Mrs Matthews could get Jess assigned to her.

Egbert tried to sound knowledgeable. "I have no cottages vacant. I paid them their dues and released them. I was under no other obligation to them, so they have gone." He then stood up, signalling the meeting was at an end.

Marcus said, "I shall send the carriage back for Lady Elkin's things in an hour. I believe there will be more at Crawley as they were only here for a short stay; I shall send a carriage there in three days." Marcus gave him no option to reply; he bowed and left. He walked into the hallway, collecting his hat and cane on the way out. As the door shut behind him, he saw a strange sight. A man at the end of the street was beckoning him. As his carriage was waiting for him, he hopped in and took off, aware he was being observed from indoors. He headed down towards the stranger, pausing at the corner and calling for him to hop in quickly.

As they drove off, the man greeted him by name. "Mr Ryan, I'm Rex Harris. I left you the letter about Lady Elkin. I have been watching the house, hoping that you would come."

Marcus was genuinely thrilled. "Well, sir, you saved me a lot of trouble. I thought I was going to have to hunt for you too. Can you tell me exactly what occurred right from the beginning?"

"If we may, sir, I will, but could we possibly collect Mrs Matthews and Mr Le Beau? We are staying at the Albion Inn, and it's not a nice place at all, sir. I'd like to get her out of there." Rex looked anxious. "Sir, I have no right to ask this of you. Mrs Jessica said that you might help; even if you could get us to the country, it would be safer than here."

Marcus smiled. "Relax, Rex, we four are now in cahoots against the fop that I have just met. Hopefully, you will be going on a trip to the country soon. You see, you are going to Crawley to collect Lady Elkin's personal things. In an hour, I shall be sending my carriage to collect her items from the house we have just left. I believe she may also want Miss Judith's things?" He saw Rex nod. "I gather the bear was hers?" Marcus watched the understanding dawn on Rex's face.

"You really will help her, sir? She said you would, but I did doubt." As the carriage headed to the Albion Inn, Rex then proceeded to tell Marcus precisely what happened right from the picnic.

Marcus sat spellbound as the saga unfolded. The relationship of his dark angel with her beloved Lucien broke his heart. Could she ever feel the same for him? She knew she could trust him as she had turned to him already. Then he remembered she had even sent him the jewellery box to keep safe. His heart soared. He wished he had known who she was. He had met Lucien when he sold him the Tea import branch of his business.

By the time they reached the Albion Inn, Marcus was up to date with what had unfolded for Jessica and the three staff members who protected her. Within half an hour, the four were on the way back to Queensbury Mews. No sooner had they alighted than the carriage returned for the first load of Jessica's possessions.

Marcus had not had a chance to warn his own staff about their arrival, but he knew they would cope. Marcus sent Jessica's staff to await him in the sitting room and called Mrs Busselton, and filled her in before they joined those waiting. Soon, everyone was up to date. When he told them what he had done when visiting Egbert, all were initially aghast.

Felicity giggled. "Oh sir, Mr Elkin would not have liked that. You really presumed a longstanding friendship with Sir Lucien?" she chuckled. The man in front of her certainly was one to be trusted. "How did he cope with the news that he was to forfeit all of her clothing and Miss Judith's possessions?"

Marcus smiled at the housekeeper. They had been stunned to find Marcus had met Lucien through business. She had summed up the situation well. "I didn't meet Mrs Elkin, but if the husband's clothing was anything to go by, I could not imagine his wife wearing anything tasteful. If Lady Elkin's mourning gown was anything to go by, I imagine her wardrobe is the essence of good taste."

"*Oui, monsieur,*" Jaques said proudly. He rarely spoke French, as none of the other staff understood him. Marcus had already had a few words to him in his native tongue. Jacque continued. "I am proud to say her ladyship made her clothing, um, noticeable. Many turned and gazed at her attire, as well as her beauty. She is *exquise, monsieur*. Perfect in every way." Jaques kissed his fingertips; he was proud to have been her dresser, as well as Lucien's. Jaques had already noticed the light that came into the new man's eyes when discussing his mistress. He liked him and could see why Mrs Jess trusted him.

Mrs Busselton had noticed the dramatic difference in her master. From a totally business-centred man, he changed from the moment he had brought Mrs Jessica home. She sat subtly observing his now animated countenance.

Marcus knew his housekeeper was surprised at how the day had unfolded, but he also realised she understood. He smiled at her visual interrogation, Marcus said, "I will go and get Jeffrey; he's my secretary. I won't be a moment."

Marcus left the four staff members alone, and Edwina Busselton took Felicity aside and had her fill in a little about her ladyship. The two ladies decided to become friends; both were willing to do what they could for their employers' happiness. Each acknowledged that there was some attraction between the two persons they adored.

Edwina Busselton said to Felicity, "What the next weeks will bring was in the good Lord's hands." She hoped Mr Marcus would not have to go to the colony to save her, but Felicity had already promised her new friend that the three of them had already agreed to accompany him should the need arise. Edwina knew that if Mr Marcus went to the Antipodes, his tiger, Giles, and valet, Colin, would not be far behind him. His party onboard would be six persons, even before he had plans to go.

That afternoon, Marcus, Rex, and Felicity made the trip to the local lock-up, only to find that Jessica had already been transferred to Newgate Prison in London.

Marcus was distraught. He had never been so close to weeping. He was determined to return to London and see her as soon as possible. On arriving home, he walked the three blocks to his sister's home and filled them in on the week's happening. He took his farewells and hugged his mother, sister, and new niece, promising that he would write.

On his arrival home, Rex was the one to soothe him. "Sir, even if you were to find her, you would not see her as you have no relationship with her. Mrs Matthews would be allowed in, as she is a friend as well as a servant. Sir, therefore, if we do go to London, she will have to come." Rex had always had a soft spot for the comely lady he had worked so closely with for many years. However, being servants, they had not thought about marriage. He was aware of Felicity's eyes on him often while working in the same room. Over the loss of their master and Miss Judith, their friendship had developed to be a little freer with each other. When the child had died, he took Felicity into his arms, allowing her to weep on his shoulder. He adored the little girl, and they mourned her loss together. Then the master passed away too; she had been there for him. Rex had been standing in the butler's room, numb at his loss. She had entered without knocking, and they embraced. Rex also knew that if ma'am was to be saved, this man and Felicity were her only chance. He would be with them as closely as possible.

~

Before they left Brighton, Marcus had one request to make of Rex and Felicity. He took them aside just before they departed to Crawley and said, "Having travelled to New South Wales before, I know of a shortage of women. Mrs Matthews, I presume, is a courtesy title?

Felicity nodded, she had never been married, but it was common for a housekeeper to adopt the honorific title of Mrs.

Marcus saw the nod, so he continued, "If you were to be married, you would be safe once we arrive in the colony." He left the rest unsaid but looked at Rex with an eyebrow raised. He had seen the closeness of the two retainers. Not that they were that old. Both were probably in their early forties if that.

"Could we, sir? Really? We never thought that we would be allowed to marry." Rex was delighted. He reached out and took Felicity's hand. "Flick, what do you think?"

"I think it's a grand idea, Rexy." Her fingers tightened on his confirming his question.

Marcus saw that the smile on their faces was genuine. "Good! I am not aristocratic, so I prefer my staff to be happy rather than conform to society's archaic rules. The archbishop has just arrived in town, and I know his family. I can get you a special licence, and you can marry before you go to Crawley. From there, go directly to my apartment in London, where we shall be awaiting you."

Twenty-four hours later, Mr and Mrs Harris were pronounced man and wife, and they left on a rather unusual honeymoon. They headed to Crawley to collect luggage and their own possessions from the Elizabethan Manor House where they had recently lived. They also packed up all the personal possessions of both Jessica and Judith. It took longer than expected as much of the clothing had been distributed to the new staff, and Felicity was determined to get as much back as possible. They arrived in London on June 17th.

By the time the contents of Judith and Jessica's wardrobes had arrived from Crawley, it was mid-June. Judith's clothes were stored at Marcus's house, and Jessica's were packed in six ornate travelling cases. The group had made arrangements to stay in Marcus's London apartments. Marcus would arrive first and take the first of Jessica's clothes from their Brighton home with him. Felicity and Rex would follow with the remainder of the personal possessions. Felicity also wished to collect some of Miss Judith's things for her mistress; keepsakes, toys, etc.

Marcus had been in town for a few days and searched for Jessica Elkin only to find she was not listed on any prison or passenger records. He presumed that she would have been arrested under the name of Elkin, but there was no record of any person by that name. Jaques was as blindsided as he was.

It was only when Felicity arrived that he uncovered the story. She mentioned that Mr Elkin had refused to have his name muddied by a family conviction and insisted that she be arrested under her maiden name. Jessica was therefore charged as Jess Bates.

When Marcus heard this, he let out a howl of anguish. He had seen that name three times. Once in prison, once on the hulks list and then again on the passenger list of convicts to be transported on the *Mary*. It had sailed to New South Wales only ten days ago. He had missed her. To himself, he said, "Oh, my love, I am so sorry!"

Felicity turned to her new husband with tears in her eyes. Her lovely mistress was incarcerated with foul-smelling convicts and goodness knows what else. She straightened and said, "Rexy, it looks like we're heading to the Antipodes after all."

Chapter 5   Chasing the Wind

It took Marcus the best part of a month to find another suitable ship that was departing London for Sydney Cove. They had missed two other convict ships that had set sail earlier, as none had spare cabins. However, in that time, he had to arrange for his secretary, Jeffrey, to take over his business affairs for goodness knows how long. He did most of the work for the board anyway, but persuading the chairman that Jeffrey had his complete confidence and had the authority to make final decisions in his absence, took some persuading. It was only when he pointed out that the idea had initially been his anyway that the crusty old gentleman relented.

Marcus only dropped the bombshell that he could be gone for five or more years. Eventually, they reached an agreement. "Cyril, Mother, will be here too, but she's with my sister and their new daughter in Brighton, so I don't expect her to be in town much. Jeffrey will be your go-to man."

Cyril Hargenhour, his chairman, was extremely good at his job and employing him had been one of Marcus's best business decisions, but Cyril annoyed him frequently. They had clashed often over the years, but Marcus was the boss, and Cyril knew it. Jeffrey was duly signed in as Power-of-Attorney in Marcus's absence.

Marcus had known Jeffrey all his life. They had met at school at Christ's Hospital. Jeffrey had been there at his father's request, but as he said, "I'm a base-born son of an Earl. What do you think life will allow me to do? Being your secretary will do me nicely, Marc. Also, I know your work and will have a roof over my head for life. What more could I ask?"

Marcus was the son of a wealthy business owner and employed Jeffrey as soon as they had left school. His trust in his friend was absolute, as they worked closely in all aspects of the business. Much of its success was due to Jeffrey's suggestions.

Marcus finally was able to get berths on a dubious-looking ship. *The Jupiter* was not the most seaworthy vessel, but it was heading in the right direction and at the right time. The sailing date was July 2nd. The ship was a merchant vessel carrying some passengers, most of whom were wives travelling to join their husbands, and cargo for the colony. Marcus had eventually sought out a merchant vessel rather than a convict transport. Having travelled on such a horrendous craft before, he knew the abhorrent stench from below decks. He also did not wish for daily reminders of what Jessica was enduring. All he could do for her now was pray she was kept safe. He had no idea how God would do that, but that was not his job. He asked, and God answered. It had happened too often for it to be a coincidence. He now called them God-incidents.

As the now-laden merchant craft finally left the pier in London, the ebbing tide carried the ship slowly down the Thames River. There was little wind, and the trip downstream to the sea could take up to a week, depending on how many crafts wished to leave the overcrowded river. All vessels must go with the flow, travelling only as fast as the tides would take them. When the tide changed, all must anchor out of the channel, and the flood tide would take in the next round of watercraft.

On his first trip years ago, a sailor had explained the system to Marcus. He now imparted this knowledge to his travelling companions. There was a twenty-four-foot tide differential, and the ebb tide would take from six to nine hours before they needed to anchor. The flood tide was much faster, so all craft were required to be well out of the way of the incoming vessels as this tide created a swift current and occasional side eddies. The flood tide only took about five hours. It was the six hours being stationary that rankled with Marcus. He wished to be on the way. He had often done this part of the trip, and it never changed. However, this trip, he wished it were over already, and he wasn't even one day onboard. The only good thing about the first stop was that it gave the passengers time to settle into their cabins and unpack.

Rex and Felicity were still adjusting to their newly married status. She discovered that Rex snored when he lay on his back. This normally didn't worry her too much as she just pushed him over, but the bed in the cabin was smaller than at Mr Marcus's house and a few times, she'd given up turning him and gone to sleep on the settee in the adjoining dressing room with the door closed.

Knowing their expedited marriage, Mr Marcus had kindly booked them a cabin with a small side dressing room. Felicity still didn't like undressing in front of her husband, but what marriage entailed had taken her breath away, and she discovered a new depth to the enjoyment of marital bliss.

Rex was a kind and loving husband whom she adored. She had done for some time, but both had thought that mutual friendship was all they would ever be permitted to have. She would not countenance any other illicit liaison, so it was marriage or nothing, and she had been resigned to the nothing, as had Rex. On the third night on the river, they retired to their cabin soon after dinner. A misty rain had set in, and although it was summer, it was too miserable to sit out on the deck.

As Rex opened the door for her, she saw a glint in his eyes. "Now, Mrs Harris, I wonder how we can occupy our time? Do you have any suggestions?" As he was in the process of shedding his clothing, she giggled.

"I have a suggestion or two, as I'm not in the least tired." She was trying hard not to smile as he was now only wearing his drawers. He was approaching her with a silly smile on his face knowing the next hour would be thoroughly enjoyable, for she didn't try to stop him from catching her. Felicity knew the cabin walls were not well insulated from sound and tried hard not to laugh too loudly; however, she thoroughly enjoyed being inducted into the joys of married life.

Marcus was, unfortunately, in the next-door cabin to the honeymooners. He could frequently hear their mirth and amorous chuckles. He groaned to himself, wishing that time could move faster than it did. He wanted to get to Jessica. He wanted to hold her in his arms again but, this time, pour out to her his deepest feelings. They were only three days into a many month-long trip via the Cape of Good Hope, then via Van Diemen's Land, to Sydney Cove. They had about five months ahead of them, and being next to a newly married couple enjoying themselves would be hard. He decided that he would have to have a quiet word with Rex about keeping the noise down. Their conversation could also be heard in the passageway by all who passed by.

Marcus donned his sealskin overcoat and went to stand in the rain for an hour or so. He needed to cool his ardour, and that should do the trick. Never before had he experienced these deep desires that he had for Jessica. He had no right even to know her name, let alone use it. He had seen her exquisite figure through the gossamer-thin night rail she had worn. Her figure was perfect, considering she had born a child. Her figure had returned to a minute waist. He understood the words in the Song of Solomon in chapter seven, as he had never done before. *How beautiful you are and how pleasing, O love, with your delights! Your stature is like that of the palm, and your breasts like clusters of fruit, and your mouth like the best wine.* When Marcus thought about Jessica's mouth and what her lips were like when she spoke, he groaned with lust for her. "I must not lust; I must control my thoughts. She will not want me even to touch her when I do see her. I am but a stranger who helped her." Marcus walked to the ship's bow and stood at the ropes thinking of his love and what she was enduring. He had never believed in love at first sight until he met Jessica.

He enjoyed the misty rain, knowing how vastly different the weather was in the colony. The searing heat and flooding rain were different from the quiet green softness of England. He had liked the rawness of the Australian country; he was hoping to see more of the sheep in the colony and see what improvements they had made in the ten years since he had first seen the wool clip from Sydney Cove. He had diversified the business from the tea his father had started to now exclusively importing wool. To think he had sold that branch to Lucien was another God-incident. The wool trade was a lucrative business idea and pulled in more money than he ever dreamed. He had bought one defunct factory, refurbished it and was in the process of building another. The thing he liked about the colony was that a man was not tied to his class. It was almost a classless society with those born free and the convicts. He had not been to Van Diemen's Land before and was interested in seeing if sheep could do well there too. He had heard it was much more like England. He had been thinking about investing in a large plot of land and installing a manager. With these thoughts running through his mind, his body was quietening. He didn't hear the footsteps drawing near until he heard a voice.

"Good evening, sir; making the most of the stillness?" Marcus turned and saw it was the captain who was now standing beside him.

Marcus was not really in the mood for chatting but knowing that a return to his cabin would not be possible for at least half an hour, he decided to get to know Master Jonathan Park, the captain. "I suppose you could say I am. I have done this trip a few times over the past decade. The softness of this rain is not what they have in New South Wales; it is violent and flooding. I love the rawness of that country and the softness of this one. Each with its own beauty and loveliness." Marcus looked at the slowly fading lights of the onshore lights. Soon the darkness would encompass them. If a fog fell, they would not move at night. That would be another day lost.

The captain looked into the gloom at the land. "I love the sea, sir, but as you say, you land-lubbers see beauty in the most everyday things. I love the wildness of the oceans and seas. I love the tempest that throws us around like a bobbing cork. I love the blackness of the night skies and the magic of the sea lights. Have you seen those, sir?"

Marcus had seen only glimpses of the fabulous sea fireworks on previous voyages. One day he wished to show Jessica. His thoughts once again turned to his beloved. These words ran through his mind, "One day, my love! One day I shall show you the most beautiful sights in Christendom." He groaned with agony at the thought of missing her by a mere whisker.

The captain saw a wave of sadness cross Marcus's face. "Sir, are you in pain?"

A false smile hovered now on Marcus's lips. "Only of the heart, Master Park, I seek a lost love." The half-smile he gave the man beside him was not a real answer. Marcus gave a deep sigh. "As we are on board for the next five months or so, it will be nice to have a friend to listen to my woes." Marcus glanced at the man, now standing in the glow of the riding lamps above them. He expected to see the exasperation on his face, but instead, he saw compassion.

"Before you continue, I, too, could use a friendly ear. It is often lonely at the helm, and I can't make friends with the crew I am in charge of, so please call me Jon. But continue…" Captain Jonathan Park often bemoaned that the one drawback of his job was a severe lack of true friends. For some reason, he felt that he could talk to this man.

Marcus nodded; he intended to say little but found himself pouring out the entire saga of the past month. "I have discovered that a lot can happen in a very little time. Two months ago, I was a money-obsessed businessman who thought of little else other than profit. Then in May, I hit a woman while she was crossing the road. She was wearing black, and Jon, I didn't see her. Honestly! The long and the short of it is she was on her way back from burying her husband and daughter after they died from eating mushrooms, which by the way, I shall never eat again." Marcus still found that so tragic.

After a moment, he continued. "In the space of two days, while nursing her back to health, I fell deeply and irrevocably in love. It would have ended happily if the story had finished there, but it didn't. When she awoke, she returned home to find herself cast out by the new owners. All her possessions were confiscated, and then to add insult to injury, when she did get a carpetbag of clothing back, this same popinjay accused her of stealing her husband's Bible. As it was a leather-bound volume and worth a pretty penny, she was charged with theft and has now been transported." Marcus was astounded to find his eyes watering. He rested his head on the stay holding up the mast.

Jon looked at his new friend with understanding. "So, you go to seek her? Do you know which ship she was on?"

Marcus nodded. "I am, and I do. She travelled on the *Mary III*. It only left a few weeks before us. But to think of my beautiful Jessica in with the rabble and loose women from the slums and docklands, I am horrified."

Jon's next question astounded Marcus. "Do you believe in God? Not the little man-sized deity, but the real God who sees all and is in all? The being who many blame for all wrongs."

"I do, Jon. Why?" Marcus's attention was now pulled from his own thoughts.

Jon put a caring hand on Marcus's arm before saying, "On board that said convict ship is one Doctor Harmon Cochrane. He's a godly man who truly cares. If any doctor will keep her well, it's him, and Captain JT Steel is also well known to me as a kindly gentleman.

As convict ship captains go, he's one of the best. He's kind and considerate to his, um, passengers and often, if not usually, allowed them to roam freely on deck. On many other ships, the felons are locked below decks for weeks on end, not so on the *Mary*." Jon paused to make sure Marcus was listening.

Marcus merely acknowledged he was by saying, "Go on."

Jon gave a nod before continuing. "As I said, God is in control. One special person came and visited the *Mary* before she departed. Have you heard about the amazing woman Elizabeth Fry? She is a Quaker lady, but her heart and compassion for the felons astounded me. She visits each female prisoner and gives them a parting gift, clothing, fabric, haberdashery and such. I do not know how often she had done this before, but I happened to be heading for my ship, and the lady and I were waiting on the jetty together. She was on the way to another ship that was waiting in the river to sail. The *Mary* had been anchored for months and was awaiting a final load of convicts. They had just embarked when she went aboard. Marcus, I shall repeat the words she said to me. I memorised them as I was impressed. She said, *I lately have had a deeply interesting visit to a female convict ship, surrounded as I am at such times by poor sailors and convicts, it is impossible not to feel the contrast of the circumstances in which I am placed. The last time I was on the ship* Mary, *there was such a scene around me - parting from them, probably forever. So many tears were shed, so much feeling displayed - and almost all present the low and the poor. Then, within a few days, I was in such a scene of gaiety, though the object in view was good, surrounded by royalty and the great of this earth. The contrast was striking and instructive. I ought surely to profit from the uncommon variety that I see and the wonderful changes that I have experienced in being raised up and cast down. Oh! May it not prove in vain for myself and others.*"

Jon heard Marcus gasp.

Continuing, Jon said, "Marcus, Mrs Fry's compassion was so profound that it has really made me think deeply about how we treat these convicts. For your lady love to be on that particular ship is a blessing. Harmon will do his best to see that they all arrive in good health. Mrs Fry obviously saw her as she added the words *almost all* to her assessment of the convicts. If Jessica stood out amongst the rabble to Mrs Fry, then Harmon will surely seek her out and bring her above decks to act as a servant to the ill passenger I know he has on board. It's his way of helping. If your Jess is lucky, she will be assigned to serve one of them. I know he was already dealing with a lady with a toothache. Two or three others onboard were also ill, and mayhap she will be assigned to Mrs Rapsey."

Marcus had such a lump in his throat that he could only nod. Eventually, he managed to say, "All I can do for her is pray."

Jon said, glancing at Marcus's face, "Sometimes that is all that is needed."

Marcus thought he might as well tell the captain who his travelling companions were. "I am travelling with three of her staff. Two, her housekeeper and butler, are newlywed and… and well, it's why I'm out here; the walls are quite thin."

"Bulkheads, Marc," Jon chuckled. "We have to get the terminology correctly used. The ship's floors are called decks, the walls are called bulkheads, and the stairs are called ladders. The kitchen is called a galley, rooms are cabins, and the dining room is the mess and food is cooked in the galley." Jon's laugh and explanation made Marcus relax.

"Well, your blasted bulkheads are damned thin!" Again, Marcus gave his new friend a shy smile. "The third person travelling with me was her husband's valet. He's French. He would have come by himself if I had not brought him. All three were dismissed for aiding her in her time of need. Jaques LeBeau was rescued from a French battlefield as an adolescent. He has been with his master for nearly a decade and would do anything for his mistress; such is his adoration for the family. I could not have stopped them coming even if I had not wished to bring them." He sighed. "They will be good company anyway. They all get along well and have opened my eyes to many things already that I have never noticed before. And I have discovered that all also have a strong faith."

Jon smiled. He could see the compassion in this man. He would also see if there was a spare cabin into which he could move.

Marcus knew that worrying about Jess did not help. "I have handed her into God's care, Jon; I can't do anything else. I know worry won't help her or me and that He knows best, but Jon, it's so hard to let her go."

They stood in silence for some time. The misty rain felt like oil being poured on troubled water.

Jon's following words summed that up exactly. "Release her to God, Marc. Imagine her in the cabin with the female passenger that Harmon said had a toothache. Let's imagine that she was the convict chosen for this role. Let's release her now."

Marcus knew this was what he had to do. "Okay, I know I won't even find her without His help." Marcus pointed to the heavens.

Standing shoulder to shoulder at the bow, the two men bowed their heads and released Jessica into God's care. They noticed that most of the foreshore was in complete darkness when they finished praying.

Marcus pulled out his fob watch and checked the time. It was close to midnight. He was astounded to see that they talked for over two hours. The prayer time had, however, given him some peace.

With a little more conversation, the captain also checked his watch. "I'm on middle watch soon, Marc, so I have to leave you. Don't hesitate to seek me out if you need a chat. Tomorrow night will be my time to unload. It's only about loneliness, so nothing too heavy! But I really could do with a friend, just that, no more."

Jon again placed a caring hand on his new friend's arm. How many times in his career had the first few days of a trip started with the befriending of a saddened passenger? This time, however, he felt it would be more enjoyable. The story Marcus had told him was not one he had come across before. This man hardly knew the woman but was prepared to sail across the world to try to rescue her. Only God could put such a strong feeling in a man's heart. Jon retired to the helm with a smile on his face and took over his watch, leaving Marcus standing at the bow. As they were stationary, there would be little to do until the tide changed. He would be able to get some sleep after they anchored at the next flood tide.

Marcus stayed only for a few minutes more before returning to his cabin. Hopefully, Felicity and Rex would be asleep by now. Rex's snoring was not nearly as disturbing. With another sigh, he decided to sleep while he could. Within minutes, he crawled into the crisp, clean sheets and settled for the night.

Marcus was woken by the sounds of the anchor being drawn up. It was before dawn, but he could see a dim light coming in the porthole. As he lay in his bunk, he felt the ship get underway. He didn't move, as he didn't have to get up. Colin would bring him tea and toast as usual when it was ready. He did not know how long that luxury would last, but while they were in the smooth waters of the Thames River, he would make the most of that bit of pandering.

He lay with his arms behind his head; his thoughts turned again to Jessica. She would be eating porridge or gruel if she was lucky. Hopefully, she will be allocated the position of looking after Mrs Rapsey. He wondered if Jessica knew how to nurse anyone or if she had always left everything to her servants. He would ask her staff and attempt to get to know her in absentia. At least he had access to them for information; he could learn much about Jessica until he found her, and find her he certainly would.

Chapter 6   Mary, Mary, Not So Scary

*J*essica could not believe that her wanting Lucien's Bible led her to Newgate prison. The week she spent in the gaol hoping and praying that someone would visit her only increased her fear. Eventually, a lady called Elizabeth Fry came for a visit. She brought each of the convicts a care parcel. These parcels contained clothing and activities too, fabrics, needles and thread, and the like. As Jessica was skilled with the needle, this was a delight. Having some sewing to do too while away her time was a blessing.

Her incarceration in Newgate was for less than a week, and the cells had been virtually empty. From there, she was taken directly on board the transportation vessel as it neared sailing time. She realised that a bucket of water was brought into the hold for washing purposes each morning. She was one of a few who knew how to clean herself and took the opportunity every chance she found. The food was far better than she expected, but it was still just slops, gruel or porridge, but it was both tasty and filling, though she found herself craving a roast beef with delicious baked vegetables. Releasing a deep sigh, Jess realised that the week she had been in Newgate was short compared to some girls. Some had been there for weeks before being sent to hulks in the river. After sometimes years there, they finally transferred them onto this ship. For her to have been moved out of gaol and onboard a boat in the Thames River was a great surprise. Less than a week later, that same ship had weighed anchor and got underway.

Once they were moving and before they had reached the sea, the doctor had come and asked her to pack her things and follow him. He had noticed how clean she kept herself, and he had chosen her to be assigned to one of the passengers.

Jess hastily grabbed all her possessions and followed the doctor. When out of earshot of the rabble below, he said, "I've been watching you. You keep yourself clean and as tidy as you can. Are you prepared to care for an ill lady with a child? It's more to watch the small child for the mother."

"No, sir, I am not."

As soon as Jess spoke, the doctor swung around and looked intently at her. "Who are you? You are certainly no guttersnipe."

She retold her story to his sympathetic ear. She didn't mention her real name or title, but enough to give him a gist of her life.

"Ma'am, I shall do what I can for you while you are on board. You are certainly going to be in the small cabin upstairs now. I will need you to scrub and if you have a cleaner gown put that on, then join me in the sick bay." He opened the door to a tiny room, but it was clean and hers.

She could sleep in peace and unmolested. Captain Steel had been strict on the sailors not being allowed below decks for liaisons, but some street women had found ways to encourage their attention for extra rations. She turned to thank the kind doctor and saw him turn into a door just down the passageway. Lifting her eyes and giving thanks to the Lord for watching over her, Jess put her carpetbag on the bunk and dug into it to find a clean gown. Felicity had packed a selection of dresses, all of which were far too glamorous for prison. She pulled out a sprigged muslin gown, its matching shoes and a shawl and lay them on her new narrow bunk. She poured some water into the basin and had a complete wash. As much as she tried to keep herself clean below decks, she was horrified that the water had taken a murky brown hue. She quickly brushed her curls with a wide-tooth comb and tied her hair up in a quick bun. The result was a very exotic bunch of dark curls that sat in a cluster on the top of her head. Now clean and in her own clothing again, she was ready for whatever was in front of her. Taking a deep breath, she went to find the doctor.

She knocked and then entered at his command.

The doctor looked surprised when he saw a stunningly beautiful woman enter the sick bay. It took him a few moments to realise this was the convict woman. She had taken off the severe black gown and looked as fresh as spring. "Oh yes, you'll do nicely," he said admiringly with a huge grin.

Mrs Rapsey was in a bad way. Initially, Jessica thought that she had the same disease that Lucien had years before. Her face was severely swollen, and it was red down to her throat. "It's just a toothache, and I think I may have to pull the tooth, but she's fighting me. I've been treating her for a month already; maybe with your help, she will see some sense." The doctor introduced the two women. He didn't tell Mrs Rapsey who Jess was; she could discover that for herself later.

Charlotte took a look at the lady entering her cabin hard on the doctor's heels. She looked fresh as a daisy and even happy. Meanwhile, she groaned in pain. Her face hurt, her head was swimming, and she was miserable.

Jess took one look at the poor lady, and her compassion for her pain instantly overtook her. Without waiting for the doctor's introduction, she went straight to the poor lady's side.

"Hello, ma'am, my name is Jess Bates; I'm also a passenger, and our learned friend here has mentioned that you are poorly. I can see that you have a bad tooth. Thankfully that is easily fixed. If it were mumps like my husband had or some other disease, I might not be able to assist with that, but a tooth we can easily dispose of." Jess's eyes had never left the lady's face. She fully intended to let the lady know her actual status later, but for now, the rotting tooth must be removed before the abscess broke.

"I'm scared, Mrs Bates. I know it will hurt." Charlotte was weeping.

"Of course, it will hurt for a while, but the tooth should come out easily because of the swelling. If you don't, it can kill you. The doctor said you have a child, so you must think of it." Jess had no idea if what she said was true or not, but she sounded as though she knew what she was saying.

Charlotte tried to smile but grimaced instead. "Oh, okay, doctor, do your worst, sir. Remove the offending item." She flopped back on her pillows, resigned to her fate. The pain of the tooth was debilitating as it was. This new lady's presence gave her confidence.

"Will you stay with me?" she mumbled as she held out her hand.

Jess, meanwhile, was nervous. She, too, hated the idea of a firmly embedded tooth being extracted. Lucien had to have one removed, but she was there when the doctor pulled it, and there was a sack of puss hanging from the bottom of the offending appendage. Hopefully, this lady would be as lucky.

An hour later, the lady was lying on her bed with hot towels held to her cheek. The tooth had been removed, and the sack had not broken. All she had to do now was recover. Jess promised to stay near her and help in any way she could. As they were still in the river, Jess asked if they could bring some fresh milk, eggs and soft foods for her patient. She spoke to the cook, and soon Charlotte was enjoying a bowl of syllabub. Jess also had a bowl of junket setting in the galley cool room, and she could have scrambled eggs for supper. For now, her patient was asleep. She sat guarding her and nursing the sleeping child. She was relaxing and praising God for her release from below deck. She would do everything she could to stay in her tiny cabin. She was determined to confess her actual position on board as soon as the lady roused.

Within days Charlotte was sitting up in bed and feeling much better. She watched Jess tidy the cabin and fluff up her pillows, making her more comfortable. Charlotte was intrigued by this woman who had attended to her in her hour of need. Where had the doctor found her? Surely another passenger would not spend so much time looking after another. "You're a convict, aren't you?" Charlotte blurted out.

Without embarrassment, Jess turned to her patient. "Yes, ma'am. Dr Cochrane has asked me if I could assist you. I nursed both my husband and daughter, so am *eu fait* with nursing. Are you happy for me to stay with you?" Jess had stopped flitting and gave the lady her total attendance. The next moments would define her trip.

Charlotte gazed at the beautiful woman. She was currently in a blue gown that added a lovely splash of colour to the starkness of the timber-lined cabin. "Stay with me? As if I'd let you go. You are an angel in disguise. Would you tell me your story, for I can see you are not an ordinary convict? Well, at least, not like the rest of the rabble below." She patted the side of her bed, and Jess sat and poured out her story.

Marcus didn't get a mention, other than Jess referring to him as a rescuer. Jess wept when she talked about the death of Judith and Lucien. She could not believe that all this had occurred within the last month.

Charlotte was *en route* to her husband, who had gone to the colony the year before. She was stunned when she heard of Jess's crime. "You stole a Bible? Really? Do you believe in all that stuff?"

Jess's interest in her questions' ridiculing nature piqued her interest. "I do, ma'am; absolutely I do. Lucien and I would read from our Bible each day then study and discuss it often. We read it together every night and often had a book of maps at hand to see where the stories were set. I miss being able to do this. Below decks, there was no light, so even if I had had it with me, I could not have read it." She glanced at Charlotte's face before adding, "I miss it, ma'am."

Charlotte was astounded; she had been dragged to church by her grandmother after her parents died. Church was not something she had really considered to be true or essential. Her husband Peter was a soldier and had stolen her heart. Their whirlwind romance and marriage occurred shortly before he sailed away for the first time. He had returned after a time of service, and they had two years together before he was sent to New South Wales. "I'm not up too much discussion now, but as we have months together, I foresee many interesting discussions ahead, Jess." Charlotte saw her smile and gave a slight nod. "Jess, will you call me Charlotte? I wish to be friends. Yes, yes, I know, it's not usual, but I am not usual either."

Jess was astounded. "Really, ma'am, I mean Charlotte? You don't mind my status?"

Charlotte shook her head. She was beginning to feel tired. "Truly, Jess, but I wish to sleep now. We'll chat later."

Jess settled her new friend down for a nap. The following months onboard looked rosy. The tiny baby was a delight and very different from Judith, and looking after him did not hurt as much as it could have done.

Charlotte was asleep quickly, and Jess thought she'd report to the doctor about her condition. Exiting the cabin, she bumped into the captain.

"Ma'am," he said with a bow as he was about to walk past her. He spun around and said, "You're not a passenger; who are you? A stowaway?" He walked back and stood a little too close to her.

Jess stood her ground and confidently replied, "No sir, I

mean captain. I am not a passenger but a convict assigned by Doctor Cochrane to care for Mrs Rapsey. She has been poorly and needed assistance. The doctor retrieved me from below decks and told me to clean myself up. Thankfully, I had not been incarcerated too long and had managed to keep my possessions with me." She waved a hand over her gown, showing that it was her own. "The doctor has allocated me a dressing-room cabin just down the passageway from Mrs Rapsey. I have been with her for the last three days, sir."

"Hmm, well, you don't look like a convict, and if I may say, you don't sound like one either." He looked her up and down. "Where were you heading?"

"To the sick bay, sir; I was just going to report to the doctor," Jess said. She realised she should have bobbed a curtsey but had forgotten. Normally, they would have curtseyed to her.

"Follow me." The captain led her to the doctor and ushered her into the well-stocked room.

Doctor Cochrane greeted the captain and then Jess. "Morning, Captain, Mrs Bates." He gave a nod of acknowledgement to both. He was busy sewing up a cut on a sailor's leg.

The two new arrivals waited until he was finished. He doused the wound with brandy and bandaged the wound. "Stay off it as much as you can, and no climbing the rigging until the stitches come out. Come back in a week unless it starts paining you." The seaman hurriedly left the room. He knew the drill; the doctor was making sure the captain knew he was to be on light duties and that he wasn't shirking his responsibilities.

Once he washed his hands, the doctor turned to the captain, "Now, Captain, I see you have met Mrs Bates. She has done wonders in assisting me with your passenger Mrs Rapsey. That lady fought me for a month to have her tooth pulled, and Mrs Bates achieved it in less than a day." The doctor was drying his hands thoroughly. "You did tell me to choose a servant for the passengers; this is the one I chose for Mrs Rapsey."

Jess didn't realise she was holding her breath, awaiting the outcome of this conversation.

The captain turned and looked at her; she was better dressed than any of the passengers. "Don't look so apprehensive, my dear, you will be staying, but to waylay suspicion of your status, you can have the servant's cabin next door to Mrs Rapsey." He paused, considering his following words. "I trust that whatever your crime, it was minor and that you will behave?"

Jess released her breath; she was safe. "Sir, I was charged with theft. I admitted my so-called guilt as all I took was my husband, Lucien's Bible after he died. His cousin charged me with stealing his property, and because it was a leather-bound, gilt-edged one and worth more than a few shillings, I have been transported." She lifted her head a little as she spoke.

Captain Steel could see she was telling the truth from how she spoke, but he would check her story with the convict log in his cabin. Somehow, he didn't think her real name was Bates and challenged her. "What name were you convicted under? I gather it is not your real one."

Again, her well-modulated voice answered his questions without hesitation. "It was, sir, as Bates was my maiden name, I am widowed, but my husband's cousin refused to allow his name to be tainted with a conviction. He insisted that the name of Elkin be reverted to my maiden name."

At the mention of the name Elkin the Captain's head jerked up. "Elkin, you are Lucien's wife? He's dead?" The captain sat down quickly.

Jess looked puzzled. "I was, sir, and he is. He and our daughter died within a day of each other at the end of May. I was tried in the Sussex courts, then taken to London, and transported within two weeks. Did you know my husband, sir?"

The captain nodded. "Luc and I served together at Waterloo. When I sold out, I am the captain who carried his tea from the East. He's truly dead?"

The doctor ushered Jess to a seat and perched himself on the hospital bed. He wouldn't miss this revelation for the world.

Jess had teared up, so she answered the captain's question with a nod. After a sniff, she said, "I'm still in shock myself, sir."

The captain sat thinking for a while. He was obviously digesting the situation. "Convicted for stealing Luc's Bible, eh? I teased him mercilessly about believing in that until he took the time to explain his faith. It was as though the scales had fallen off my eyes. I've not been able to do enough for him since. For each trip I made, I asked if he had any stock needing transportation. I carried tea for another merchant until he turned to wool." The captain smiled at the memory of Luc's friendship. "You know, Harmon here was the same, scoffing at his faith. We have been working together to ease the conditions of the convicts ever since. Once we are out of the river, the convicts will be given free access to the lower deck when they wish. The hatches will not be locked, and the ladies will be treated with dignity, at least as much as we can. They will still be under guard, but the passage should be reasonable for them. You, however, will be moved into not the servants' cabin but a passenger cabin. I gather Mrs Rapsey knows your status?" She was about to reply when he added that he knew Luc was knighted after Waterloo. He said, "So you're really Lady Elkin?"

Jess smiled and then nodded. "I told her, sir, well, not the title bit. She laughed when I told her why I was convicted." Jess smiled; she looked forward to more conversations with her. Mayhap, these two men could assist with that project; the captain's words just hit home. Turning to the doctor, she asked, "You knew Lucien too? How?"

The doctor nodded. "I was a field medic at Waterloo. Luc and JT would bring in their wounded and expect blooming miracles. One was a little French boy Luc found. He'd just witnessed his parents' murder at the hands of French soldiers, and then they burned his home. I can't remember his name, some froggy name."

Jess knew the story well. "His name is Jaques Le Beau. Lucien kept him close." Jess had prayed that she would be kept safe; these two friends of Lucien's would make sure that happened.

Chapter 7 Van Diemen's Land

*J*ess was standing at the captain's side as they turned into the mouth of the Derwent River. "JT, I shouldn't be here. I should be with Charlotte." Her friendship with her husband's two war compatriots had developed into an easy one. The three would often seek each other out and tell Jess war stories about Lucien; all three were grieving his loss. She couldn't talk much about Judith as her death was still far too raw to discuss. Jess would tear up and turn away from the men. They learnt to avoid the topic. If Jess wished to discuss her, they would leave it up to her to bring up in conversation.

Charlotte recovered from her toothache quickly, only to fall victim to *mal-de-mer*. Jess stayed by her side and nursed her until she finally got her sea legs. Jess escorted her up on deck and found a place out of the stiff breeze. It had taken nearly six weeks before this occurred, and they were heading down the West coast of Africa before she finally emerged from her cabin. At Jess's insistence, Charlotte dressed in a scarf rather than a bonnet and realised the benefit of this once outside. She also needed her fur overcoat as the wind was icy. "It's summer; why is it so cold?" she complained.

Jess had said much the same to JT earlier. He had replied, "It may be summer in England, but we're nearing the southern tip of Africa. Here the seasons are reversed, so it's mid-winter. You will have to get used to that in the colony."

Jess had added when repeating the information to Charlotte, "I believe that we are due to dock in Africa somewhere, and it will be frigid. I have been told you will need to rug up warmly."

Lucien had told her about a trip he had taken to India to seek tea, and his stop-over in Africa had been eye-opening. "Charlotte, my husband told me of this place, and he was horrified that they mistreat people. So, be warned that we will see some bad sights. We see black people as enslaved people at home, but this is one of the towns they come from. I don't know what to expect myself, but I'm not looking forward to it."

Their first sight was of a group of primarily naked black men waiting on the foreshore. The wind was frigid and bit hard into the well-clad ladies watching the onshore activities. These poor men must have been freezing. One slip of a boy was rubbing his arms to warm up when one of the older men walked to him and pulled him close. Jess knew the benefits of shared body warmth. A melancholy thought crossed her mind. Even after nearly three months, she still missed Lucien. Her bed was lonely and cold. Only when alone did she let her tears for her lost family fall.

Thankfully they did not stay long in that port. Charlotte refused to disembark without Jess, and Jess was not permitted to leave.

Both watched from on deck and saw the mistreatment of the near-naked men who were loading cargo and fresh food onboard. They sailed away from the foreign shore, pushed by a stiff breeze. The final but longest leg of the journey was yet ahead of them.

~

Jess was still not sure if she should thank God for her cook Maria tasting the food and getting sick, thus saving her, or blaming herself for wanting the picnic in the first place, thus leading to her family's demise. Sometimes she felt God was far away, yet she knew He wasn't. JT had loaned her a spare Bible from the ship's library, and she took comfort in reading a passage each night before bed, but she missed the discussion afterwards.

Harmon had seen her quandary over her survival, and they had discussed this often. It didn't ease her guilt.

~

As they came in sight of Van Diemen Land's main inlet, Jess had stood beside Charlotte, watching the wild and rugged shore draw near. The two had grown close in the months since sailing. Jess expressed her appreciation for Charlotte's friendship and acceptance, knowing her true lot in life as a convict.

Jess said, "Charlotte, I presume that I shall be rounded up and sent back with the ladies below decks once we reach the shore. I wish to say thank you for your extreme kindness."

Charlotte looked puzzled. "Jess, you're staying with me. Surely the captain told you?"

Jess was stunned. "How? Don't I have to be assigned along with the others?"

Charlotte chuckled. "You just have been, dear. You're coming to Sydney Cove with me. The captain and doctor spoke to the Major, and you have been assigned already." Charlotte was almost jumping for joy. "Jess, you will almost be a free person. I certainly won't be telling anyone about your status. I shall introduce you as my travelling companion," she giggled at the private joke. "Well, you have been, haven't you? You have taught me so much, and I have so much more to learn. Do you know, not one person has ever told me the Bible, and everything in it is actually true history?" Charlotte was still amazed at what Jess had told her about Jesus and his taking her sins upon Himself, and therefore she was washed clean of them. No, she would fight tooth and nail to make sure Jess stayed with her for as long as possible. She gave her friend a sly glance. "Jess, the only problem may be that Peter may already have staff, but I'm sure we will work something out. But Jess, know this; you will only leave my side if I'm sure you will be better off."

Jess was unable to see the land through her tears of joy.

Charlotte saw and enfolded her in her arms. "Did you think I would forget you?" she asked.

She felt Jess nod against her shoulder. "I dared not presume, Charlotte. I'm a confessed criminal," Jess said in a soft voice. Others were standing nearby, and she didn't want them to hear.

Neither heard approaching footsteps. "Hello, ladies, enjoying the view?" Harmon saw Jess's distress and came to offer his assistance. Jess pulled away from Charlotte's arms as he spoke, and she mopped her tears. Unsure of what he'd asked, she nodded anyway.

Early in the voyage, they had agreed that Jess would continue to use the name of Bates. Charlotte had still not discovered the secret of her title, and Jess hoped that no one would. Harmon and JT were wonderful. Protecting her from a distance but seeking her out in private when they knew others were occupied elsewhere. Often the doctor would ask for her assistance in the sick-bay. There the three would sit and discuss Lucien and drink tea. Both men admired Jess for how she coped with what life had thrown at her.

The doctor looked at the tears in Jess's eyes. "Mrs Bates, are you not well?"

Charlotte answered for her in a soft voice that didn't travel far. "I have just had the pleasure of letting Jess know that she's been assigned to us at least until we reach Sydney. Thank you, doctor, for speaking to the Major. I will do anything to help my friend, and this way, she will be kept safe." Charlotte handed Jess a clean handkerchief. "Blow, dear; only I don't want it back until it's clean!"

That brought a smile to Jess's lips. "Yes, ma'am!" she replied with a laugh.

It took two days to sail up the Derwent River as the wind dropped, and they sat becalmed. At least the weather was nicer; not too hot and not too cold. The doctor explained that October in the colony was spring, and as Hobart could be darned hot in summer, it was best not to be there at that time. He then told them that they would unload half of the convicts in Hobart. The Major had chosen the worst offenders for this drop, and the remainder would travel to Sydney Cove.

As they sailed up the harbour entrance, he pointed to where a new convict prison was being constructed. "Over that headland is a point called Eagle Hawk neck. The thin wisp of land is the only way to and from where the new barracks and gaol will house the worst offenders. Most people here are into timber felling to clear an area for the planned development. Once the trees are gone, they will dig stone quarries and brick pits. The next stage will be the construction. The sixty women we are leaving here will be assigned immediately. Life will be tough for these naughty ladies, so I have chosen the strongest ones." They stood looking at the rugged land they were passing. "When we leave, we will pass the new site and Eagle Hawk Neck and all Maria Island, where there are plans to put the worst offenders." He shuddered.

As Jess was now officially assigned to Charlotte, and both men trusted her, she was allowed to accompany the doctor and Charlotte and her son on an area tour. The doctor pointed out various sights and said that this new town would soon become a significant receptacle of convicts. However, the foundations still needed to be built. Once around, the small hamlet was enough to see everything. Jess was relieved that she didn't have to stay there.

Ten days later, the ship weighed anchor, and they waved farewell to Hobart. The tides had assisted their departure, and soon they turned north and headed for Sydney Cove. With a light breeze behind them, they were able to reach the sea in less than a day.

~

As the *Mary* was dropping anchor in Sydney Cove, the *Jupiter* was approaching the western coast of their destination land. They should reach Hobart in two weeks. They had to deposit a load of building materials there for the town developments. The iron girders had to be carefully manhandled out of the hold, and then the pig iron and other construction equipment needed to be unloaded. The double-handed saws, known as misery whips, were vital to the felling of the enormous trees.

Once in Hobart, it took ten days before they could be underway. Marcus found out that half the convicts from the *Mary* had been unloaded and taken to the Macquarie Street Gaol, but he could not find a single one of them who had known Jessica by any name. He was puzzled. How could she be unknown by any one of them? He visited the Major in charge, and no Jessica Elkin had been unloaded in town.

Marcus had watched while the cargo was manhandled from the hold. He was frustrated that he could find no trace of Jessica. Shackled convicts did most of the work, and the uniformed soldiers stood guard over them. Their muskets were always at hand, and they never offered assistance. Marcus watched as a whip activated a lazy man who was taking a quick breather.

Jaques, Felicity, Rex, Giles, and Colin had taken the opportunity to investigate the tiny hamlet thoroughly. There was not much to see, considering there had been over twenty years of habitation. There were a few stone buildings and many timber cottages. They did, however, return with some rosy apples.

Marcus visited the site where the new female prison was being constructed, but other than the foundations of a large building, it offered no answers. Jessica was not known there either. He asked around with any female convict he passed, but she was unknown. Had she died at sea? What had happened to her?

Marcus returned to the ship and waited in his cabin in peace. Jon had been as good as his word. The day after that first conversation and before they reached the sea, Marcus was transferred to a different cabin.

Colin, Giles, and Jaques had moved everything over the first luncheon on board. Marcus had discovered there was a spare room on either side of him, so from then on, he slept well. He was also thankful that he did not need to embarrass Rex or Felicity, but after he had bashed on the bulkhead that second night, he was sure they realised that sound travelled through the adjoining wall. He had seen Felicity blush that following day, but no further mention of their activities had been made.

In the middle of a small storm, Marcus had made friends with the Major for the Royal Artillery regiment travelling on the lower deck. Being military, they were given free access to the entire ship. Yet, most evenings, it was to Jon that Marcus turned for companionship. The ease of their friendship had surprised them both. Other than the fact that Jon teased Marcus for being a landlubber, they were remarkably similar in many things. Today, Marcus didn't want to see anyone due to his frustration. Marcus understood Jon's loneliness; only he'd never realised that was what it was. He had focused his frustrations on his work. Jessica would hopefully fill that void. Oh, how he hoped.

Chapter 8   Port Jackson

Charlotte, Harmon, and Jess stood on the deck, watching the towering cliffs. They could see the waves crashing against the rocks, but they could see no opening in the headland that any ship could pass through. Ahead were more towering cliffs. Harmon pointed to the new lighthouse and watched their faces, knowing that he would soon hear a gasp. Sure enough, he did; then he heard the tacking call, and as the ship neared the shore, it was as though the cliffs magically opened.

Charlotte stood watching. "There's a middle headland! Look, Jess, I can see two bays now. Doctor Cochrane, which one are we heading into?"

Harmon pointed to the southern bay, "This is Port Jackson. Captain Phillip chose this instead of Botany Bay as it is a much bigger and safer harbour. Wait until you see the vast size of it." He had done this trip a few times, and each visit saw the difference in the colony. During Governor Macquarie's time, the most significant change occurred. The ramshackle slab huts were slowly demolished to make way for permanent buildings. It was still not the Albion that Governor Phillip had envisaged, but it was well on the way to being a decent place to live. Phillip's Albion was supposed to be long straight streets with white cottages. Up until Macquarie, it was a filthy higgledy-de-piggledy collection of hastily erected hovels. Back then, the streets flowed with excrement, and there was nowhere clean to sit without becoming overwhelmed by the stench. Within weeks of

Macquarie's arrival in 1808, things started to change. Harmon didn't come back for ten years, and when he did, he found that the town was almost unrecognisable. In the intervening years, every visit brought new buildings to completion. He excitedly pointed out some of the more prominent buildings. He mentioned that when he arrived on the last trip, he heard a sky observatory was being built in Parramatta. He was hoping to be able to get out to see it.

The doctor announced his departure. "Ladies, we will have a few hours until we dock, or I should say anchor, as there is no place to draw up to a sturdy jetty, so I need to have the final things arranged to lodge with the Colonial Secretary. Will you please excuse me?" He squeezed Jess's hand and tipped his head, showing he wished to speak to her.

Jess made her excuses and soon followed him.

When she entered the sick bay, Harmon said, "Jess, I have written a character reference letter for you. JT has also enclosed one. I have written to Governor Brisbane and explained your situation. I'm not sure what society Peter Rapsey will circulate in, but I feel sure there will be better placements than him. If you get offered one by the Governor or his representative, would you please consider it?"

Jess was almost overwhelmed. "You wrote to the Governor for me? Thank you so much, Harmon! I so appreciate it. Charlotte said there is a strong possibility that I may not be able to stay with them for long. Just knowing that I could get here safely was enough. It has been wonderful. Lucien and I had heard horrible things about some of the convict trips. I presume it must have been from the two of you."

Harmon nodded. "I have also made sure that your assignment to Mrs Rapsey is official but trust the Lord that He will get you in the right place, Jess."

Jess could hardly wipe the smile from her face. "Harmon, can I hug you? I won't be able to see either of you once we berth. I'm sad that I will miss saying a proper farewell to JT."

As she spoke, the door opened, she had expected it to be a needy person, but JT was standing behind her, grinning. "This was planned, Jess. You get to say farewell properly to us both. I claim a farewell hug, too," he said while laughing.

Soon after, the three parted. Jess was carrying her precious character references. They were both written in the name of Bates, but Harmon had also added a countersigned letter saying what her real name was and that her husband was knighted, and she was, therefore, Jessica, Lady Elkin. JT also had a farewell gift for her. He told her to keep the Bible she had been using; however, Jess refused. "JT, it's more important that you have this on board. I trust that somehow. I will come across one and will be permitted to use it. These letters are enough for me but thank you." Jess went to place her precious letters in her carpetbag. She then had to finish Charlotte's packing and make sure all the washing she had done was dry enough to pack away. What would happen when she landed would be out of her hands. Hopefully, Charlotte's husband would allow her to stay with them. Taking a deep breath, she shook her head. "It's no use worrying about any of this," she said positively to herself.

She clipped the last locks shut on Charlotte's bags and sat on the bed to wait. Charlotte had her son with her, so she didn't even need to worry about him.

~

As Jess was awaiting to disembark in Sydney Town, Marcus was watching the towering cliffs of the Great Bight pass. Marcus thought that she didn't know that she was even being followed, let alone by Marcus and her faithful friends. He did know that he had handed her to the protection of the good Lord. He must now trust that the Lord would see her somewhere safe.

Marcus knew that the *Mary* had gained time compared to their trip. They were now six weeks ahead of them.

Jon had done all he could to coax the *Jupiter* forward, but as he said, "They give me a leaky boat to sail across the seas and expect me to make a record time. One day this tub will sink. I'm thinking of changing ships, Marc."

Marcus knew that Jon was far more than lonely.

Jon shared his overwhelming emptiness. "I'll take the *Jupiter* home and rethink my life. After this trip with you, I may even look for a wife. If I can find one like your Jessica, then that's what I'll do. I'll see if any of the return passengers are single. Who knows, I may not have to look too hard." Jon chuckled.

Marcus and Jon had spent much time digging deep into their feelings. Neither had done this before, and the profound sincerity of what they shared surprised them both. "Jessica isn't mine, you know, and Jon, what I shared with you is private; please remember that. I know she trusts me as she sent me her jewellery box to care for. She will not be expecting me or know that I would sail halfway around the world to see her. My welcome will be unknown. I only know that Felicity, Rex and Jaques said Jessica trusted me, but I flounder beyond that. I want to pull her into my arms and kiss her silly. Remember Jon, that most of the time she stayed at my house, she was unresponsive. I freely gazed upon her beauty, and my heart thawed a little more with each moment. Soon all I could think of was her. Am I nervous? Oh yes, but she may see me and not wish to know me. Remember, she had also recently lost her husband and child."

After they unloaded cargo destined for Hobart, the *Jupiter* once again got underway. It was now mid-November, and the weather was hot. Jon hopefully would get a tailwind as they headed northward; if not, they would have to tack and wear all the way up the coast. This wind would extend the sailing time from a few days to up to ten. He knew Marc was anxious, but there was little he could do to change the winds.

Marcus looked puzzled, "I thought it was tacking and weaving?"

Jon shook his head, smiled and walked off, saying, "Nope, wearing, not weaving. You'll learn the cant, Marcus."

A week on, and the tailwind had not eventuated. They were now off Green Cape, having passed Cape Howe the day before.

If all went well, the change of angle of the land would mean that they could sail to the wind without tacking so much. Jon could see a squall coming and hoped the wind would change.

The seas became choppy, and the leaky vessel sloshed heavily in the now heavy seas.

Marcus joined Jon at the helm. "Any more water on board, and I'll have to run her aground on a beach, Marcus. She's heavy to steer as it is. Can you get the first mate and head below decks to ensure the pumps are being worked at full pace? I can't leave the wheel." Marcus was about to leave when Jon shouted, "BRACE." They had heard this often enough over the past months, but the size of the wave that approached was monumental.

Marcus clung to the mast. He felt it shudder as the old ship slid down the monster wave. "Cor, Jon, where did that come from?"

Jon was battling to hold the wheel. "I don't know Marc, but I hope there are no more following. I don't think we'll make it over more than one or two more of those." Jon steered the shuddering vessel over the set of waves then the sea quietened. "If I didn't know better, I'd say that was a tidal wave, Marc. It should be safe for you to go below decks now. We're still sluggish, so we need to pump out that water."

Marcus had still been clinging to the mast. "Okay, I'm going! You can keep this sea life; I'm proud to be a landlubber." Marcus went as quickly as possible and headed below decks.

He found that only three of the pumps were being manned, and in a short space of time, the rest of the pumps were working at full pace.

The squall passed, the sea calmed, and the bilge emptied. With the wind now behind them, they made quick progress.

Sydney Heads was sighted two days later. Marcus's heart was pounding. Hopefully, his search for Jessica would soon be over. He felt like he was playing cat and mouse across the world. Would she be in Sydney or somewhere else? She had arrived over six weeks ago, and she could have been sent anywhere in that time.

~

As soon as the *Mary* anchored, a boat pulled up to the ship's side. They had let down a rope ladder, and soon they were boarded by the local surgeon. Harmon had told them this would happen. The surgeon would inspect the passengers to make sure the ship was disease-free. None on board had died from any sort of infectious condition. Sadly, six children had perished. Two were sickly twins aged eighteen months old when they embarked. Both succumbed due to natural causes. Four others died of either misadventure or non-infectious illness. Harmon was congratulated by the surgeon who had come on board.

They were given the all-clear to disembark.

Now they started processing the convicts. Only sixty-five women had come from Hobart. All but Jess were to be sent to the Female Factory in Parramatta. Jess watched them depart; she knew she should have been with them. She had been checked off the convict list, and her assignment to Charlotte duly noted.

Charlotte's husband, Peter, had arrived and stood waiting on the foreshore. Charlotte was the first to disembark, and once seated, her child was carefully lowered to her.

Jess stood and observed the passionate welcome of her new mistress. Peter was obviously pleased to have her arrive safely. She could see Charlotte pointing to the ship and then Peter shaking his head. Jess's heart sank. If she couldn't go there, what would happen to her? Hopefully, she could stay at least a night or two with them. It would give her time to sort things out. She was so busy watching the interaction between her friend and her husband that she didn't notice someone approaching. When she did hear the footsteps, she thought it was JT or Harmon.

When a very cultured voice said. "Mrs Bates, I wondered if you could accompany me, please," she started.

Jess turned and saw a tall, fair-haired soldier standing next to her. "Pardon, sir? Did you speak?"

"I did, ma'am. Would you accompany me, please?" He didn't await an answer but walked towards the cabins below. Neither JT nor Harmon were in sight. The blonde soldier held the door open for her, and she knew she had no choice but to go below. "In here, please, ma'am." He held open the door to the sick bay.

He followed as she entered and then quietly closed the door. Initially, she panicked, but she saw JT and Harmon waiting for her. Her fear evaporated.

"JT, Harmon, what's happened? I presume Charlotte can no longer take me?" Jess looked at the three men in the sick bay. The young soldier returned her glance with a warm smile.

Harmon stood and approached her. "Jess, you suppose correctly. Peter, her husband, has just had a new allocation of convicts and is not allowed more. Major Grace here had seen the discrepancy and alerted JT to it. I saw you watching them meet and realised you understood what they said."

Jess nodded; she turned her attention to the tall soldier. "Do you have a suggestion, sir? I have a feeling you may do."

The gentle smile that crossed his face was comforting. "I do, Ma'am. I have met these two gentlemen before and trust their judgement. I have been sent from Parramatta to find a suitable convict to become a nursemaid or even a governess for a small child. Your doctor tells me that you had a child and are experienced with caring for one, let alone well educated." Ned Grace raised his eyebrow enquiringly.

Jess nodded. "We had a daughter who died, sir, as did my husband." She didn't elaborate, but she was sure Harmon or JT had filled in the handsome soldier. She shook her head to shake away the sad thought. Her loved ones were gone. What was this man going to suggest?

Ned spoke. "The needy person is Reverend George Augustus Middleton, and he has a young son, also named George. His wife died in childbirth. Ma'am, he lives further north in the Hunter Valley. Other staff are assigned to him, but you would be exclusively for the child's care. Will you accept this position?" He saw a flick of concern cross her face. "Ma'am, let me assure you that most convicts do not get a choice. They are assigned where I say. Your friends here assure me that you are not whom you seem. Your paperwork says Mrs Bates, but JT said there is something you need to tell me." His gaze did not leave her face.

Jess glanced from JT's face to Harmon's, who said, "Tell him, Jess, he needs to know."

She turned back to the young Major, and with a straightening of her stance, she said, "You know I was convicted for theft, but not what I stole; it was my husband's Bible. His cousin refused to allow me to use my married name; Bates was my maiden name, sir. I am really Jessica, Lady Elkin." She stood a little taller as she spoke. "My husband, Lucien, was knighted after Waterloo, and these two men served with him."

Major Grace nodded; her story correlated with theirs. She certainly had the look and bearing of a Lady. He stared at her and said, "So you'll go?"

Jess met his gaze. "Yes, sir, I'll go! I have only these two friends here, and they can't stay. I'll go, and I will care for this child like I loved my own Judith." Jess was close to tears.

Ned relaxed. "Please don't think I will pressure you, but if what your friends say is so, this placement will keep you safe. I can't keep you protected any other way. If you go to the Female Factory… No, please don't even consider that. It is not suitable for decent females, I can assure you. Sadly, it's my duty to attend there, and I have seen the unwashed bodies and unsanitary conditions. I am working with people to improve things, but it has a long way to go. It is also terribly overcrowded. Until we are given a warning when more ships are due, things will be unlikely to improve."

Jess was astounded. "Are things truly that bad?"

Ned frowned, "Worse, much worse, ma'am. So please be assured that this placement is for your safety."

"Then, when do I leave?" Jess realised she had little option. She would become a governess in a rectory. Then she smiled and turned to the captain. "JT, I told you God would provide me with access to a Bible. There should be one or two I could borrow in a church residence." Jess threw back her head and laughed. The three men gasped. She had no idea how beautiful she was. Her lips were hard not to watch as she talked. Her beauty was more than just a pretty face, exquisite though it was; her loveliness was in the regal acceptance of how she accepted what life threw at her.

Jess was allowed to stay on board until the coastal trader took her to Newcastle. Charlotte said she would come back on board, but Major Ned suggested that she wait until his shift was over, and he would accompany her to their home where she could say her farewells in private. Harmon offered to accompany them, and Ned accepted his offer. Tears were shared, and hugs were given, but no excuses were needed; Major Ned had explained in detail the new rules, and Jess told Charlotte about her new placement.

The *Mary* would stay at anchor for some weeks as she would need to source cargo for the return trip. JT and Harmon were frequently onshore, so she was on deck virtually alone. Occasionally, they took Jess with them if they were on a visit where she would not be in the way, but she was often left to twiddle her thumbs onboard. After her few trips ashore, she realised that the ship was both clean and comfortable compared to town. Harmon said that the town had been cleaned up; however, it was still filthy compared to how she and Lucien had kept their properties. If this was clean, what was Newcastle going to be like? All she knew about the place was that it was a new coal town. She imagined there would be more filth, soot, and squalor.

After a week onboard, Major Ned arrived and gave Jess the news that he had arranged her transport, and she was to leave in a week on a coastal trader that she had seen anchored in the harbour. This ship would be met in Newcastle by Reverend Middleton, and she would then meet her charge, little George. Ned apologised that he could not accompany her.

It was now the end of October, and on the day she sailed, Major Ned returned. He joined Harmon and JT to escort her to a cutter that she had seen sail from around the inner bay and anchor near the *Mary*. She saw the name of the vessel was the *H M Sally*. JT had told her all about it when it anchored beside them. It was a colonial cutter, and JT said that her rig was a gaff cutter so that the *Sally* would make the trip a speedy one. The three men introduced her to the captain and escorted her into a cabin, and saw her settled.

With a major, a captain and a doctor to give her credence, the new captain welcomed her on board. Ned had to provide him with her convict paperwork, so the man knew her actual status, but it was done in the privacy of his cabin. Hopefully, the wind would be a tailwind and take her to her final destination in twenty-four hours.

Late morning, the three men stood on the deck of the *Mary*, watching the *Sally* weigh anchor and hoist its sails.

Jess stood waving a farewell from the stern until they were out of sight. She was on the final leg of her incredible journey.

Although the captain knew her status, he treated her like a paying passenger. She appreciated his courtesy as it made her trip more comfortable. The other passengers treated her with unexpected politeness. She had nearly two half-days onboard and hoped they would be pleasant. With time on her hands, she spent much of the afternoon outdoors, watching the coastline pass by. The weather was perfect, dolphins joined the bow waves now and then, and they played leapfrog over one another for some time before departing as fast as they appeared. Other passengers joined her, watching the birds overhead and the action of the waves.

She shared a meal in the ship's small mess with the ten other passengers and the captain, after which Jess again decided to sit outdoors and watch the sunset. Again, some of the other travellers joined her. The dynamic colours made them gasp. Pinks, purples and vibrant orange was painted across the sky by the master hand of the Maker. Many commented that no two sunsets were alike, and she agreed. It would be the last one she would enjoy before she went into service for the minister. The group stayed out on the deck until a chill wind made them retire for the night. The sloshing of the waves was more audible in this small craft, but after five months at sea already, the sound and movement were now familiar to her. She slept well.

Jess was woken to the familiar sounds of the sailors' calling instructions; only the voices were unfamiliar, as were her surroundings. It took only a moment or two before she became aware of where she was. She stretched, rubbed her eyes and made an effort to rise. She hoped they would reach Newcastle harbour today, smiling to herself; Jess knew she wouldn't know unless she rose.

The smells emanating from the galley were less delicious than on previous mornings. In Sydney Cove, the cook had managed to find fresh eggs and some bacon. With only the crew, captain, doctor and herself on board, he had cooked special breakfasts for them. One morning, the cook had made French toast with crispy bacon; her mouth was watering for it again. Here it smelled like porridge and dried fish. Her stomach roiled. The unappetising smell made her linger over her dressing. Tea and toast would have to do, as she didn't wish to be lightheaded when she met her new master.

After an unappetising meal of overcooked, hard toast and lumpy marmalade followed by a tin mug of tepid over-sweetened black tea, she returned to her cabin and packed. The steward told her that they had had a stiff breeze behind them all night and would be arriving at the harbour mid-morning.

Nerves set in. There was no JT, Harmon, or even Major Ned to ease her pathway this time. Her thoughts of Lucien were less now, and she could often think of her lost family without tears. There was, however, another face that had more frequently come to mind. His gentle smiling countenance and honest face had given her confidence even through the short time she had known him. Marcus Ryan had been the first name to come to mind when she needed assistance. She had asked Felicity to take him her jewellery box for safekeeping. She knew it would be not only kept safe but also returned should she be permitted to go home. Home, where was home now? Her memories of Marcus were vivid. She remembered his deep well-modulated voice. She had heard him talking to her in the depth of her mind. He told her of a lovely Elizabethan country home with many different styles all jumbled together. He talked of his business and other homely things. She fought to recall his words over breakfast and remembered that he had said he was in the wool trade. Lucien had purchased the import rights for Black Oolong tea from a man now concentrating on the wool trade. She smiled; it would be so like God if that man had been Marcus Ryan. Nothing surprised her now; her safe journey had proven that. She knew that other women below decks and in the Female Factory had a horrific time. Major Ned had elaborated in private about the condition of the Factory. Knowing her status, he wished to spare her from that.

Chapter 9   Jupiter's Arrival

*M*arcus stood at the bow, watching the coastline pass.

They were close enough to hear the waves crashing against the towering cliffs. Sydney Heads would be a surprise to his three new travelling companions.

Giles and Colin had been here before. Colin was already packed and ready to disembark and was still in the cabin.

All of Jessica's luggage had also been brought up from the hold, and Jaques and Colin had meticulously gone through every item and made sure it was ready for her use. One case had become damp, and the gowns needed washing. Felicity, Jaques, and Colin had spent three days repairing the damage to her dresses. Sadly, a beautiful ball gown was beyond repair, but Marcus knew she would have little use for it in the colony anyway, so he was not very upset. Some of the fabric could be reused for reticules or even a shawl.

Marcus could see the towering cliffs of Sydney Heads, and his heart jumped with excitement.

Rex and Felicity were at the ropes with the other three men nearby. Would their journey be nearly at an end?

Marcus felt almost empty, as though he knew she wasn't there, but where was she? Marcus heard the soft gasp from his three new travelling companions as the towering cliffs parted before them. The harbour that opened before them was a sight he never tired of seeing.

Jon steered the sluggish vessel into the designated bay and

dropped anchor. Marcus noted that they were in the next bay from where he had previously anchored. The ship carried cargo, and Marcus realised that the cargo vessels would have to give way to passenger craft, especially as there were six ships already at anchor off the main cove.

With the efficiency of one used to his job, Jon had his vessel secured and welcomed aboard the surgeon and officials. He reported that there was no illness on board and no convicts. His cargo was mainly building products, pig iron, and food.

Knowing that Jon would be in port for a couple of months, Marcus only said a cursory farewell and disembarked with his shipmates.

The six friends now had to climb down a wobbly rope ladder and into a rocking boat.

Felicity was not good with heights; she was still feeling seasick and was often dizzy and tired.

Rex enjoyed holding her behind as she bravely made the descent. Their luggage would stay on board until they had things sorted.

Marcus was first ashore and went to seek information. A storekeeper told him that he would need to see Major Downes up at Hyde Park Barracks to find a particular convict. Marcus then enquired at the quartermasters' office in the Argyle store complex for more information and directions. They were just as evasive.

The quartermaster said, "Follow the smell of baking bread; it will lead you up the hill. You will see a tall building with a big stone fence. Go in there; the Major's office is to the left of the bakery." The man pointed up the hill.

Marcus could already see the large building he spoke about, so he rounded up the others. Felicity, Rex, and Jaques set off, leaving Colin and Giles to inquire about accommodation on shore and possibly find a suitable conveyance for their use while there.

After so long at sea, all needed to regain their land legs.

Felicity still didn't feel well but stayed quiet.

They had discovered the need to get land legs when in Cape Town and then again in Hobart. A good walk was something all relished, but it was so very hot.

Soon all four could smell the delectable aroma of freshly baked bread. The man was not wrong; they followed their noses and soon saw the tall building and the fence he mentioned.

Marcus approached the guard and was told he could enter, but the others had to wait outside.

The guard called another soldier over, and Marcus was escorted to a sandstone building and into the office that stood beside the bakehouse. The quartermaster had been correct, after all. He was surprised to see a young soldier, who would have been not much more than twenty, seated behind the desk.

The Major stood as Marcus entered and shook his hand; typically, a greeting would be a bow each. However, a firm grip took Marcus's hand; then, the Major offered Marcus a seat and tea. As the day was stifling hot, tea was the last thing Marcus wished for. He noted that the Major was in a red woollen uniform and must be swelteringly hot. Why would they want tea?

As Marcus's reply was some time coming, the Major said, "In this hot climate, we need to keep our fluid levels up. Strange as it may seem, hot sweet tea does the trick. If you stay here for any length of time, you will find this is correct. There is a delicious cordial that some make that is also good, but one has to be careful as unless it's kept cool, it can ferment quickly and becomes unpleasant. The fruit tastes much like apple juice, but it is made with native berries they call lilli pillies. Delicious stuff if I say so myself." With that, the Major handed Marcus a tin mug of black tea. "Sorry, we're an army barracks, no fancy china here." He served himself and then inquired, "Now, sir, what can I assist you with?"

Marcus had taken a sip of the sweet brew. "I'm looking for someone. She is a convict who arrived on the *Mary* last month. I know she was not off-loaded in Hobart, as we have just come from there, but none of the convicts on board seemed to know of her. I'm hoping to find some trace of her here."

Major Downes lay back in his chair and reached for a ledger behind him. "What's her name?" he asked as he lay the massive book on his desk and flicked it open.

"Jessica Elkin, but she may be under Bates." Marcus watched as the Major flicked open the pages.

The man found the *Mary*, and his finger paused. "Ahh, she did arrive and had been assigned to Mrs Charlotte Rapsey, but as her husband had his quota of convicts, your lady was reassigned. Major Grace at Parramatta arranged a private assignment for her. He is stationed at the Barracks at Parramatta with the 48th Foot, so you will have to go there." The young Major smiled at Marcus, then said,

"It's all above board, but just not sure whom he's let know about the special placement."

Marcus was not sure if his heart soared or sank. Another journey, but at least she had been safe and well. Jon had been correct that she'd had a more comfortable trip than she could have had. After another sip of the flavoured tea nectar, after which he grimaced, he asked, "How do I get there?"

"Ahh, well, I'd catch the ferry if I were you. It is irregular as it goes up a tidal river. If you go out there, stay at the *Rear Admiral Duncan Inn*. It's the best in town and is the place that makes that juice I told you about. Molly Miller is a fabulous cook, Bill runs a friendly inn, and you won't have any trouble there. They are reasonably new to town, having only been here a few years, but I've stayed there a few times myself rather than the barracks. The beds are clean, and no bugs. If they are full, then stay at the *Jolly Sailor*. Also, it's a tightly run inn and no funny business, but you'll probably be in hammocks there. Sal is a brilliant cook. They are all friends so you will be safe at either one. I'll write you a letter for the Major out there, name of Ned Grace. If I know Ned, he'll take you up to the Factory, and you can see the place for yourself. He and some of the other innkeepers, including the two I mentioned, are doing what they can for the felons under lock and key in the town." The Major checked his watch. "Actually, sir, if you're quick, you will have about an hour until the government barge departs, so I will quickly write you a note for Ned and a pass for the government barge. Please send my regards to him. He was only in town a few weeks ago, but I catch up with him when I can. Nice man, you can't miss him; tall, blonde, and a true gentleman. When you meet him, you will know what I mean." He set to writing the other Major a note. He sanded the paper, added his seal, and handed the letter to Marcus.

Marcus looked at the name on the front, Major Edward Grace. He said, "Thank you, sir," as he took the note, then put down the partially drunk tea and left. The Major followed, and they walked together to the gates.

Felicity had been escorted to the shade of a tree. She knew the heat was getting to her as she really didn't feel well. Rex and Jaques stood watching the gates. Soon they saw Marcus returning, followed by a uniformed man. Halfway across the courtyard, the soldier stopped and called for a carriage.

Marcus waved a farewell and walked to join them. "Sorry I

was so long; we have another leg of the journey westward to Parramatta. Major Downes is sending the carriage for us, as he has a delivery for the ferry that we are to catch." Marcus saw Felicity was not her bright and chirpy self. "Felicity, are you not well?"

She felt quite ill now. "I could be better, sir. I think the heat is getting to me. I shall certainly relish the carriage ride back down the hill again. The smell of the bread turned my stomach for some reason."

They were not left waiting long as the carriage arrived while Felicity was speaking.

Marcus knew that they had a little time and suggested a return by another street. It was no further and would save the carriage from turning around.

Leaving the barracks, then proceeded down the road, past a church, and an assortment of other buildings, *en route* to the bay. No structures were vastly distinguished from another until they came to a hospital and one next door, with guards outside. With no signs to tell them what it was, they refrained from guessing. There were windmills and other slate-topped sandstone buildings.

The carriage pulled up to the harbour, and they finally saw a small sign saying Phoenix Wharf. This was their departure point.

Marcus had previously known this bay as Sydney Cove, but a new ferry wharf certainly made accessing a craft easier. There was a large tree with a bench seat, and they seated Felicity in the shade with the slightly cooler breeze blowing on her. Rex stayed by her side as the other men meandered around the waterfront.

They were no sooner out of sight than Felicity needed to throw up. "Rexy, I do feel poorly." Not one to usually show affection in public, Felicity rested against his shoulder. "I hope it's just the heat. I would hate to get ill at this stage of the trip."

Felicity recovered a little and was pleased to see a small craft approach the shore. They were somewhat aghast to see that this boat was not a passenger vessel but more of a barge. A wagon was unloading goods onto it. Felicity saw Giles and Colin with three of their bags, which meant they were staying overnight.

Rex assisted her up, and they joined their fellow travellers. Another man was waiting for the boat. He was a tall blonde gentleman dressed in poor clothing, but he was clean and well-spoken.

Marcus introduced himself, and the three joined the craft for the trip. The fair-haired man reciprocated. "Charles Lockley, from Government Stores at Parramatta and innkeeper of the *Jolly Sailor* in Parramatta, at your service, sirs, ma'am." He bowed appropriately and explained that he was collecting stock for Government Stores that had arrived on the *Jupiter*.

Marcus had nearly jumped when the man introduced himself.

Colin noted, but remained silent. This man was the image of some of Marcus's friends from home, and they were Lockleys too.

The craft was soon loaded and underway.

Felicity was seated in the only shady place available, and that was in the wheelhouse. She was feeling much better since she had been able to have a glass of cider. While they waited, Marcus had purchased a bottle of grog from the bond store and a mug, which they shared. The apple cider settled her stomach quickly.

Marcus was intrigued by this man and struck up a conversation with Charles.

Charles said, "You are fortunate that Major Downes allowed you on the government barge, sir. The passenger ferry is a log."

Marcus didn't know how to answer him, but the frown he gave Charles made the man add, "Sorry sir, by that, I mean that it is slow. It can sometimes take a week to do the full circuit run as it stops at every nook and cranny along the route. This barge will go directly to Parramatta and unload at my jetty. We should be there in a few hours as the wind is blowing from the East. Sometimes it can take all day, but we're lucky today." Charles was itching to know who they were and why they were there, but Marcus Ryan had mentioned that he had a letter for Ned, so he knew he would eventually find out. Ned would be coming to dinner tomorrow night, so it would be one of the first questions he would ask.

Marcus had never ventured this far down the river before. He had gone to a few farms further south, including Macarthur's farm down at Camden Park, for he had wanted to see their Spanish merinos and check the quality of the fleece. He had offered to buy their wool clip, and it had been accepted. The sale price of that first shipment alone had made that business a tidy profit. More had followed, and he was keen to source other suppliers for the warehouse in London. But he also wished to buy some of his flock to start his own farm. Marcus had refurbished his grandfather's small woollen mill and wished to expand the business, hence the proposed trip to New South Wales. By the time he arrived home, the new factory should be completed, and a recently purchased mill should be in full production. If he could get the business out of the way immediately, he would be able to send word back with Jon that would satisfy the Chairman. Once he found Jessica, then he would look for land. He knew the Macarthurs had a town residence in Parramatta. Marcus had heard that Reverend Marsden also had sheep in the area, although not of the same quality. So, while in town, he would make an appointment to see the cleric, and then he wouldn't have to return later.

A few hours later, the craft was heading directly to a massive clump of mangroves.

Felicity was now lying on the only bench seat available, and Rex had removed his coat for her to use as a pillow. She was once again feeling ill.

Jaques watched where they were heading and shouted to the skipper, "Hey, captain, you will hit the trees."

Charles laughed. "No, watch, sir. We go around this bend, and there is a river opening. It's tidal, so we can only safely enter at high tide." The craft was now in the tide flow, and although the wind dropped once they slipped behind the mangroves, there was enough breeze and current to carry them upstream at a decent speed. After a few more twists and turns, a small jetty came into view. A fair-haired lady with two small children was waiting, and Charles waved.

As the barge docked, Marcus saw a contingent of soldiers guarding a cluster of men who were walking towards the arriving boat.

Charles explained that they were convicts who would unload the cargo and take it to the Government Stores building.

Once onshore, Charles introduced everyone to his wife, Sal, then hoisted both young boys up into his arms. When the soldiers arrived, Charles asked that their luggage be taken to Miller's inn. He then said for the men to follow him. They headed off uphill towards a large building that looked like the barracks in Sydney.

Rex reluctantly followed them, glancing over his shoulder at Felicity.

Felicity stood, watching them go. She was left alone and still feeling ill, and she was left with the convict woman.

When the men were out of earshot, Sal took one look at Felicity and asked, "When are you due, ma'am? I have just had our third. She's asleep in the inn with a friend looking after her."

Felicity looked at the woman, horrified at the suggestion, and said, "I'm not…" she paused mid-sentence, then said, "Oh, no! No wonder I'm ill." She blanched and giggled. "Rexy and I only married shortly before we departed. Mrs Lockley, I'm over forty; I can't be having a child."

"Call me Sal, please; everyone does, and you most certainly can. How long have you been ill?" Sal inquired as they walked.

Felicity thought back. "Off and on for about eight weeks. However, I was so seasick at times that I put it down to that." Felicity sat her hands on her stomach. She had been feeling flutters for some time. Since Hobart, actually, but put it down to nerves. Puzzled, Felicity asked, "How did you know, Sal?"

Sal smiled at the older lady. "Two things, first, the dark patches on your face, and second, you are positively glowing. Are you feeling butterflies in your stomach?"

Felicity nodded with a smile. "So, not nerves?"

Sal shook her head. "No, they are baby flutters." They walked towards a two-story building at the top of a grassy slope. "Molly Miller is at our house watching Liza. She's expecting one soon too. They run the *Rear Admiral Duncan Inn,* where Charles has sent your luggage, but first, I'll make sure you can stay there. Otherwise, you can have our second room. All the other inns in town are far too rough for any decent person. The *Freemasons Arms* is virtually a brothel with things even going on outdoors, and we steer clear of it. Molly and I keep clean establishments, but their inn is better suited for travellers; ours is for sailors, soldiers, and male travellers." Her chatter continued until they reached the building.

Felicity was still in awe at her discovery. She was almost in denial, too; she was having a baby! Any doubt of her condition vanished when she met Molly Miller.

"Hello, I'm Molly," the merry lady grinned, then enquired how far along she was. The extremely expectant lady had the same blotches on her face as she did. She had never noticed this condition in a lady before, but then, she had never had much to do with expectant mothers other than Mrs Jess, and her magnolia-like skin didn't alter. However, she had been so busy nursing Mr Lucien and his swelling illness that she might not have noticed even if Mrs Jess's face had changed.

Felicity was flustered at the question. "Um, I'm not quite sure, four or five months possibly. Sal has just pointed out why I have been feeling ill." Felicity was suddenly feeling lightheaded. "I thought I was seasick." She clutched her head with one hand and the table with the other.

"Ma'am, you need a drink." Molly handed Felicity a large tumbler of pink fluid. "Sal, I made some punch while you were gone."

"Thanks, Mol; the men have gone along to the military barracks to see Major Ned. They have taken the boys." Sal collected more glasses.

Felicity tentatively sipped the pink concoction Molly handed to her. It tasted like apples, with a hint of both lemon and honey, but joy above joy; it was cool. "Oh, this is delicious, Mrs Miller. What is it?" She thirstily downed the contents.

Sal smiled at her reaction. "It's lilli pilli punch with a hint of honey and lemon. It's the best thing for a hot day. The men like ale or cider, but we prefer this." Sal poured more into all their glasses. "Molly makes the best version of it and won't share her secret. Mine never tastes quite so good."

As soon as Sal's back was turned, Molly whispered, "The secret is the honey, dear. I only use White Box or Clover honey; Sal uses Ironbark." She put her finger to her lips and smiled.

The house was blessedly cool, and Sal suggested that Felicity put her feet up for a while. She said it would take the men at least half an hour before they returned.

Felicity accepted her offer and was asleep before Sal left the room.

The crunching sound of boots on the verandah woke Felicity. She was feeling much refreshed but needed to find the facilities.

Sal heard her get up and showed her to an outhouse. "The men are now in the taproom having an ale. It is closing time in thirty minutes, and Charles has to take over and close up."

On her return, Felicity joined Sal in the kitchen, sat on the stool, and waited for Rex to return.

Sal chatted as she cooked. "Molly said she would prepare rooms for you all. They have no one else staying at the moment, so there's plenty of room for you all." Sal was pulling the meat off a long joint that looked like a tail. Felicity watched, intrigued. Once she had removed all the meat from the bone, Sal put it back onto the pot and added diced vegetables and a few hands full of grains. "This stew is meals for the hungry. Some don't get a good meal, and on Saturday nights, I make them a good healthy stew. The meat is only a kangaroo tail; it is nourishing but needs a lot of cooking to make it tender. Old Tom will be along first, and others will follow when they see him leave. He used to always eat at Bill and Molly's place, but since she fell with child, he's been eating here. The smell of meat has been turning her stomach." The giant vat of stew was soon bubbling away, and it thickened as the grain cooked. She ladled a huge serving onto a tin plate and added two slices of liberally buttered, thick fresh bread. She walked to the kitchen door and passed it out to a pair of gnarled and twisted waiting hands. When he had gone, Sal explained. "Bill Miller arrived in the same ship as old Tom. We really shouldn't call him that, as he's not much older than us. However, he's been living a tough life, and time has not been good to him."

The pungent aroma of the visitor assailed Felicity's nostrils. She quickly put a handkerchief to her nose.

Sal noticed and, after checking that he was no longer nearby, said, "That's the other reason that it's better he eats down here now. Her patrons are much more upper class."

The noise from the front room soon dissipated, and Felicity saw the men reappear.

Rex came to her side and asked how she was feeling.

Sal motioned for her to take him to the back verandah while she told him her news.

Marcus and Jaques waited for them in the courtyard. Marcus had not said a word since leaving the Major's office. He had missed Jessica by a mere three weeks. She had already left the town and gone further north. As if that was not enough, he had recognised the Major from his school days. The recognition was mutual as the Major had just put his finger to his lips and mouthed, "Later," to him. What revelation would follow? Why was Lord Edward Lockley here as Ned Grace, for that's who Marcus knew him to be?

Marcus gazed at the river in the late afternoon sunlight. The searing heat of the day was easing, and the evening would soon approach, but it was still hot. They had yet to get to the inn and settle for the night. He noticed Rex was taking a darned long time to collect Felicity. Then he heard an almost gleeful shout.

Jaques spun around at the sound. They didn't have long to wait until they found out the cause.

Rex appeared beaming, and Felicity snuggled up to his side.

She looked embarrassed. "Tell them, love, go on," Rex said with glee.

Felicity was shy at admitting their nocturnal activities had born fruit or soon would. "I'm…, I mean, we…, I'm…" She mumbled, somewhat tongue-tied.

Rex could not contain himself. "We're having a child; it's why she's been so ill. It wasn't seasickness at all." He was beaming, and Felicity blushed scarlet.

Congratulations were issued as they strolled up the hill to the *Rear Admiral Duncan Inn.*

Marcus took his bearings so he knew where to come later that evening. Ned said he would meet him at the end of Charles' street. He could see the barracks just up the hill, but there would be no light once night fell.

Molly welcomed them and showed them to their rooms. She had cleared their room and finished the laundry in their absence. The inn was large with many sizeable guest rooms, so all could have not just a bed but their own room. Marcus was in the single front room, and Rex and Felicity were in the back double room.

Molly didn't have to cook for them as they had eaten the delicious stew that Sal had made. After dinner, Molly took Felicity aside and discussed babies and imparted various bits of information she would need to know. Molly handed her a jar of white powder and suggested that she have a spoonful of it whenever she felt ill. "It is just a mix of loaf sugar and bicarbonate of soda, and you should try to mix it with some lemon juice; this helps with the sickness."

Felicity looked forward to a lazy day as the men were going to have a look around town tomorrow after church; the service was at seven in the morning. Now that she knew what was wrong with her and that it should soon pass, she began to relax.

Marcus made his excuses to his travelling companions and said he was going for a walk as he needed to clear his head.

Knowing that they had missed Jess by only a few weeks, they all understood his anguish. None, however, realised his real reason for wishing to walk alone tonight. He walked down the hill again in the fast-fading light. Having checked his watch and seen that it was nearly eight o'clock, he knew Ned should be waiting for him already. He picked up his pace. He saw his old school friend in the dim light and the familiar shock of almost white hair.

When Ned had first started at his old school when he had been just six, each new junior boy had been buddied with a senior student, and Ned had been placed under Marcus's care. Over the years, a friendship grew between the two. When Marcus left school five years later, the firm friendship remained. They would catch up frequently until Ned turned nineteen. Then, Marcus lost contact with him. It had been the year of Ned's presentation Levee at court. Marcus had not been invited as he was only in trade, but he soon heard of Ned's betrothal. Then silence; Ned had vanished; obviously, the engagement had been called off as his now ex-fiancé, Elouise Wickham, had married Ned's older brother, David, who was the future Duke. For over five years, Marcus wondered what had become of his young friend. Hopefully, tonight he would find out.

Ned turned as the footsteps approached. He recognised the familiar gait of his friend and smiled a welcome. "Walk with me, Marc. There is a log down here; we can talk uninterrupted and not be overheard." Ned led them to an extremely large log that had been placed under a tree down near the wharf.

Once seated, Marcus said, "What's with the moniker change, Ned? And why Grace of all names? Also, is Charles related?"

Ned smiled. "Hello, to you too, Marc, and enough of the twenty questions. I shall reveal all; just bide your time. First, you heard of my engagement?" He saw Marcus nod, so he continued, "Well, she decided she wanted a full-blown Duke, not his younger brother, she dumped me, so I left. Well, there's far more to it, but that will suffice. I came at David's bidding, though, not hers. It suited me not to be around as I found she has the morals of an alley cat, and David didn't believe me. So, my sponsor for my enlistment was not my father but Duke James from Malvern Hall near you at Billingshurst. I believe he's only about two properties away from your country house?"

Marcus nodded. "Yes, I'm on the other side of the Earl of Meldon, next to Duke James."

Ned continued. "The Duke had overheard the words she threw at me, and knowing her reputation better than I, he told me I was well out of it. Two weeks after our engagement was announced, I found her in a compromising position with another man. I stayed at home long enough to try to warn David of what I had discovered before then buying my commission and fleeing here. I told my mother what had occurred and where I was going, but not under what name. Father was ill at the time. As you know, Duke James is one of Father's good friends. It was Duke James who offered me an escape." Ned glanced at his friend, who motioned to continue. With a nod, Ned did so, "I enlisted under the first name that came to mind." Ned still chuckled at the name chosen. "As you know, mother's nickname is 'Grace', and it is so appropriate for her." Ned chuckled at the thought as she was known as "Her Grace, 'Grace' instead of Gracemere." Ned gave a resigned sigh. "You have met her, Marc; you know how regal she is. Well, I chose that." He took a deep breath, then said, "Regarding your third question regarding Charles. I'm stumped to know how he could be. Marc, however, with his surname and looks, there must be a connection somewhere."

Marcus looked stunned. "Connection! Neddie, darn it, he could well be your brother. He's the image of both Doug and David." He saw Ned give a nod in agreement.

Ned glanced at Marcus. "But Marc, that means Father cheated on Mother, and I'm not going there. I've never seen two people more in love than them. Charles is the same age as Paul, and as you know, Paul's twin, also named Charles, by the way, died soon after he was born. Father's name is Charles, too, so I can't help but wonder. Damn it, Marc, I just don't know, and I dare say I never will. Here, we are friends, good friends. Many may wonder, but as I don't know, we can't say anything, can we? So, we say nothing. Charles doesn't even know my real name; he might well ask more questions if he did. He's never even mentioned our similarity." Ned fell silent; he so wished he knew the answer to this puzzling question. If he ever went back to England, he would try to find out. "Anyway, enough of this! Tell me about this woman you are seeking. I met her a few times, you know. She was travelling with JT and Harmon. I think they were in the year above me at school."

Marcus gasped, then said, "I remember them too; both were nice lads. Now, re Jessica…" Marcus told Ned the entire saga and his search for her.

Ned filled in a few gaps as to why she was not known by the rabble and told him of Jess's change of assignment. "Marc, she is safely ensconced with Reverend Middleton and his young son in Newcastle. It was a suitable position for her and the best I could arrange. I kept it quiet as they are trying to keep convict numbers down in the town. I had no idea of your connection, though." Ned explained how he had been charged to find the minister's young son a governess, and there had been no suitable convicts in the Female Factory. So, Ned had gone directly onboard and had discovered that

JT had the perfect candidate.

For the first time in nearly six months, Marcus relaxed. "Ned, I'm going to marry her if she'll have me. Will you stand up with me as a witness? I'd like a friend to be by my side."

Ned smiled; Charles and Sal had been as smitten. His heart still hurt from Elouise's callous treatment of him. He wasn't ready to look for a wife. He wasn't sure he ever would be. He said, "Yes, Marc, I'd be honoured, but I'll have to sign as Grace, just so you know. You'll have to ask permission, so send me the paperwork when it occurs. I will fast-track it if I can; benefits of being a friend of the magistrate. Oh, that reminds me, Harry Moffatt is here too, so he knows who I am, just in case you run into him. He's the magistrate in Parramatta," Ned chuckled, as did Marcus. More and more students from their old school seemed to have escaped to the Antipodes.

The men sat talking of other things for a while before Ned said he had a dawn parade before church and had to retire. "See you at church tomorrow, Marc. You'll find that Jess is quite safe. Trust Him in this." He pointed heavenward.

By now, Marcus couldn't see his action but knew he would have made it. "I do, Ned, or I would not have got this far."

Their mutual faith had been the essential thing that drew the two together. Neither joined the debauched society of the peerage, not that Marcus was a peer, but his family was wealthy. Marcus knew that Ned had a group of other friends whom he also liked. Being their senior, he had not had much to do with them other than rescuing them from the repercussions of a few silly pranks that had spun out of control.

They parted with a brotherly hug as they often did and went their separate ways.

Chapter 10   Newcastle Bound

*J*ess adored her new charge. Georgie was a delightful little boy who had never known a mother's love. He now relished the hugs and kisses she showered upon him. He returned them with adoration. Teaching him was like pouring water into a dry sponge. He absorbed everything he could, but it had not been so in the beginning.

She had been with him for nearly a month, and Reverend Middleton had quickly grown to trust her. The first week she arrived, the child had pulled away from her, and she wondered if she would ever break through to the lonely boy. He was so different from Judith. Her dark curly hair and outgoing, sunny nature were the opposite of the surly fair-haired child that showed little affection for anything or anyone. The breakthrough came when he had thrown a tantrum and poured the drink she had just brought him onto the floor. He sulkily shouted, "You're not to tell me what to do."

She had retreated to the garden in tears. She had sat weeping, and unbeknownst to her, he watched her from the window. He crept outside and pulled himself up beside her. He put a pudgy hand on her knee and said, "I'm sorry, but you're not my mama."

"And I'm sorry Georgie, but you're not my daughter because she died, just like your mama did." Jess's weeping continued.

George watched her weep. A frown was now plastered on his childish face. "You lost her too?" he asked.

Jess nodded, "And my husband died the day after our little

girl." Jess was unable to say more as the words she wanted to say stuck in her throat. The little boy sat looking at her for some time. Jess's tears did not abate. A sob escaped her, though.

Georgie understood her sadness; he climbed up into her lap and hugged her, making her cry even harder. His chubby hugs were so like Judith's.

She said, "I need this so much, Georgie. I need your hugs and your love because I miss my little girl so much."

From then on, Georgie saw her differently. She needed him as much as he needed her. Every day they shared many hugs. Jess explained that she wasn't trying to replace his mama, just like he could never replace her daughter, but they could care for each other and make a special hole in each of their hearts for the other.

Jess explained that loving or missing one person didn't stop you from having more room or love. It did not stop you from fitting many more people into your lives. Marcus's face came to Jess's mind when they spoke about this. She was uncertain what her feelings were for this man, but she trusted him, that much she knew. She still loved Lucien, but he was gone as Judith was.

Over the next weeks, reading time was a delight to them both, as he would again climb up into her lap, and she would read him a story. He would often try to read a word, and it didn't take long before he recognised small words like 'the', 'love', 'cat' or 'hug'. She ran her finger under the words so he could follow. Another of Georgie's favourite things to do was go down the foreshore and watch any ship that was arriving. Reverend Middleton insisted that they were accompanied by Vincent, his paid groom, whenever they roamed, as there were still fifty convicts in the colony.

Jess had corrected the minister gently when he had mentioned the number of convicts by quietly adding, "Fifty-one, sir, for I am one too." Her gentle smile and the ability to fit into his busy life had made him forget her status.

Reverend Middleton had replied only with a nod and a smile. She was not a paid employee but a government servant. Reverend Middleton's one rule for the outings was that she was not to take Georgie on board any ship. Vincent may, but she was not to board any vessel. "It's for your own safety, Miss Jess. I don't trust the sailors." He looked slightly embarrassed. "Miss Jess, let me just say that all men admire a pretty face and a well-turned ankle, but not all men will respect you."

When Reverend Middleton found out the reason for her conviction, he treated her more like a friend. He had been so astounded that he said, "You were convicted for stealing a Bible? Really? Who would do such a preposterous thing?"

The entire story unfolded; Jess held nothing back. Even to staying at Marcus's house unaccompanied for the two days after the funerals when she was insensible. She confessed everything to him, even acknowledging a soft spot for the handsome man she barely knew. She also told him of her trust in Marcus. His behaviour over his care of her had instilled confidence. He had many opportunities to touch or manhandle her, but he did not. He had held her hand and kept her covered when holding a glass to her lips. But he had never been inappropriate, although she remembered his words of affection for her. He showed her only care and compassion.

Reverend Middleton was dumbfounded and consequentially allowed her freedoms that no other convict enjoyed. The only condition was for the groom to accompany them where she wished to go. This didn't worry Jess, as Vincent often had to carry Georgie back up the hill to the church. They attended the markets and parks. Vince carried any shopping they purchased if he wasn't carrying Georgie.

Three weeks after her arrival, towards the end of December, they had planned to head to Morpeth for the week when one of the local people died. Reverend Middleton was required to take the funeral, and the minister cancelled their trip. The funeral service was on Wednesday, and it was, therefore, too late in the week to head west. On Thursday afternoon, Georgie had spied a mast coming around the headland and begged that they go and watch the small supply ship come in. It was the regular coastal trader that would bring mail, newspapers from Sydney and news from further afield. The three ambled down the slope to the river mouth. They kept their eyes on the approaching ship, but Georgie wished to have a flying ride from Vince first.

Jess was seated on a seat on the grassy foreshore while the groom watched the little boy running in circles around a playful seagull. A few birds would take off and land as the small child ran around. His squeals of delight made her chuckle. She had not even noticed that the cutter was already tied up and unloading. A rider had met the boat and taken mail with him as he quickly departed unnoticed.

Out of the corner of her eye, Jess saw someone approaching, but there was room for them to pass by her, so she remained seated in the tree's shade. She turned back to watch Georgie. Vince was now spinning the boy around with one hand and a foot. The joyous giggles the child emitted as he was twirled in Vince's arms reminded her of Judith again. Lucien used to do this for their daughter. He had done it at the picnic. Judith had shouted, "Look, Mummy; I'm flying." Jess's eyes filled with tears at the sudden memory. In her sadness, she had not noticed that the person had stopped at her side. She tried quickly to wipe away tears when she heard a familiar voice call her name.

"Jessica, oh my Jessica, I found you." Marcus stood gazing down at the love of his life. He knew he should have addressed her properly, but he had only ever thought of her by her Christian name. He watched anxiously, wondering what she would do. As she looked up and him, he noticed her tear-filled eyes. He saw she was sad. He dearly wished to gather her into his arms, but he held back. However, he dropped onto his knees before her.

Hardly believing who she saw before her, she cried, "Marcus, you came!" Rather than shy away from him, she reached out and touched his cheek with her knuckles. "Are you real? You are not in my dreams this time?" Her caress was so soft he hardly felt it.

He released a sigh of delight. "I came because you are here. I would chase you all the way around the world if I had to, but halfway is far enough." He looked intently at her face; it was exactly as he remembered. He had gazed on it every moment he could for those two days that she had lain unresponsive in his house.

A tear rolled down her cheek. He thumbed it away. He watched her rosebud-like lips turn into a smile at his endearing, and gentle act. Her following words made his heart sing. Her musical voice gave him far more than hope; the following actions fulfilled a dream. She gave a gurgle of laughter. "As long as you don't bowl me over with your carriage this time." Then, unexpectedly, she reached out for him.

He was still on his knees as he gathered her into his arms. He felt her shoulders shaking, then realised she was weeping again. It was with mixed relief, joy, and happiness. She was no longer so alone.

"Thank you for coming," she murmured against his neck.

He drank in her delicious scent again as he held her. He had first noticed the smell of roses as he had first carried her. He whispered, "No more, my love, will you be without me, for I will follow you wherever you go. Dare I call you that? It is how I have thought of you since you awoke on that fateful day. Back then, I discovered that you had only recently lost your family; even now, I know it is far too soon to declare myself. However, I so wish to protect you. I searched high and low for you when you left that day. I even went to London on a false trail, and I was not around until too late. I would have stood up for you in court and spoken for you. Jessica, even then, I was hopelessly in love with you. That occurred before you even woke." Marcus released her slightly and pointed to the bench. "May I?" He didn't care about the grass marks on his trousers; he only cared that he had found Jessica.

Jess nodded. He sat close to her, almost too close. Her emotions were in turmoil. Moments ago, she had been weeping over the loss of her husband and child and, yes, thinking of this man. Now here she was in his arms. She gave him an embarrassed smile. "Hopeless? Not so, Marcus! As to the endearment, yes, you may, whenever you wish. But why are you here? What about your woollen business? Doctor Wayne said you were a hard-headed businessman who looked neither left nor right from the profit side of your work."

Reluctantly, Marcus moved away from her a little more as propriety demanded, then chuckled as he said, "God dealt with that by throwing a dark-haired angel literally in my path." He dared not kiss her, but he did kiss the palm of her hand, which he had not yet released. He was about to make some banal conversation when he noticed the arrival of three more persons and moved even further away from her. "Jessica is there somewhere we can all stay?" He gave a slight nod for her to see who had arrived. As the ship arrived, he saw that the town was minute. There were no inns evident that would be suitable for long-term accommodation. The drinking hole was, quite literally, a bark hut.

Jess turned her head and saw her three beloved servants slowly approaching her. She noticed Felicity was walking with her arm on Rex's. Marcus assisted Jess to stand.

Jess called out to Vince and requested that he keep a close eye on Georgie. He nodded, and she went to greet her friends. She embraced each in turn, leaving Felicity to last. The mistress and servant ranks had vanished long ago. Jess put her hands on Felicity's cheeks and said, "Thank you so much, Felicity, thank you for coming and…" she shyly glanced at Marcus, dropping her voice, "Thank you for bringing him. You have no idea how much I need you all."

Felicity drew her former mistress into her arms again. Life had changed drastically for them all. Felicity saw Jess had not noticed her wedding ring and raised her eyebrows with a smile. There would be time to tell her of that and other news later. They knew the story of the chase across the seas would follow. For now, Miss Jess was found.

Jess's heart was light for the first time in a long time.

Marcus offered her his arm, and she willingly took it, clinging to him with both hands. She clasped it much tighter than she should have done. As they were no longer alone, she said, "Mr Ryan, in answer to your earlier question, there is no suitable place to stay but with us. Reverend Middleton has rooms available." She dropped her voice so only he could hear and said, "And sir, he knows all. Even about you," Jess shyly looked up at him before continuing. "I'm sure he will be content if you stay. The rectory is vast, and few are staying with us. Shortly before I arrived, most of the convicts were transported to Port Macquarie. The rooms were occupied by some supervising soldiers who have accompanied them, so the rooms are empty." She whispered again, "Please stay."

His heart was pounding with joy. He squeezed her hand gently for a reply. "Until I can buy somewhere, I will."

"You'll stay in the colony?" she said, astonished at his words.

Marcus replied in a soft voice, "I told you, no more will you be alone. I will stay here, in this town, or wherever you are and watch over you. However, we shall talk more of this in private at a later date." Marcus could see Vincent and the little boy drawing near.

Jessica dropped his arm and went to pick up the child. "Georgie, I want to introduce you to some of my special friends from England. You will need to add them to your heart too. They have just come on the coastal cutter we saw arrive and need somewhere to stay. How about we all go and see your Papa and ask him?"

Georgie looked at the newcomers. He frowned, then hid his head against her shoulder, but he was nodding.

"Are you tired, or would you like to walk?" Jess asked.

Georgie ignored her question. "Did they come in on that ship? Can we have a look onboard? I know Papa said that you couldn't go on deck, but Vince can. Please, Miss Jess, please, can we look on board?" He had pulled back in her arms and was pleading with her.

Jess looked to Vince, who shrugged and then nodded. She then asked Marcus, "Mr Ryan, do you think you would be prepared to show a small boy and Vincent over the ship?"

Marcus grinned; if Jessica wanted him to make friends with this child, he would do anything for her. Marcus bowed to the child. "I would be delighted to, young sir. Mayhap you would like to view the harbour from an elevated height?" He passed his hat to Rex. Marcus took hold of the boy in Jess's arms and slipped him onto his shoulders.

The squeal of delight from the child made them all smile.

Georgie was elated. "Miss Jess, look, I can see everythink. Oh, Mr Ryan, thank you so muchly; this is wonderful. Vince, I like it up here. Can you carries me like this sometime?"

They walked across the grassy foreshore towards the ship.

Rex and Felicity had fallen slightly behind. He watched Marcus with the child and whispered to Felicity, "Flick, I still can't believe that we are to be parents. I wonder what jobs we will do while here; I will have to get a position doing something as we will need the money. I don't imagine there will be many calls for butlers or housekeepers here. Jaques and I have been in deep discussion about this quandary."

Felicity glanced at her husband. "Rexy, do you really think God hasn't gotten that sorted already? Why we may even become farmers. Don't worry about it; I'm not. God will provide, you know that." Rex gave her hand a loving squeeze.

Giles and Colin were waiting on deck for instructions. They had packed but not moved the luggage from the cabins.

Marcus waved hello, and they saw his smile, and both realised he had found her.

Marcus noticed the hand-bump the two men shared in acknowledgement of the success of their search. His own smile showed the delight he felt. Not only had he found her, but she wanted him to stay close. She had been thinking of him and had already confessed his existence to the minister. This astounded him as they had spent so little time together, let alone talk. She had only just lost her family, so he had not expected any response at all. He realised with some embarrassment that he should not have confessed his feelings as he did. He glanced at her, and their eyes met briefly.

Jess stayed with Rex and Felicity while Marcus, Vincent and

Jaques showed Georgie through the ship.

Rex noticed an empty wagon just about to leave the foreshore. It had just finished unloading cargo into the hold. He asked the driver if he was able to drive them to the church and then return for a load of passengers and luggage. He held up a shilling.

The grinning man said, "Eh, mister, for a shillin', I'll drive you to Morpeth if you wants! Hop on, and I'll drop you at the Reverend's house in a jiffy."

While the others were still giving Georgie his tour, Jess and Felicity were assisted up beside him while Rex hopped on the back. The half-mile uphill was accomplished in a very short space of time.

Jess asked her friends to wait outside while she went and spoke to the minister.

Jess returned moments later with a huge smile. "Reverend Middleton said you are all welcome. Rex, bring Felicity inside, and you can both help with the rooms; I will go and collect everyone else." She was almost bouncing with joy.

They found out the driver's name was Henry, and with the promise of another shilling, he was prepared to drive up and down the hill as often as they wished. Henry arrived back at the ship with Jess as Marcus and Vincent escorted a young boy bouncing down the gangplank.

Georgie spied Jess and cannonballed into her waiting arms, full of everything he'd seen. "I gotted to steered the big wheel and turn the tiller. Then Mr Marcus tooked me down to the cabins and showed me the tiny rooms. Oh, Miss Jess, I've had the bestest day ever."

Jess met Marcus's eyes and smiled at the boy's joy. "Oh, then I don't suppose you want a ride back home on the back of Mr Henry's wagon with Mr Marcus and the rest of our new friends?"

George was over the moon. "Really? A ride too? And I can go on the back? Will Vince hold me tight, so I don't fall off?"

"He will," Marcus added, chuckling.

Soon the many cases were being unloaded, and they placed some on the back of the wagon.

Marcus gave directions to his staff. "Colin, Giles, I will take Miss Jess and Georgie home and send the wagon back for you two. Jaques, you can come with us and start the unpacking. Felicity and Rex will also need assistance." Marcus lifted Georgie onto the back of the wagon. Vince and Jaques climbed up on either side of him, and Marcus sat next to Jess. He wished to take her hand but restrained himself.

Soon after they arrived at the single-story, stuccoed brick parsonage, Marcus gave Henry a one-pound note. Henry had just unloaded the first few bags when Marcus said, "This is for keeping you late, sir, but you have saved us no end of effort in the heat."

"Golly gosh, mister, you can hire me any day for that amount. I don't make that in a month." Henry shook Marcus's hand so hard that Marcus laughed.

Marcus realised the benefit of having transportation. "Give me your direction, and I may well do that, Henry. I'll be staying in the area and looking for a place to buy, so let me know if you hear of a house or a property for rent or sale. I shall also require a vehicle of sorts and a beast to draw it. In the meantime, we may require your services."

Henry grinned. "Will do, mister. You take care now. I'll be back in a jiffy with the others and the luggage." Henry said, "Gee-up" to his old horse and headed off downhill again.

Jess slid her hand down to Marcus's and gave it a quick squeeze before she led them indoors.

Reverend Middleton greeted them at the door. He had seen the quick action Jess had made, and he smiled. He was pleased she had told him about Marcus Ryan. If this man was prepared to chase her halfway around the world, he really must care. "Welcome, Mr Ryan. I have your rooms nearly ready, so come in out of the heat."

His son interrupted him. "Papa, Mr Ryan tookded me on the ship, and I steered and did the tiller, and then I seended downstairs."

Reverend Middleton hoisted his young son up and hugged him. "Again, thank you, Mr Ryan; I dare say we shall all hear about this excitement for some time. He's been aching to get on board again."

The child clasped his father's face and demanded his attention. "Papa, Mr Ryan made me promise I won't get on board by myself, but I've seen it now, so I won't do that."

Reverend Middleton said, "Good boy," then turned to Marcus. "Come inside out of the heat, please." He led the way indoors while Jaques and Vincent carried the bags inside after them. "Georgie, go find Miss Jess and see where she's put everyone. Then go to Cook and have a drink."

The rest of the baggage had arrived and been carried into the rectory within an hour. When the last load arrived, Jess recognised her monogrammed cases. She stood with her mouth open and turned to Felicity and Marcus. "How did you get all this? I left it at Crawley."

Marcus was expecting this. He had made sure that Reverend Middleton was at hand when Marcus handed over a special gift for Jess. He didn't explain what would follow. "Miss Jessica, your luggage is not all we got, I shall tell you the story of this later, but I wish to return your property to you." He handed over a parcel tied in a gold ribbon.

The moment Jess took the parcel from his hand, she knew what it would be. "How?" was all she managed to say before she was tearing the wrapping and hugging Lucien's Bible. With everyone watching, she walked into Marcus's arms. "You have no idea what this means to me, Marcus." She reached up and kissed his cheek.

Reverend Middleton asked, "Is that the Bible Miss Jess was accused of stealing?"

Marcus smiled at him and acknowledged that it was. His smile at Jess's reaction spoke volumes. "I must confess, I told a fudge to Mr Egbert, sir." Instead of looking guilty, Marcus was grinning broadly. "It's quite a story but well worth telling."

The reverend nodded. "Good, then let us retire to the office while everyone is settling and tell me all about it." He led the way into his den and offered Marcus a seat.

Felicity took this opportunity to take Jess aside and let her former mistress know of her status change. "Miss Jess, Mr Marcus only allowed me to come if Rex and I married. He arranged it all, and we married by special licence just before we sailed."

Jess hugged her and gave her a kiss, then said, "I had no idea you had feelings for each other."

Felicity smiled. "Neither did we until all your troubles started. When Miss Judith died, I turned to Rex. Then we found ourselves drawn to each other more and more. When we met you in the park, I knew then that I didn't wish to leave him. He was being sent to Crawley, and I had been dismissed. Jaques had already been sent away. Mr Marcus knew I wished to come and gave us an ultimatum: marry quickly. It wasn't a hard decision, but it has had an unexpected consequence; you see, I am with child." Felicity blushed and glanced shyly at Jess.

Jess got the giggles and told Felicity that she was delighted.

Life was now looking up. These three people were almost family. She yet had to speak to Marcus, but she was sure that she knew what he wanted. She was still astounded he had come looking for her, let alone bring her senior staff. They were already friends and had been before their tragic picnic.

In the meantime, Felicity and Rex were unpacking in their room, in-between kisses of delight from Rex and chuckles from Felicity. The room downstairs may originally have been a store room, but long ago, it was transformed into a guest room with a big bed. What was best, they had no one sharing their area.

Jaques was unpacking some of Jess's clothes into her wardrobe, although most of her fancy gowns would remain in her cases. Jess thanked Jaques as she saw what he was doing. It would be nice to have a few options other than the gowns she had almost lived in for six months. Giles and Colin were doing the same for Marcus. Once done, Giles went down to the kitchen to see if he could assist. As a groom, he was content to leave Colin to his work.

With five unexpected extra persons for dinner, the cook and the kitchen hand were overwhelmed. Vincent was already there peeling potatoes. He was courting Milly, the maid. Any chance he could, he would offer his assistance. As they only had one horse, he had very little stable work to do, so he helped her at any opportunity. Giles joined them, picked up a paring knife and was soon assisting Vince.

Marcus and George Middleton were getting to know each other in the office. The discussion started with Marcus confessing the lies he told to Egbert. The physical description of the man and his attire set George laughing. The more Marcus described the man and his reaction to his visit, the more George chortled. "I know it's not Christian of me to laugh at someone, but I can envisage such a man. I have met them before. They used to be referred to as macaroni or a tulip of fashion. I have sometimes found that it is a knee-jerk reaction to weak self-esteem. Which is so funny, as to wear such attire one would think just the opposite."

Marcus was beginning to like this man a lot. "Sir, I can see our good Lord led Mrs Jessica to a place of safety. She is in good hands. However, sir, I will tell you now that I intend to do all I can to marry her. I chased her halfway around the world, and it was not without reason. I have not had much time to talk to her yet, so I am asking permission to have a private conversation with her this evening on the verandah. We have much to discuss." Marcus was determined to talk to her anyway, permission or not, but he wished to pave the way to a smooth future for her sake. She had already had enough trauma. Marcus waited for George to answer his request.

George lay back in his office chair and twiddled his thumbs. "Mr Ryan, no, Marcus, if she had not already told me about you, I would have wondered. However, from the moment she arrived, she was truthful. She told me her entire story. From the picnic, the mushrooms, then the funeral and accident, and the two nights at your place. She told me she felt something for you already, which astounded her, considering her recent loss and the love she held for Lucien. She wondered if you had feelings for her. Did you know she wasn't asleep some of the times you spoke to her? Listening to you speak of mundane things eased the pain of her loss. Your vivid descriptions of your home took her mind from her own sadness." George watched the look of bewilderment cross Marcus's face. "I gather you also spoke to her of your budding feelings."

Marcus shook his head, unable to speak. He had no idea she had heard his words at her bedside. His heart was pounding with a mix of excitement and concern. She had heard his words of endearment to her. He merely nodded.

George continued with his story. "Then, when she was cast out from her home, the only person she could think of was you. She knew her uncle would not help. You were her only hope. Even on so little acquaintance, she knew she could trust you. I presume you brought her jewellery box too."

Marcus nodded. "…And all her clothing. There are other things of Judith's too, but they are at home. Egbert rightly inherited all of Lucien's things but not Judith's or Jessica's, so I collected everything I could. The three who accompanied me were her staff. They were all dismissed for assisting her, so they were my allies from the start. Mrs Felicity Harris was her housekeeper, and she knew what to bring; Rex was her butler, and Jaques was Lucien's tiger and valet. I'll tell you his story one day." Marcus gave George a wry smile. "The new owners were not impressed that I claimed everything of hers. I left Judith's things at my London home, though."

George sat thinking that this situation was not entirely to his liking. He did not wish to lose Jess. Georgie was finally happy and beginning to come out of his shell, and she had achieved all this in just a matter of weeks. "I will agree on one condition. Marcus, she is to be courted properly, no hasty marriage by special licence. And then when you do marry, I do not want you far away. I won't relinquish her assignment until I know Georgie is settled. There has been a profound change in my son in the few weeks that Miss Jess has been here. Are you prepared to do that?" George sat watching the face of the man across his desk. He expected anger, but he saw excitement.

Marcus was ecstatic. "You mean it, sir? I intend to move as close as possible to her. I knew I would need to woo her, but sir, I'm not sure she will need much of that if my welcome on the foreshore is anything to go by. If you permit us to marry, I will not remove her from Georgie until you give her leave, or should I say, give us leave." Again, Marcus waited anxiously for his reply.

George gave him a slow nod as he lay back in his chair now with the tips of his fingers bouncing together. He thought deeply. "Marcus, I will lay all my cards on the table. My priority must be Georgie. Marcus, Miss Jess has achieved more in the few weeks she has been with us than any other help I have employed for him since his mother died. For my sake and his, I can't risk her leaving for a while." He glanced at Marcus to gauge his reaction. Still studying his face, he continued, "Now, when I say all my cards, I confess I am also getting remarried. I have just received her acceptance." He tapped the letter sitting on his desk. "Georgie needs a mother and hopefully siblings; I have met a young lady, and we have been corresponding. With her official acceptance, I shall write back and tell her I will begin to call banns. I shall start them this Sunday. If possible, I would like a February wedding, but that will be at her home in Liverpool. I would have preferred earlier, but her parents said I had to wait. Georgie has been my stumbling block; he had rejected every other person I have had to care for him, so the way he has responded to Miss Jess is amazing. If I tell him she will leave, he will withdraw again. So do you think we can work together?"

Marcus stood smiling so hard that his heart was thumping with anticipation. He reached over to shake his hand. "I think we have a deal, Reverend, but I warn you, as I said, I intend to propose as soon as I can find somewhere for us to rent or live. As soon as that is arranged, I shall marry her."

George knew there was a fly in Marcus's ointment. "Marcus, there is something else to consider. Miss Jess is a convict. Like it or not, she must have permission from Sydney to marry. This can sometimes take months, so I would propose sooner rather than later if I were you. I think you are correct in not having to woo her, but still, take it easy. God has protected her from what other convict women endured, but that doesn't mean she doesn't carry emotional scars. Then, of course, she is still grieving the loss of her husband and daughter. I catch her sometimes looking at Georgie with tear-filled eyes. My heart grieves for her, but she shrugs off her melancholy and gets on with life." George had found her weeping for her loss and the following consequences. "Marcus, things in the colony are not strict, so you won't need to move out once engaged. However, as you are to be living in a church residence, I trust that you will abide by all the normal rules. Take her out on the verandah this evening after our meal. And, Marcus, please call me George."

Marcus had been warned about this by Ned. "Thank you, sir; I promise that all your rules, and we will both see that society's rules, too, are followed."

At that moment, Jess knocked on the door and called them for dinner.

George gave them a minute alone to arrange their rendezvous later that evening.

Marcus gently took her hand and prevented her from leaving. "Jessica, we will need to arrange a few moments to have our chat. Would you be happy sitting on the verandah with me later this evening? We have permission from George."

Jess was suddenly shy, but she knew that now he was here; the sooner they spoke, the better. She also wished to hear how he was able to get all her things from Egbert. He had chased her; knowing of her conviction, she was pretty sure what he wanted to talk to her about, so she stepped close and kissed his cheek to reassure him. "I'd love that, Marcus." She took his hand and led him from the room.

Dinner was a jovial event, and as the sun sank, the temperature dropped.

As soon as Georgie was bathed and put to bed, she hoped she would get a chance to have some private conversation with Marcus.

Chapter 11 Planning the Future

With dinner over and his son in bed, George motioned for Marcus to take Jess outside. The house had a wide verandah that wrapped right along the front. From one end, the verandah tapered onto a single step down into the spacious gardens. Marcus knew what he wanted to do and knew what he should do. He had promised that he would behave appropriately, and kissing Jessica on the parson's verandah in full view of the town was inappropriate.

For dinner, she had changed into one of the gowns he had brought her. The gown was cinched in at the waist and had triple frills along the hem. It was not the typical high-waisted gown that many women in the colony wore, but Jessica was far from ordinary. She was special. The dress was both simple and modest and suited her to a tee.

Marcus could not wait to give her the other surprise he had for her. He intended to hand her the jewellery box she left with him; however, that would have to wait until tomorrow as it had not yet been unpacked.

From its elevated vantage point of the elevated verandah that overlooked the small town, they sat on a double bench seat in relative privacy. Here, Jess and Marcus could sit together and not be overheard. The wide verandah picked up the evening sea breeze, and Marcus could smell the salt in the air. He had now found her but discovered that he was tongue-tied. He needed to figure out where to start. He stood looking out over the town but could also see some of the outbuildings and immense kitchen gardens. He swallowed, knowing he must speak.

Jess took his hand and interlinked her fingers with his. "Marcus, you have chased me halfway across the world; I think I know the reason for your presence here. Be assured that you were never far from my thoughts." She took his other hand, "Talk to me, Marcus; tell me why you came?"

Marcus lifted his eyes from her hands. He could still see her face illuminated in the quickly fading twilight. He swallowed nervously before launching into the words he had rehearsed for months. "Jessica, I find I am unsure of where to start. It is just six months since your double loss, and I know it is too soon to say anything, but I want to, no, I need to, for various reasons. So I will open my heart to you and hope you treat it kindly. To put it simply, I love you; I wish to marry you, and soon. I have already told George that; however, he insisted that I must woo you; and he suggested we take things slowly. To give you time to adjust to everything." He paused for a moment as if to catch his breath.

She smiled but waited for him to finish. Her eyes were bright with happiness.

Marcus said, somewhat embarrassed, "Yes, I have followed you, and I intend to stay as close to you as possible if you allow me to. I will fight tooth and nail against anyone who hurts you. I will defend you to the hilt. I am already far too free with your name, but our introduction was unusual. Jessica, I need you as part of my life, but I will try to be patient. George has told me that even if we become engaged, we still have to have permission before we marry. I know this to be true, as my friend Ned mentioned the same thing."

He saw a micro frown cross her brow. He wondered if she would laugh at his bumbling words. Marcus paused for a moment before asking her, "Jessica, is it too soon to speak of these things?" He had never been short of the right words before, but he also had not expected to be able to go on his knee before this woman and propose on the day he found her. Hopefully, that will follow soon.

Jess brought one of his hands to her lips, kissed it, and then placed it on her cheek. "No, Marcus, it isn't too early, and no wooing is required."

To his relief, she gave a chuckle.

Her adorable smile gave him confidence, but it was her words that made his heart sing. "I have been through so much in the past six months that it seems like far more time has passed. I still miss Lucien and Judith, and I always shall, but that won't bring them back. It's how and why we met, and for that, they will always remain part of our story. So, it's not too soon for you to speak. I need you as much as I hope you want me. So, ask me, Marcus. Ask me what you have come so far to do."

Marcus slid off the seat and was on one knee before her; he then laid bare his heart, and he now offered it to her for life. Gazing up at her in the dim light, he added, "No more will you be alone, my love. No more will I bury myself in business, trying hard to hide my loneliness. No more will either of us wonder if we are loved and cared for. So, no more, my lovely one, for I want you to be mine forever. Will you marry me? Will you be my wife and hopefully bear my children?" He could see the smile that tipped her beautiful cupid lips. His heart was pounding in anticipation.

Jess could not believe that this was happening. "Yes, I will, Marcus; I will marry you with all my heart and soul. Yes, I most certainly will." Jess leaned forward and kissed him, then pulled back, realising they were fully visible to all in the town.

Marcus enjoyed her brief caress but moved to sit beside her again. This time, keeping her hand clasped in his. "Oh, my Jessica, my beloved, I promised that I would behave. We are so visible here, but I do wish to kiss you properly."

She also wished to be in his arms. "Come," she stood and took his hand to lead him around the verandah to the other side of the building. "Around here, we are not visible from town, and no one should be around."

Once out of sight, she turned and walked into his waiting arms. As they were engaged, she felt no embarrassment in being held so close to him.

She lifted her lips to his, but he stood gazing down at her soaking the realisation that she would soon be his.

Marcus was fighting the desire to crush her to him and drag her somewhere private; however, he would not. He was now finally holding her as he had dreamed. Finally, he bent his head and felt the response of her lips to his. He had not expected her to step closer to him or wrap her arms around his neck, drawing him closer still. She pressed her body so snugly to his that it felt like they were moulded as one; then, she opened her mouth as she was kissing him.

As their kiss deepened, her tongue touched his, and he reached a point he almost lost control. "Oh, golly gosh, Jessica!" He had temporarily forgotten that she had been married before, whereas this was all new to him. He had kept himself from intimate relations with anyone until marriage; therefore, he was unaware of the passion that awaited him. Now he held his beloved; he found it hard to release her. Sanity finally prevailed, and Marcus broke the embrace. He was breathing rapidly, and he was so close to breaking his promise to George. He pushed her away gently; his resolve was stretched almost beyond his power to stop. "Oh, Jessica, I never knew the power of just a kiss."

Jess understood; she also knew the battle he was having and moved from his grasp. "I'm sorry, Marcus," she finally said. "I won't put you in such temptation again, at least not until we are wed, but please send through the request for our marriage quickly."

With his raging emotions coming under control, he took her gently in his arms again. He gave a quick laugh, then said, "I will not kiss you like that again, my beloved Jess, or I shall come fully undone. I, too, wish that our request will be granted soon."

Now in control of his rampaging emotions, he remembered he had not yet given her the ring he had purchased in London. Pulling the small box from his back pocket, he took her hand and placed a small hook-locked box onto it. He flipped it open, and she saw a gem twinkling in the scant moonlight.

He could hear the joy in her voice as she said, "I can't see it properly, but put it on Marcus, and then it's official." She held the open box to him. She had put her other wedding ring in the jewellery box before Felicity had given them to Marcus to mind.

He took the ring and slipped it on her ringless finger.

Marcus knew the size was right, as when she was at his house, Mrs Busselton had, at one stage, removed her wedding rings and handed them to him to hold while she washed the mud from Jess's hands. Both hands had been muddied when she fell. So as not to drop the gold bands, he slipped them onto his little finger. It had sat on the first joint of his knuckle. He had not opened her jewellery box, so had not realised her other rings were in there. He had chosen a diamond and two yellow topaz stones for an engagement ring, knowing it would suit her. He still had a wedding band in his luggage. Hopefully, that would sit next to these gems very soon.

With her engagement ring now in place, he gave her a quick kiss. "Let us go in and share our good news. I do not trust myself out here with you any longer."

George and the rest of Marcus's travelling companions were waiting for them in the sitting room.

As they entered, Jess went straight into Felicity's arms.

The men all crowded around a grinning Marcus. He could scarcely tear his eyes from his beloved as she spoke to her old staff. He was still shocked at finding her, let alone getting engaged the day he arrived.

Colin, Giles, Jaques, and Rex each nearly shook his hand off. All were pleased with the outcome of their hastily planned trip.

George smiled; he, too, knew this joy. He wished Sarah was nearer so he could embrace her for the first time. Being so young, they had not been allowed any time alone at all. Even when he proposed, her mother was in the room as she was too young to be unchaperoned. That time would come in the not-too-distant future. He was thrilled that the ship today had brought a letter of Sarah's official acceptance. When he proposed, she whispered to him that she had agreed, but her father had insisted they wait until after her birthday. So, as there had been two official engagements in one day, it was a good reason for celebrations. Currently, only Marcus knew of his joy, but soon word would spread, so he thought he might as well announce his news too.

He called in Cook, Milly, and Vince and shared his news. He knew that Georgie also had to know, but that would be better coming from Jess tomorrow. He hoped to visit his betrothed sometime after the Christmas services next week. When he broke his news, a second round of congratulations ensued before everyone eventually retired for the night.

Marcus received a chaste kiss on the cheek as he headed to his room. Jess's room was not in this building but next door to Cook's and Milly's in the staff quarters.

~

Christmas Day broke sunny and bright. All the residents of the parsonage were all up early as there was much to arrange before services.

Jess had Georgie dressed and was feeding him his favourite breakfast. Dippy eggs with toast fingers were a special day treat. This morning she had made it even more special. She had collected an enormous double-yolk egg a few days before and had hidden it from him. On Christmas morning, Cook had prepared it for him. His eyes nearly popped when he saw the enormous size of his breakfast treat. Cook had also toasted an extra slice of thinly cut toast, buttered them thickly, and then cut them into fingers for him; this set the morning mood. Delightful sounds of adoration emanated from the young lad as he sat in the kitchen consuming his treat.

When Marcus had purchased the rings, he had also bought Jess a matching topaz and diamond necklace and looked forward to presenting it to her as her Christmas gift.

During the week, Jess had seen a beautiful leather wallet at the market and had managed to get Marcus's initials embossed on the front. She, too, looked forward to handing it to him when they swapped gifts after luncheon. She had embroidered some handkerchiefs for Reverend Middleton and had purchased small trinkets in the market for everyone else. She had found a pull-along toy horse for Georgie, and for Felicity, she found a lovely baby shawl. Hopefully, they would all love their gifts.

After an early breakfast, Marcus and George left for the church as George had asked for assistance.

In the days between their arrival and Christmas, Marcus had spent time with George, doing the rounds of the village. It was quite small, so had not taken long. Marcus was also kept occupied assisting in the preparation for the Christmas services. The question of their ages had arisen during that week, and Marcus was surprised to learn that George was only a year older than him.

George was impressed with Marcus's biblical knowledge, and the two were often found sitting on the verandah in some deep theological discussion while looking hard into the depths of their tea, not that there were any answers there.

By the time Christmas Day had arrived, George had sounded Marcus out to see if he would like to assist with some catechist's work for him. Earlier in the week, George showed Marcus around the church. George had risen early and prepared for his Morning Prayer service.

Marcus joined him but poked around the back of the church and got the feel of the place. There was little to see; however, he found a wooden box hidden under a rear seat. He was just about to haul it out when the service started. During the noisy parts of the service, he nudged it out and found it was full of hymnals.

Three evenings a week, George also held Evensong, but his household was the only attendees.

Marcus liked the way George ran services and was surprised that George asked Marcus for a critique of his sermons. He was astonished that the Evensong was not conducted each day, but George admitted that few ever came. Plus, with no musical instrument, all singing was *a cappella*. Marcus had a strong baritone and carried a tune well, so he enjoyed the opportunity to exercise his lungs. His school years had given him a love of singing. Marcus had not sung a great deal in recent years, but he and Jeffrey had loved singing in the church choir when boys. Both had been boy sopranos, and both were booted from the choir when their voices had broken. He knew Ned and his friends also had been in the choir after he left school.

After only a week in town, Marcus realised that finding somewhere to live would be more problematic than he realised. He discovered that he would probably have to build their home, and with only fifty convicts in town and no building teams, his plans were going to take far more time than he realised. There was just nothing suitable for rental, let alone for sale. Admittedly, he could build a minute cabin or even a small brick cottage, but the residence he was currently in was comfortable and spacious. He was close to Jessica and able to give her assistance if required. They were chaperoned at all times, so he could see her when he wished.

George was in no hurry to have his visitors leave. They were like a breath of fresh air. Marcus had willingly become a sounding board for his musings, and therefore his sermons had more vim and vigour than ever before. Marcus did not hesitate to ask him questions or request clarification of some topics, and sometimes he even challenged his facts. Consequently, George put more effort into his words, and others noticed too. He could see the attention on their faces. Previously they had often even gone to sleep in his long-learned dissertations.

One hint Marcus gave him was some words of wisdom. "If you can't say what you need to in ten minutes, stop anyway. For after that time, you have lost your congregation's attention."

George had watched the congregation and saw that after that time, their minds wandered. He could see it in their faces. A ten-minute sermon was much easier to prepare than a one-hour lecture.

Marcus's second gem of wisdom was something he already

knew but had forgotten. The Bible was the inspired word of God; if the congregation only heard the Bible readings, then they had heard God. George realised that his words were only a pale shadow of the Bible. In just one week, George's vitality for his work had returned. Miss Jess's arrival had been a blessing, but now he knew he was no longer alone. Marcus's words gave him moral support, and now he was eager to be married again.

After Mary had died when Georgie was born, he found himself to be a hollow shell. The midwife found a wet nurse for his tiny son, and although the child had never known his mother, Georgie had become attached to the wet nurse. The boy had grieved when aged just two; they sailed for Sydney Cove and had withdrawn from everyone except his father. Georgie had cried as soon as he was out of sight until Miss Jess arrived. He had felt sorry for his son but floundered at how to assist him. The child had been passed from carer to carer for over three years. At one stage, George did not even see him for some months. Now freed from the constant burden of his care, he was looking forward to the ten days off in the new year and seeing Sarah Rose again. Georgie had willingly volunteered to stay with Miss Jess while he went away. He even refused a trip on the boat.

The week had brought two more long letters from his betrothed. George had only managed to find time to write one that week. Marcus's ideas of new ventures planned to start after his marriage excited him. He started the busy day ahead of him with joy. With his friend beside him, they entered the vestry door in the side of the brick church and then busied themselves in preparing for the influx of parishioners that would arrive shortly. Marcus had adopted the role of verger and went to sort out the prayer books required for the service. Today they would sing carols; Marcus had found a massive pile of music in a box in the vestry. Inside the box were some thirty copies of John Newton's and William Cowper's Olney Hymnal.

Both George and Marcus knew some of the carols and hymns they had chosen; it would be a surprise for the congregation. All would be invited to join in the singing. Marcus would stand at the back and sing from there; he nervously wondered if he could carry this off. He stood and welcomed the congregation.

George stood beside him and introduced him as a friend from England. No one needed to know differently. Jessica and

Georgie were sitting in the second front pew as Georgie loved to watch his father.

Once the convicts were seated and locked into the boxed pews, George started the service by explaining that the service would be a little different because of Christmas. There was a momentary pause before George gave a nod.

Marcus's voice rang out from the back of the church, singing *O Come, O Come Emmanuel.* There was a collective gasp as his strong, clear voice rang out. After the initial shock, others joined in the joyous Christmas chorus.

Jess knew who it was as soon as she heard the first notes. She would have loved to turn around and watch; instead, she stood and joined him. Even the convicts joined in as they picked up the chorus; each stood as they did so. George saw the smiling faces of the congregation and knew that the choice to have music included was a good one. Throughout the service, Marcus sang more carols and hymns. By the time he had sung the first line of each, many others had accompanied him.

At the end of the service, many requested that he sing more, so they had a singing time just with Christmas songs and carols. *Angels from the Realms of Glory* was followed by *Joy to the World, When Shepherds watched their Flocks by Night, Hark the Herald Angels Sing*, and to finish off, Marcus finished with his favourite Wesleyan hymn, *And Can it Be.* While not specifically a Christmas carol, it gave the message he wished them to hear. The hymn was tied firmly to the words of the earlier sermon. However, before he sang this one, he walked to the front of the church and stood at the altar steps. At the end of the hymn, he explained the meaning.

Marcus explained that Christmas and Easter were interconnected. One was not possible without the other. Marcus then held out his hand and called Georgie to him. The child ran to him and was hoisted up into Marcus's arms. With Georgie now listening intently to his words, Marcus explained the Christmas Nativity in simple language. It was almost like a children's talk, but his words were suitable for every person there. Marcus explained, "The link between the two celebrations was not tenuous, as many think, but, in fact, they are totally interconnected. Christmas and the birth of Christ are forerunners of Easter. It is about the birth of the Saviour of the world, and Easter was all about His death and particularly His resurrection, where Jesus took our sins and wiped them away. He obliterated every stain and crime that we have made and taken them on himself…" There was an audible gasp heard from the convict stalls, but he continued, "…where Jesus opened a new pathway for all humankind back to God. Jesus needed to come to earth as one of us to be able to complete His God-given role as Redeemer and Saviour of mankind after the fall in Genesis. Easter would never have happened if Christmas didn't come first. We are washed clean because He died for us. No one is too bad to be forgiven." His simple children's talk at the end of the service brought tears to Jess's eyes.

Jess knew that Georgie would not be the only one there today who understood his story and absorbed it in a way that they had not done before.

From his chair in the sanctuary, George also listened, absolutely spellbound at the simplicity of the story. He knew his words reached only a few educated listeners; however, Marcus's words were understood by them all, convict and free alike. Old and young alike comprehended what he had said. Marcus, still carrying the child, left through the vestry side door at the end of the service. He did not want the accolades, so he quietly left by the side door and took Georgie onto the grassy hill outside. They walked down to the windmill and watched the wooden sails slowly turning in the wind. There was no grinding done on Christmas Day, but the cooling sea breeze still turned the enormous fan.

Inside the church, Jess watched the reverend give the final blessing, then moved to follow him down the aisle. Her friends followed on her heels. Normally she would have her charge with her, but she realised Marcus had disappeared so as to avoid drawing attention from the minister. It was one more thing she loved about her betrothed; his humility was endearing. They had been able to spend time together each day. Marcus had escorted her, with Vincent accompanying Georgie, as they walked to the foreshore. These outings gave them time to talk without finding themselves in a compromising situation.

They had discussed the possibility of Marcus building something. Still, with word of the cleric's upcoming marriage announced, Marcus knew that staying in the rectory after his wedding would be difficult for the new bride. Marcus realised he would have to make a decision reasonably quickly. Having no other options currently available, they decided to leave it in the Lord's hands.

George felt that by the first week of January, he could leave the midweek services in Marcus's hands. He arranged that one of the lieutenants of the 48th regiment would conduct the Sunday Service, with Marcus giving the message. It was really the Major's role to undertake to do this; however, he declined. The soldiers usually did a service without a sermon. After his oratory excellence on Christmas Day, George had no qualms about what Marcus would say. Their discussions about the doctrinal beliefs had shown that they agreed with much. Marcus was more inclined to treat all equally, which somewhat surprised George.

By now, George had discovered Marcus's extreme wealth. He had a knack for knowing how to invest and turn an idea into a profit. George was wanting to invest in some land and turned to Marcus for advice. With so few people in the town, Marcus suggested that they look a little further up the valley for new supporters. Being the only church in the valley was a benefit, as most official ceremonies needed to be held in a consecrated church.

Before George had departed to see Sarah, he travelled to Morpeth to conduct a funeral. Marcus had accompanied him. They had come down the river in a small sloop and were met at the wharf close to Morpeth. A horse and sulky were waiting for them, and they were soon heading southwest through the most beautiful countryside. The undulating hills were well stocked with an assortment of beasts. They passed vines, crops, and barns at nearly every turn.

Marcus saw the beauty of the valley they passed through. "George, I would seriously consider land out this way. You know I am a wool merchant; I have my head office in London, and my friend, who is my secretary, is running things while I am here, but if I get some land and run stock myself, that will save me thousands of pounds. I saw John Macarthur's merinos last visit, and I'd be interested in buying some of those."

George was incredulous. "You really mean to stay, don't you?"

Marcus smiled at his question. He had been in much trepidation himself, but having seen the lush valleys around him, the decision to stay in Australia had just become a lot easier. "Of course! Jessica cannot leave for nearly seven years, I shall be here at least that long, and in that time, I will petition whomever I can to have her come home with me at the end of her term. I know Governor Brisbane is not favouring emancipists leaving, nor is he allowing large grants to be issued. So, I intend to see if I can purchase what I require, and this valley seems perfect for sheep." Thankfully, he was very warm in the pocket, so financing this new wool venture would not be a problem. He sat back in the sulky they were now in and took in as much of the area as possible.

George could see his intent scrutiny and gave him a running commentary as they drove. "Macarthur won't sell you any stock, you know. His amazing wife deserves the credit, though. He willingly takes the credit for her years of hard work and selective breeding. I hear she worked like a Trojan living in a bark shack at Camden before returning to Parramatta to recuperate after the shearing was completed. I've not heard a bad word about her, you know."

Marcus knew of the reputation of both Macarthurs. "I met John in London at the time of his banishment. Then some years ago, on one of my first visits here, his wife and her overseer showed me their stock. I know of John's reputation and that he is supposed to stay well out of the political argument, but I foresee that he won't sit too far from the action." He fell silent, watching the verdant pastures go by.

Miles passed when Marcus started. He saw a magnificent black stallion in a lush green pasture and exclaimed, "Oh, George, he's magnificent!"

The reverend smiled. "He belongs to the people we are going to see, so you may get a chance to see him up close. He is a cantankerous beast, and he threw the owner, causing his demise. They may wish to get rid of him."

Marcus smiled. "I will make an offer for him, George. Even if he can't be ridden, he would make the most wonderful sire. I hope he will become the first of my beasts for my new farm." With that, Marcus folded his arms and gazed at the horse as they drew near.

Chapter 12 Exciting Times

*T*he wedding of George Middleton and Sarah Rose occurred in Liverpool near the end of February 1824. They had a short honeymoon and arrived back in Newcastle on the coastal cutter in early March. Sarah had not visited Newcastle before and was surprised at how small the community was.

Jessica and Marcus were astounded when they heard that Sarah was just sixteen, but on the newly married couple's return, it was evident that she was both very much in love and in awe of her new husband. She was confident and willing to assist George in his work, but she was young, so very young.

George, on the other hand, was smitten. Sarah was no simpering miss, though. He was nearly thirty-three, and as he had been married before, he was very careful not to scare or overwhelm her. Therefore, he had told her a little of what was ahead of her.

The two weeks away together had been blissful, but Sarah was now to meet her stepson for the first time. She was nervous; as was expected, she also now knew others would be sharing their house. Also, she realised she was expected to take over the running of the parsonage and knew she had to step into the role of minister's wife immediately.

George had mentioned Jessica, but only as a governess who was assigned to his son. He had not mentioned that she was a titled Lady. He had discussed this and asked Jess to tell Sarah herself if she felt it was necessary. George had only informed Marcus and Jessica about the remarkably young age of his future wife when he left to get married in mid-February. George admitted this small titbit of information on the way down to catch the boat *en route* to the wedding. He said, "I wished to marry earlier, but her parents insisted that we wait until she turned sixteen. Her nature is sweet and compliant, but she has energy to burn. Hopefully, Georgie will adore her as I do."

Since his father's departure, Jessica had spent the past two weeks preparing Georgie for his new stepmother. The following week would be interesting, for no one knew how these two would get on. Jess had done all she could. They decided that they should meet on neutral ground for the first time. Therefore, the excitement of the boat returning was chosen as the venue. Georgie would already be distracted by the ship, so hopefully, he would take to the new person without mishap.

The small ship berthed without a problem, though a mishap did occur soon afterwards. Georgie was dancing with excitement about his father's return home and overlooked the gangplank being slid across the wharf behind him. The cacophony of noise all around him masked any sound. He was so busy watching the sailors on deck furl and tie off the sails, coil the ropes and make the small craft shipshape that he didn't even notice that his father had alighted. When the last of the ropes were coiled, he spun around and tripped over the end of the gangplank. With a grazed knee and hurt pride, the small boy lay still on the ground in some shock. Then he started weeping.

A young lady sat beside him on the end of the ramp and drew the sad child into her arms.

Georgie didn't look up; he just felt loving arms cradle him and bring him comfort. The gentle hug she gave him was returned when his little arms slid around her waist. Soon the tears ceased. He looked up and saw a smiling face looking down at him. Without asking, she dabbed at the blood on his knee with a clean handkerchief. "You are a big brave soldier, aren't you? I would have wept for much longer if I had done that."

Georgie looked down at the blood and was about to cry again. It didn't look too good. He watched the blood trickle down his leg and drip onto the wharf. He was about to cry again when he remembered her loving words. He frowned. "Are you my new mama?

I haven't had one before, and you smell of flowers like Miss Jess sometimes does, but she normally smells like roses. I like flowers." The child's innocent question made all those watching wait in anticipation of how he would react.

The gentle voice replied, "I'd like to be your mama, but that's up to you; I could just be a friend. You can work out what you'd like to call me later. In the meantime, how about you say hello to your Papa?" Only then did she look up and see smiling eyes on her as she sat on the wharf with her new stepson.

Georgie had not released his hold on her waist. He usually would have cannonballed into his father's arms. He had become used to hugs, and he liked them. "Hello, Papa. I missed you, and I'm glad you are home."

George had watched the way Sarah had taken control of the situation. Usually, he would have picked up his son and told him that he should watch his step. Sarah had broken through without even trying. A twinkle appeared in his eyes when they flicked from his son's face to his wife's. "Hello, son; I see you have found a way to introduce yourself in a very unique way," George laughed.

Ignoring his father, Georgie turned back to his protector. "You smell nice; what are your flowers?"

Sarah chuckled. "Violets, Georgie. Do you like them?"

The small head nodded against her chest. "I do, 'n' I like all pretty flowers too. I think I'll like you as a mama. Is that all right?" the small boy asked in earnest.

Sarah smiled and flicked the tip of his nose affectionately. "If you want me to be; otherwise, as I said, I shall just be your friend as I said."

Georgie tipped his head as he looked at her. "No, I think I will keep you as my mama," he hugged her again.

With introductions completed to everyone else, Henry appeared from nowhere with his wagon. With the banns being read in church, everyone knew the young minister had left to get married. Henry had been watching for the ship's return and hoped they would have luggage to bring to the parsonage and he'd get a good tip. He wasn't wrong. He collected the passengers, and they were the reverend, his son and his wife. Marcus and the rest of the group would arrange for the luggage to be loaded into the cart and follow on the second trip.

Rex greeted them at the parsonage and put on his best

butler's voice. He welcomed the new mistress of the house.

George felt Sarah cling a little tighter. She had never seen a butler in real life and was somewhat overawed at the debonair man in her house. Everything was so new. She wished her family had at least come for a visit first, but she was so alone. After introducing Sarah, George asked Felicity to take Georgie into the kitchen for a biscuit, leaving his parents alone. George showed Sarah into his office and shut the door. He took both her hands and kissed her. "Sweet Sarah, you have done so well with Georgie. Sitting with him on the ramp was wonderful. Hopefully, he will accept you now. I just wanted to say welcome home in private."

She stepped into his arms and returned his kiss. "I'll try my hardest, George, but he's such a sweet little boy; I'm sure he'll be wonderful." By the time the wagon arrived, George had shown Sarah through the house and outbuildings. She had already met Felicity, and when Sarah realised Rex and Felicity were visitors and not staff, she relaxed.

Within a week, Sarah had settled into her new role. On the day she arrived, Jessica had willingly handed over the chatelaine of keys to everything, then had explained she was a convict and assigned to them as the governess. However, Jess decided not to reveal her status immediately. She offered her assistance for anything Sarah needed. As George had not previously told Sarah that Jess was also a titled Lady, that fact had come as a huge shock for the new bride when he let it slip.

Sarah froze and looked at Jess in shock. She had never met anyone like Jess before. She felt inadequate as it was, but the poise of this lady left Sarah gasping. Her governess had the most amazing dignity and presence, but yes was approachable and a delight to talk to, just like a titled lady should be.

Shortly after their return, Jess often caught Sarah watching her as she worked. After some days, Sarah asked her to sit and have tea with her.

As Jess had been watching her and could see the young bride was in some physical discomfort. Obviously, George had told her that Jess had been married before, and with no mother around, Sarah turned to her.

Making sure no one was listening, Sarah asked Jess something that was distressing her. "Jess, I knew about the marriage side of things, what happened on the honeymoon and, well, you know… but

I didn't know everything." Sarah blushed and glanced at Jess. "I get sore and itchy."

Jess smiled; she knew precisely what her problem was. "Sarah, you are going to have to ask your husband not to use soap *down there*. It contains things that burn ladies. I found out that when I first married too. Men don't realise and think they are cleansing themselves for us, but it is more than inconvenient. It's one of the more uncomfortable things one has to do in marriage, discussing private things with your husband. I was only a year older than you when I first married. But if you don't talk to him, it will continue. To ease your discomfort, you will have to sit in a basin of warm, very salty water to remove pain."

"You mean it's not me?" Sarah wept with relief.

Jess felt like hugging her mistress. "No, dear girl, it's not you." Jess took her hand and commiserated. "If you don't address the situation, you will find you don't enjoy that side of things."

Sarah's eyes opened even wider; she blurted out, "You mean I'm allowed to enjoy it? It's not wrong?" She clapped her hand over her mouth, but her eyes twinkled with glee.

Jess was thanking her mother for their pre-wedding talk. She gave a small chuckle. "Yes, dear girl! They are not called the *joys of marriage* for nothing. Many women think they have to lie back and do nothing but let the man have his way with them. Sarah, respond how you wish if you really love him. It will not just be enjoyable but very desirable too. Trust me; it works both ways. I will get Marcus to talk to George. However, as Marcus has not been married before, so he will not understand. Sarah, you are very young, but that will be a benefit. Please, know you can talk to me about anything."

The two young women broke down the final barrier to their friendship with that conversation. Sarah mopped her eyes. "If I can talk to you about soap and my itch, I feel that there will be no more barriers between us." She gave Jess a big hug.

Jess said, "Come to me with any questions, especially when you think you may be with child. Your first sign is that your monthly flow will be late, then your breasts may get tender, and you will find some foods will turn your stomach. However, every woman has different symptoms. Mine were soft eggs and cooked meat making me ill. So, I know what this is like too. Thankfully my mother was still alive when I fell with Judith. However, Sarah, your mama is not here, and I have been through it, so don't hesitate to ask about that either."

Sarah gave her hand a gentle squeeze as thanks.

Jess explained, "Sarah, Felicity is in much the same situation. She did not even know she was with child. She is due in a few months. Trust me; she asked me many questions. The soap problem was one of her first, too. They have now sorted themselves out. These sorts of things often occur in new marriages. One of the benefits of a many-generational household is having people to turn to. Here you just have us, ma'am."

Sarah jumped at the term. "Call me Sarah, please, Jess. You may be a convict, but you have a title. I'm just a frightened young girl." Sarah hugged her again. She smiled shyly. "I've never liked being called ma'am."

Jess ended up chatting to Marcus about this problem as Sarah confessed that she couldn't possibly discuss such intimate things with George. Considering Marcus and Jess were not married, the topic was inappropriate for them to discuss; however, she knew she had to help Sarah.

Marcus also did not know that soap was a potential problem and took Jess's words to heart; however, he brought up the topic with George. When Marcus mentioned the soap problem, George was upset that he had caused distress to his new wife. That problem quickly sorted itself.

~

Weeks passed, and Marcus still had not heard back from Ned. He had written requesting permission to marry and hoped that Ned could fast-track their application. By Easter time, they still were waiting. Marcus discovered that during the private time he spent with Jess, he found it harder and harder not to touch her. Once or twice, he had kissed her on the back verandah. Both had been somewhat carried away as they had been the first time. They realised that they had broken their own rules. Marcus knew that living in the same house as Jess made it more difficult. With Sarah now installed in the home, George spent his spare time with her. Marcus was seriously at a loose end.

Two weeks before Easter, Marcus was sitting reading the newspaper that had just come in from Sydney. He didn't feel like reading anything heavy like one of George's theology books, so he was even reading through the classified advertising in the paper. Jess was sitting further along the verandah and was reading to Georgie when she heard Marcus shout.

Jess looked up as she heard his footsteps approach.

Marcus was excited. "Jess, sweetheart, listen to this." He read aloud the advertisement.

"*NOTICE. Tenders will be received at this office, up to the 20th Day of April, from such Persons as are desirous of Renting the large GOVERNMENT WINDMILL and HOUSE adjoining, at Newcastle, with the use of such fixtures as belong thereto, for One Year, from the above Date.*"

Marcus continued, "Jess, I could move next door. When we marry, we will still be close to Georgie. Rex has been looking for something to do, and he could run the mill or at least butler the house."

Jess's face lit up with excitement.

Marcus reread the advertisement and then said, "Sweetie, this is an old paper; I will have to go and see Major Morriset now and let him know. The lease is only for a year, but we'll see what happens then." He had handed Jess the paper, and she looked up, and he saw that she was happy about the prospect. He bent and gave her a quick kiss. "Jess, I'll go down directly; this is wonderful. And Georgie boy, this means you can visit when you want and that even when we marry, Miss Jess won't be far away." He ruffled the little boy's hair. He was astounded that this small boy had become so important to him. He adored him.

Georgie had heard Marcus. "So you won't leave me, Miss Jess? You'll stay and... and..." He threw himself into her arms. "Don't leave me, Miss Jess. Please, don't go far away." He was obviously still thinking. "Uncle Marc, if you live in the windmill, can I go and have a look inside?" It had not taken Georgie long to turn Mr Ryan into Uncle Marc. Vincent, Marcus, and Georgie were often seen out on the grass near the church, kicking a leather ball around. Jaques would occasionally join them as time was also hanging on his hands. He had almost become Marcus's little brother. They would sit talking in French to hone their skills. Jaques and Giles had also become good friends.

Marcus knew that Georgie would see everything he could in the mill when he was finally given a chance to investigate. First, Marcus had to say he wished to rent both buildings officially. "I'll be back for luncheon, Jessica. I shall go down now." He went indoors to grab his hat and cane.

Jess saw him head off down the street with his cane swinging as he walked. She watched as long as she could. The emotions that he stirred in her still sometimes overwhelmed her. When she came on him unexpectedly, he set her heart racing.

Major Morriset and George had already gone head-to-head about allowing the convicts to come to church. Also, he accused the Major of having loose morals and setting a bad example for the convicts Middleton was trying to reform. Morriset didn't want to permit the convicts to take time off the mining on weekdays. Occasionally he had even turned a blind eye to work being done on the Sabbath. He didn't mind Christmas and Easter, but he had already vetoed weekday services for any convict under his care.

Marcus had stood outside George's office while the Major made his case. The Major eventually compromised. He would allow the convicts to come on Sundays as the government rules insisted, but not for mid-week services. George had let off steam with Marcus after the Major had departed. Marcus knew he had to tread carefully and not take sides until he secured the lease on the mill residence. He wasn't worried about the mill itself, but he would hire someone to run it if one went with the other. He realised that the community needed to have it working to grind the grain used locally. Hopefully, someone could teach him to run a grain mill. Maybe the other mill manager would be willing, or possibly Rex may be interested.

On the Thursday before Easter, the coastal cutter brought two letters. Both were life-changing for Marcus. Jess was once again sitting on the verandah with Georgie doing some reading. The first was permission for Marcus to move into the mill residence any time after April 20th and the second was permission for their marriage, including a letter from Ned. He knew Ned's exquisite calligraphy of old, as they had often written to each other at home.

Marcus flicked the seal from Ned's screed and devoured the news. He gave a shout of joy. "Jess, sweetheart, we have our reply from Ned. Listen!" He read out Ned's newsy letter, pausing towards the end; he read to emphasise the words.

"Marcus, I am working over Easter, but if you could arrange for Banns to be read prior to that, I will come for your nuptials at the end of May. May 29th will suit me if that is convenient. Let me know by return ship, and I shall get things moving on this end.

Sorry this has taken so long, but the Governor has been exceptionally busy as he is leaving in December.

Ned"

Marcus was so excited that he grabbed Jess and swung her around. Forgetting his promise not to compromise her, he kissed her while Georgie watched on.

Georgie got the giggles, and it was those chuckles that made Marcus remember where he was. "Papa does that to Mama Sarah."

With another peck on her lips, Marcus released his betrothed and went to find George. He knew George would be battling over his Good Friday sermon. Marcus knew that sometimes telling the same story differently was incredibly hard. Easter was always a joyous celebration because of Jesus's resurrection, but the sombre service of Good Friday could either be a dirge or, if done well, a time of deep reverence. Finding the fine line between the two was difficult. Preaching about death to a bunch of convicts was always hard to do. Marcus had already worked out his words for the children's talk. George had asked him to again speak to the young people in the church, although he noticed that often the convicts listened more to the simple words he spoke than the theological dissertations that George often delivered. Thankfully, George's sermons were now only about fifteen minutes long.

Marcus now did these talks quite often, and the children loved it. Amazingly, so did Marcus. He had never had much to do with children until he arrived in the colony. The talks stretched his thinking, as to have to tell the Bible stories, or whatever the topic was for the day, in a way children could understand was challenging. It also made him check the stories in the Bible rather than use presumed activities from Christmas carols. He chuckled when he saw the looks on the faces of the congregations when he mentioned that there was no evidence of there only being three wise men and none that they were kings. Also, camels were not mentioned, nor were donkeys, except that Jesus was born in a stable.

Georgie loved these story times and would now bound into Marcus's arms as he walked to the front. Marcus would tell the stories to him, but for the benefit of all listening.

Marcus knew that Major Morriset disliked these talks and had overheard his complaints about the convicts being forced to attend mid-week services and listen to silly kiddies' stories, as he called them. Also, he had not been too keen on Marcus renting the mill accommodation, but obviously, there had been no other candidates. Marcus now had the official word that he could move in. Now he could start to settle. Colin and Jaques could start packing, and as soon as they had the keys, Henry could load up his wagon and earn some more pocket money.

Good Friday service started with a hush as George walked slowly through the rear door and processed slowly up the front to the stripped and empty sanctuary. There would be no singing today at all. George led the solemn service, and his words about the death of Christ were raw. They hit home. The convicts could identify with the cruel whippings Jesus received. Many had similar scars.

George and Marcus had stripped the sanctuary of everything possible. The Communion Table was enveloped in a black shroud. Everything sat in the vestry, waiting for the late afternoon or the next day when the sanctuary would be redressed in its Easter finery. The altar cloth had been washed and was currently drying before being starched.

Georgie sat between Sarah and Marcus. Jess sat next to her beloved, and occasionally they would each drop their hands to the seat between them and hold hands. Next to Jess sat Jaques, then Rex and Felicity, holding their month-old son Damien. By rights, staff should have been at the back of the church, but only their household knew their previous status. Here they were all just friends.

Georgie took special care of the new baby. He had been devoted to the tiny child from the moment he saw him. He had still been red and wrinkly, but Georgie adored him on sight, although his first words set them all giggling. "He's not cooked real good, Mrs Flick; he's red and wrinkly."

Sarah came to the rescue. "Actually, Georgie, he's *cooked* just right. That's how babies start. Then they grow, as you have."

After the service, everyone left in silence. Marcus waited outside for the household to gather; Major Morriset had walked up to him as he left the church and handed him a huge key. "You may as well move in as soon as you wish, but the place will need a clean first." With no further comment, he marched after the shuffling chain gang of fifty convicts that were now headed down the hill to their primitive accommodations.

Marcus was overjoyed. As soon as George changed, they walked the short distance to the mill residence and had a look inside.

Marcus was almost euphoric that he had the key to their new home. Monday morning, he would set to clean the place out.

Easter Saturday arrived, and everyone joined in to clean the church and re-dress and decorate the sanctuary.

Easter morning was a joyous occasion. Marcus had gathered the household in the weeks before Easter to practise the singing. George had chosen to sing two hymns during the service. Both hymns were Charles Wesley ones and known to many. The first was to be sung before the service started and would settle everyone. The group, including Cook, Milly, Sarah, Jess, and all of Marcus's household, stood and sang, *"Christ the Lord is risen today."* The men's voices added a wonderful depth to the sound.

As George entered from the vestry and took his place in the sanctuary, the hymn paused. He gave the welcome and invited everyone to join the merry chorus. The church was alive with their song. Marcus's eyes fell on the scowling face of Major Morriset, who was standing at the back with his arms folded, almost as a defence against the church. He obviously didn't wish to be there, but duty said he must attend. Marcus would have loved to have pointed him out to the rest of the household but couldn't. His eyes moved around the rest of the congregation. Even the convicts chained together in their pews were singing at the tops of their voices. It seemed that the poor Major was seriously outnumbered.

After the last verse, they took their seats and were seated and ready for George to lead the service. George entered into the joyous service with every ounce of his heart. He had not enjoyed a service as much for a long time. He thought back to the dull liturgies he had led for the last couple of years. This was vastly different. He saw animation on the faces of the congregation as they sat wondering, not knowing what to expect. George proceeded to do a standard celebratory Easter service. They would enjoy another sample of Marcus's ingenuity after Holy Communion had finished. Marcus would do his little talk for Georgie while George cleaned up after Holy Communion. It was usually a slightly dead spot, and today they had decided to change things up a little. Marcus stepped forward, and George watched his wife lead his household and stand near Marcus. This time Georgie was standing with Sarah and holding on tight.

By now, everyone knew they could, and should, join in the wonderful Charles Wesley hymn. Again, everyone but the stern

Major was smiling. He still stood at the back with his arms folded. Marcus started the first line of the melody with his strong voice.

> *And can it be that I should gain*
> *An interest in the Saviour's blood?*
> *Died He for me, who caused his pain?*
> *For me, who Him to death pursued?*
> *Amazing love! how can it be*
> *That thou, my God, shouldst die for me?*

In the next three verses, every voice but one had joined in. Marcus smiled. He was watching the lips of a certain person who had now reluctantly joined in. Their eyes met, and Marcus smiled. He, too, had no condemnation for the man who caused George such frustration. If only he would listen to the words of the Hymn. The words of this hymn were so meaningful. Marcus knew that God's love and acceptance were open for all who asked. None were rejected, but all must repent.

> *No condemnation now I dread,*
> *Jesus, and all in him, is mine!*
> *Alive in him, my living head,*
> *And clothed in righteousness divine,*
> *Bold, I approach the eternal throne,*
> *And claim the crown, through Christ my own*

When the congregation sang the last two lines, the roof almost lifted with the joyous words. With the service now over, everyone poured in the April sunshine. Many still had the tune in their minds. Even the convicts were heard humming the wonderful Wesleyan hymn as they assembled to return to the barracks. There would be no mining today.

Major Morriset was obviously in no mood for socialising, as he was seen striding alone down the hill at a pace. His minions were left to bring the convicts back.

Sarah said, "What a wonderful way to start the day!" She was happy for Jess but wondered how they would work out her assignment after marriage. She would miss Jess's wisdom. Whenever Jess saw that Sarah was floundering in some household decision, Jess called to her and privately explained how she should do things. Sarah didn't want Jess to leave but knew that she would go with Marcus after the wedding. She couldn't be selfish, but she was sad.

Chapter 13 Wedding Bells

*T*he day of Marcus and Jessica's wedding finally arrived. It was to be just the household and Henry. He had insisted on an invitation.

Marcus had moved out of the parsonage Easter week, and he had spent the last month sourcing furnishings for their house. He would scour the Sydney papers and send word to Ned to purchase whatever items had caught his eye.

Henry was delighted as he was earning a tidy sum with each delivery. It was usually only a shilling at a time, but sometimes, he'd get flicked an extra coin or two. Once or twice it was a pound if the boxes were very large.

They had no idea how he had eked out a living before their arrival. There were deliveries of beds, tables, chairs, and numerous other items. However, shortly before the wedding, two large items needed six convicts to move the first and eight for the second. These two wooden boxes were delicately moved up to the hill very carefully.

Marcus would not say what was in them, but both boxes had big red arrows pointing upwards on the sides. You didn't have to read to know that they could not be tipped up on their sides.

One had to go to the church, and the other to the windmill

residence.

More people came to watch or assist as they transported the various loads. There was a procession now following Henry's wagon on the final leg of their journey.

Marcus had the biggest grin on his face as he whispered to Henry what was in the two immense boxes.

Henry first delivered the crate to Marcus's house.

Hopefully, George would have returned from his home visits to see the second one placed in situ. Thankfully he arrived as Marcus was giving instructions for access to the building.

"Marcus, what's this?" George was returning his Home Communion set to the church when he saw the melee at the other door.

Marcus welcomed him with a whoop of joy. "Yeah, George, you're here! In answer to your question, call it a belated wedding gift for you, George. It's not something that I could hide, so I didn't bother. But it's yours, not the church's, as I don't have permission to put it in there. But you will see when we get it inside. I hope you will like it."

It took over an hour to extract the new pump organ from its container. It took longer to work out where it was going to sit. The helpers were sworn to secrecy.

Marcus decided to leave it near the rear and see how it sounded. He quietly said to his friend, "George, we can always move it later if it's no good here."

Once the precious organ had been unpacked in the church, the larger box needed to be placed in its new home at the mill residence.

With the many hands assisting, the pianoforte was eased out of its wooden prison.

Marcus stood watching with his arms folded. It was not as good as a grand piano at home, but it was at least music. Ned had chosen both instruments for him from the store. Marcus had sent a bank draft down to Ned with the letter telling him what was required.

Thankfully, the store owner who sold these instruments had placed many advertisements in the Sydney Gazette. Along with the advertisement for the instruments, there was an advertisement for a couple looking for work. They were a dairyman and his wife skilled in cheese making. Marcus had asked Ned to interview Mr and Mrs

Tom Landy for him.

Although Marcus didn't have any cows yet, they would soon need at least one, and preferably more.

With a residence arranged in town, he could now start looking for some land to lease until he could buy what he wanted. He had seen a note in the town store for a ten-acre paddock to rent, and he had already taken the option on that but had not yet told Jessica. The black stallion was to be the first occupant.

All this was to be part of her wedding surprise.

Jaques, Felicity, and Rex had moved into the mill residence after Easter when he had. All had been busy scrubbing the place from top to tail and refurbishing it.

Rex had been given a tour through the mill and decided that he was content to do the bookwork but not actually run the mill. Felicity had him asked to find a cook, as her duties of mothering their son were far more tiring than she had ever thought. Damien was now eight weeks old and was the delight of the household.

Marcus wondered if the new couple arriving on the next boat would be willing to learn the mill. He had discovered that many in this colony were keen to learn new skills and improve their lot in life, himself included.

Marcus was content with the musical instruments now in place and well hidden. He had kept himself very busy the week before the wedding, and he anxiously waited for the best man to arrive.

Ned arrived and was greeted by Marcus.

Another man was seen striding down towards the craft, and Marcus heard Ned groan.

"Wait for it, Marc," Ned muttered under his breath and then plastered on a false smile and stood waiting for Major Morriset to arrive.

Major Morriset arrived on the foreshore, and the waiting men were not sure if he was angry that Ned had come or if he was going to dissect his faith as he usually did. The two men were both majors in the 48th foot, and both had been pleased they had been posted in different areas.

Morriset had seen Ned's uniform from his office as he disembarked and had gone to investigate. He was not expecting any new replacements.

"Hello, Major, this is a surprise," Morriset said.

Ned bowed, then saluted. "Hello, Morriset; how have things been since the convict transfer?"

Morriset grunted and said, "Better, I suppose."

Ned smiled. "I presume you know my friend Marcus Ryan? He's an old friend from England; I'm here to stand as a witness for their wedding. I had a week's leave and am spending it looking around this area." Ned thought that should satisfy the man's inquisitive nature without being pumped for the information. He knew that he usually called everyone else by their surname, and he always made it sound rude. However, even Ned's name annoyed Major Morriset, as he couldn't make the name of Grace sound abusive. Ned smiled at his private thoughts.

Morriset grunted, turned on his heel, and walked away without further comment.

Marcus had remained silent. "What was that all about, Ned? I have my own issues with him, but...?"

Ned chuckled. "I gather he's still a bone of contention with Reverend George and the frequency of services? Well, it's the same old story. We arrived on the same ship and sadly had much time to debate faith. When he discovered that I believe in God and live a Christian life, and also that I have a strong and active faith, and I became a target of his ridicule. Trust me, the discussions we had on board the journey were many, and some were quite heated. Unfortunately, as we were the same rank, we were bunking in together. Thankfully Governor Macquarie could see our differences and separated us as soon as we landed. Thanks to a mutual friend, Perry White, the Governor kept me close to him and sent Morriset away."

"Perry was here?" Marcus asked.

"Yes, but he and Katy left with the Macquaries," Ned said, forgetting that Perry would have been in Marcus's year or thereabout.

Ned and Marcus started walking up to the windmill. Henry had appeared as usual and said he would bring Ned's bag.

Ned flicked him a coin which was deftly caught.

Marcus pointed out the various buildings of interest. Halfway up the hill, Marcus realised the Landys had not arrived.

Ned grinned again. "I have told them to come when you get back from your honeymoon. Nice couple, though! Names of Tom and Mary, and they seem very capable."

Marcus found that not seeing Jess buzzing around the house

every day was hard. It was only eased as he knew she was just across the paddock, and he walked over often. They still took time to take Georgie for a walk, although Jaques now escorted them.

Vincent found that he was almost superfluous for Georgie; however, this left him more time for cleaning his beloved tack in the stable. This job had suffered, and now he was able to get the bridles and leatherwork back into pristine shape. Giles and Colin were content to play baby with the lad and wear him out playing.

~

The morning of the wedding, Jess awoke somewhat nervous. Today she would be married again.

George suggested Jess have a week off, which they willingly excepted. They were going out to Morpeth for a honeymoon. Amongst her gowns, Jessica had a lovely ivory-coloured day gown. She wore her mother's blue topaz necklace as the something old, a blue ribbon on her garter, which was borrowed from Sarah, and a sixpence in her shoe, just as the saying dictated.

It had taken three days for Marcus to remember to give her the jewellery box that she had entrusted to him. Jess stroked the box before shutting it. She put on a poke bonnet, and being May, Jaques also unpacked a lovely white lace shawl that she would use as both veil and later as a scarf.

Sarah had confided in her the day before, prior to the auspicious day of her suspicions that she may be expecting a child. Sarah pumped Jess with questions about if they could continue their close relations.

Jess had not discussed how that side of their marriage was other than to ask if she dealt with her itch.

Sarah blushed and nodded, then giggled. "It's good, Jess. I see what you mean about the joys, though." She blushed again.

Jess assured her that those joys of marriage could continue to be enjoyed as her condition progressed and that her size would need to be taken into consideration but was safe.

As Jess dressed in her wedding finery, she was both nervous and excited. Her first wedding had seen her mother making all the arrangements. She would have no family at all for this one. She was looking forward to the coming week ahead. From tonight, she and Marcus would be able to enjoy the deep passion that simmered just below the surface. Jess realised that he had busied himself elsewhere to keep distracted for the last week.

Midweek, he had come over after dinner. He had taken her for a turn around the verandah, then taken her into his arms as he had the day he proposed and kissed her. The depth of their embrace had stirred his desires again, but instead of releasing her, he held her tight while his breathing returned to normal. He whispered, "Jess, I will stay away from you for the rest of this week as I find that I am strongly tempted to take you home before the blessings of our nuptials. I can't keep my hands from your exquisite person, and soon I won't have to. I look forward to our wedding night, my beloved."

They had discussed the wedding night and where to stay. Jess suggested that he make the arrangements and surprise her. Marcus arranged that they could stay at a parishioner's place just a mile out of town, as there they would be away from prying eyes. They would have the cottage to themselves for the night, then they would head further northwest, and Marcus could not wait. Soon he would not have to.

Jess and Felicity walked the short distance from the parsonage to the church. Jess heard music.

Sarah had disappeared sometime earlier, and lovely sounds of beautiful organ music came floating out the church doors.

Jess gasped. There was an organ?

Felicity quickly told Jess of Marcus's activity during the week. She still did not mention the second instrument that she knew resided in her new home.

Felicity left Jess standing at the church door as she slowly preceded her down the aisle.

Jess saw Marcus waiting for her; Ned was beside him, smiling, dressed in his red uniform. His hat was tucked under his arm, and his fair hair was like a bright light in the church. Jess, however, had her eyes fixed on Marcus's grinning face.

Marcus was having trouble seeing her as his eyes were tear-filled. He swiped them away and stood waiting. His dreams about finally claiming her as his own were coming to fruition. He knew that when she arrived beside him, he should put his arm out for her to place her arm on it gently. Instead, he took her hand and interlaced their fingers, giving it a loving squeeze. He had managed to get his eyes cleared and looked down at his beloved, now waiting beside him. Soon she would be his wife. Soon! He now only had minutes to go.

Jess had felt like running up the aisle. As she went to bed the night before, it occurred to her that it was two days shy of a year since Lucien died. She knew that he would want her happy. She remembered Lucien saying how nice the gentleman who sold his tea business to him was. It had taken only a few conversations with Marcus to discover that it had indeed been Marcus who had sold Lucien the tea import business when he had focused on the wool importation side of his company.

Marcus had thought about that meeting many times over the past year. That the two men had met and liked each other was far more than a coincidence. Lucien and Judith would always be part of their relationship. Marcus needed to know that although her first love would never die, that didn't mean she didn't love him wholeheartedly. Now she was to be joined to him in marriage. He took her hand as she reached his side rather than offer her his arm. She knew he wanted to kiss her even then. That would soon occur.

The marriage service started, and Felicity and Ned stood on either side of them. Finally, the words they had each waited for arrived. George pronounced them man and wife and said that Marcus could now kiss his wife. With so few present in the church, Marcus did just that. He slid his arms around her waist and drew her to him. "Jessica, my beloved, we are one. No more will you be alone, that I promise," he murmured to her before covering her lips with his own. Then he kissed her as he wished.

George cleared his throat in an effort to end the long embrace. It was ineffective. Finally, he said, "Marc, really? Time for that later."

George's words sank in, and Marcus released his wife. They grinned at each other; Marcus gave her another quick peck on her reddened lips before giving his undivided attention to George. They signed the register, with Jess signing Jessica Elkin for the final time. Ned signed as Edward Grace, and Felicity Harris added her name. With the legal side now completed, Marcus led her from the church.

They were married!

However, Jess was no longer a titled lady but was now plain Mrs Marcus Ryan, and that's just how she liked it. It had not been a hard decision to make.

Marcus had, however, wondered. Most women would have clung tooth and nail to hold on to a title, but not his Jess. The more he knew her, the more he loved her. She was everything he had wanted in a wife; that she was also stunningly beautiful was a bonus.

She was confident yet humble, loving but discreet. She was skilled at many things but also willing to teach not only Sarah but others too. He had watched with delight as Jess had eased Sarah into her role of rectory wife. Jess had also prepared Georgie to accept his new mother, and after the initial incident on the wharf where Sarah had gone to the aide of the young boy, he came to love her dearly. Jess had just stepped back and let it happen, encouraging the new family to bond.

Marcus had been nearby when he overheard Georgie say to Sarah a few days after she arrived, "Miss Jess said I had to make a hole in my heart for you, Mama Sarah. But I found it was there waiting to be filled already!" His small arms had wrapped around Sarah's neck, and he had hugged her. Jess had also prepared the child for the arrival of siblings. Felicity's son had made that easy too.

Jess had pointed out that Felicity was only a visitor and wouldn't stay with the family, and when they left, they would take Damien with them. Georgie was upset until Jess quickly added that his parents might try to have a child he could keep for his own. Probably they would have even more than one. With this news, Georgie was delighted. When he saw Marcus next, the young boy had told him that he would have a brother or sister, or even both, one day. Marcus hoped he would also have some other small friends to play with.

With the service over, the merry procession left the church and made its way back to the rectory.

Cook had hurried home as she had left a roast leg of mutton cooking, and the delightful smells were wafting through the open front door as they arrived back.

By three o'clock, Marcus wanted to leave on their honeymoon. Admittedly, it was only a short trip to their accommodation, but the farewells would eat up some of that time. Vincent and Giles had vanished half an hour before. He had given them the nod, and they left to prepare a surprise for Jess.

Marcus had been storing another gift for Jess. He had purchased a buggy and bay mare. Henry had housed it with his wagon and now brought it up for their use. Vince and Giles loaded their luggage and brought it around to the front door. Marcus lifted Jess in and hopped up lightly beside her. Everyone gathered outside and stood waving farewell.

The mare was fresh, and Marcus had to give it his full

attention for a while, but he slowed the vehicle up and kissed Jess again once out of sight of everyone and the town. "My darling Jess, we are finally wed. I have booked us somewhere close to stay tonight as I cannot wait to make you mine. I need my first lesson in loving. I know that may be inappropriate to admit, but it's also true."

Jess laughed. "Not inappropriate at all, husband mine, and certainly reciprocated. Just not here, sweetheart." Jess chuckled; she had missed the intimate side of marriage. She missed sleeping, cradled in her husband's arms. She missed the loving caresses and Lucien's gentle touch. However, she realised she must never compare them. Lucien was her past and Marcus was her future, and she loved him dearly.

They pulled up a short while later at a lovely stone cottage. There was smoke coming from the chimney, and a young man appeared from a barn at the rear. He held the reins, and after Marcus retrieved their bags, he took the buggy around the back.

Marcus lifted Jess down and, carrying their two smaller bags, escorted her inside. He then shut the door behind them and followed Jess into the bedroom. There he held out his arms for his wife. Jess soon unbuttoned his shirt as he was doing the same for her ivory wedding gown. Food and even tea could wait.

Jess took her time, knowing that the next hour would be one they would remember for their entire marriage. They ignored the growing trail of discarded clothing as Marcus lifted her onto the big feather bed. Jess reached out to him and fulfilled his most vivid dream.

With their marriage now consummated, they dozed in each other's arms. Marcus awoke with Jess playing with his chest hair. Her gentle fingers awoke his desires again, and she willingly obliged to sate his need once more. He was far more confident this time, and her instructions were more explicit; she taught him how to pleasure her.

The discovery of sharing the act had been foreign to him. He had no idea that their joining could bring mutual satisfaction. He had heard the term the joys of marriage but had no understanding of what that meant until today.

Jess had opened his eyes to the exquisite delights ahead of them. Marcus said, "Jess, I finally understand why Solomon wrote those loving words in Song of Songs." As he quoted the verses, his fingers trailed across her exposed chest, "*I am my beloved's, and his desire is toward me. Come, my beloved, let us go forth into the field; let us lodge in the villages. Let us get up early to the vineyards; let us see if the vine flourish, whether the tender grape appear, and the pomegranates bud forth: there will I give thee my love."* Marcus kissed her again, then added, "We will get up and eat, and once we have taken our fill of food, we shall return here, gorge ourselves on the delights that Solomon speaks of and then tomorrow, we too shall find that vineyard and blossoms and again take our delights."

Jess looked puzzled, having no idea what he meant.

Marcus chuckled, "We are spending our honeymoon on a farm with a vineyard, my love. I won't say that we shall spend the nights outside amongst the vines, as we would freeze and surely be caught," he chuckled. "However, the house we will be in is as private as this one. Let me put it this way; I look forward to investigating the other lessons you have to teach me. I find that I am your very willing student."

Jess stroked the slightly bristly cheek of her new husband. "And I, my love, am a very willing teacher."

Chapter 14 New Arrivals

 *T*ime was drawing close for the arrival of Georgie's first sibling.

Sarah and George's child was due in the new year. Georgie, now six, had been delighted that Sarah had allowed him to feel the baby moving. He knew that he would soon have his own tiny friend and that no one could take it away from him. He told his parents that he didn't mind if it was a brother or sister but thought a brother would be better for the first one.

Sarah sadly had to stop him from climbing onto her lap as the baby would kick him. Instead, he would climb up on her bed in the mornings and cuddle her. George had always been an early riser, and when he arose and opened their door, he would lift his son onto the high bed. He laughed that his son was soon at his side no matter how early he woke. The only way he could get some peace was to allow him to take his place in the big warm bed he had just vacated.

Early on, he had caught his parents in a passionate embrace more than once and soon, new rules and boundaries had to be set. Georgie was not permitted entry while his parents were in there together or if the door was closed. He was never far away, awaiting permission for his morning cuddle with his new mother. Georgie had a disconcerting habit of standing and watching his father kiss Sarah. Far from upsetting Sarah, she would get the giggles and lift him up to include him in a group hug. She soon realised that poor George had been floundering, trying to raise the small boy himself.

Jess had been the first person to make an impact on her stepson. Sarah, however, discovered a deep love for the child. More than that, she adored him. With the imminent arrival of their own child, Sarah spent more and more time talking to Jess about what was ahead of her.

Jess came across her one day when she was obviously distraught at being alone for the birth. She had heard the screams of Felicity with Damien's birth and was aware of the pain that was before her. Sarah was scared.

Jess was upset that she had not fallen with child herself in the seven months since their marriage. She knew she could conceive, for she had produced Judith. However, she had not fallen again. Each month when her flow had returned, she became more concerned. Maybe the problem had been with her and not Lucien after all. Jess shed silent tears, not even admitting her fears to Marcus.

On the day Sarah had confided her fear, Jess had just discovered that another month had come with no child. This time she had wept in Marcus's arms before they had risen that morning.

Marcus had been all that was wonderful. "It's in God's hands, my sweet. I have you, and that's enough. I never thought of marrying, let alone having a child. For me to be blessed with you is my heart's desire." He had cradled her to him as she wept. He discovered that his words were true. Yes, of course, he would have liked a child, but may God's will be done if that were not to be.

Charles Middleton made his appearance with little problem. Sarah being only just seventeen, suffered little at birth. Jess had insisted that she stay active in the months leading up to the delivery, and this had paid off. When Felicity had delivered, as she was in her forties, she had thought she would have a difficult time. The local midwife, Gertrude Holmes, had Rex stay and hold his wife as she delivered their son in the squatting position. After what Jess went through delivering Judith, laying on her back with her legs tied up in the air, she realised how much easier this was on everyone except for the midwife.

Gertrude, or Gerty as she preferred, had become a friend to Jess through the church, and Jess found that she loved to chat about the recent deliveries she had done. She knew Jess was a convict, as she was, and they had become friends over the year. Jess realised that she was an amazing fount of knowledge about what was happening to everyone in town. Gerty attended Sarah's delivery with Jess and

Felicity assisting. George refused to enter the birthing room, and in the end, Jess had to hold Sarah as the child was born.

Felicity stood watching the entire process, and Jess had her eyes glued to her dear friend's face. She wondered if Felicity was expecting again as she kept her hands carefully sitting on her stomach. Considering she was soon to turn forty-four, she was surprised. Shaking off a wave of jealousy, she refocused on Sarah.

By the time Charles was four months old, Felicity was well advanced in her condition. She and Rex had returned from the farm to deliver their second child in time for Easter.

As the months passed, Jess lost her sparkle, and Marcus was quite worried for her. They had been married for nearly a year and still so signs of a child. He often found her weeping and was now concerned for her. To make matters a little worse, Georgie had transferred all his affections from Jess to Sarah. This, however, meant that the separation from Jess would not break the child's heart.

Marcus knew that Jess had to be his primary concern.

George had spoken to Marcus soon after Christmas about the possibility of transferring Jess's assignment to him. The paperwork had just come through.

Marcus wanted to take her away. He was sure a change was what she needed. Marcus had purchased a six-hundred-acre farm not far from Maitland in a new area called the Patterson Valley and had slowly been stocking it with sheep and refurbishing the house. The black stallion had been the first animal to move into his new pasture. He shared it with two new brood mares Marcus had recently bought. The original small farmhouse had undergone a major restoration and extension, including a wide verandah surrounding three sides of the building.

A few months after their wedding, Marcus saw an advertisement for some rams. John Macarthur has placed some of his stud rams up for sale. Marcus had bought them all. He needed more merino ewes and knew that he would probably have to head to Cape Town to purchase what he desired. Sadly, that meant a trip over there himself, as he had no contacts in the area.

Rex and Felicity had already moved to the property soon after little Charles Middleton was born. They had gone with the Landys, who had proven to be excellent farmers. Another couple had arrived and were now running the mill.

Rex had taken to farming and discovered that he loved

getting his hands dirty. The vegetable patch was his pride and joy; however, surprisingly, he also adored the sheep. He willingly put his butlering days behind him.

Marcus had kept his promise to George and had stayed nearby until Jess was no longer needed by his son. They all knew the lease on the windmill residence would expire in April, and Marcus knew he either take it up for the third year or find some new accommodation in town. A long conversation with George ensued. With Jess now reassigned to him, Marcus knew that the decision would be hers. To tell her his news, Marcus had taken Jess's hand and walked to the edge of the hill. They stood overlooking the riverside town and watched the movement of the watercraft on the bay in front of them. "Jess, George handed me a document that came in on the trader this week." He handed it to Jess. "It's your transfer papers, love. George said we can move to the farm if you wish."

Jess's answer was to turn into his arms, sobbing. He had hoped for happiness, not this. He felt her nod against his shoulder. "Yes, let's go. Mayhap a move will see my condition change." She hiccoughed, then looked at him with watery eyes. "Why, Marcus? Why can't I conceive a child? Felicity did, and she's more than ten years older than me, Sarah has, and she's ten years younger. It's just not fair." Jess had found out that Sarah was expecting again already.

Marcus cradled his weeping wife. "I don't know, love. I don't understand God's reasoning, but we must trust Him. Can you do that?" He was caressing her neck with one hand, and with the other, he rubbed up and down her back, trying to bring her some comfort.

"I don't know if I can, Marcus. I want a child so much. I want your child; no, I want our child." She pulled away slightly and sniffed in a very unladylike way. "I have empty arms that so need to hold our own flesh and blood." She lay her head against her husband's chest and wrapped her arms around his waist. His strong heartbeat gave her more comfort than words. "And it is so hard seeing Georgie with Sarah."

Marcus kissed her dark curly head and said, "Then we will leave, sweetheart. I shall let them know today and give little Georgie time to get used to the idea. However, he has known for some time that we will go. Now we will give them a date."

Within a month, Henry had completed moving everything for Marcus bar the pianoforte. It needed to be repacked in the transport box that Marcus had kept and then carefully moved out to their new home.

Vincent and Giles had transported a lot of the personal items in the buggy and a fully covered carriage that Marcus had purchased.

The excitement of moving had taken Jess's mind from her sadness. Again, the month passed with her flow returning. She shed no tears, but Marcus knew of her despair. He would see her watching Felicity and did what he could to sidetrack her.

Marcus took Jess on picnics and arranged romantic interludes whenever he could. Every opportunity they had, Marcus took.

One month passed, then two.

Still, no child had been conceived.

Jess became quieter and quieter and more distant from Felicity.

Felicity had delivered their second child, and the little girl, who they named Victoria, was adorable. However, her arrival made Jess even sadder. She reminded her so much of Judith.

Like Jess, Felicity remembered the captivating little girl and missed her joyous laughs.

~

Marcus had read about another sheep sale near Camden. He decided to take Jess along for the trip and see if they could source more ewes. It would give them a mini holiday. He planned to be away for some weeks and would only take Giles, Colin, and Jaques with them. Felicity and Rex would stay and mind the property in their absence.

The coastal cutter carried the five people out of the heads and south to Sydney. Jess stood watching the shore fade into the distance. Marcus had his arms around her waist, holding on to the ropes and steadying her. She was leaning back against him and he could feel she was tense.

It was fifteen months since they married, and he had become used to seeing the monthly tears; however, he hated knowing she was so sad. He would try anything to make her smile again. Sadly, there was little he could do about them not conceiving. They were undoubtedly doing what was required. It just didn't happen.

Marcus knew that Ned had taken Jess for a couple of drives around Sydney when she had arrived years before, but neither Marcus nor Jess had absorbed what they had seen. Hence, on this trip, they took a few days layover in Sydney. They stayed at The Kings Arms Hotel on Pitt Street, and the three accompanying men went on their own tour of discovery as Marcus and Jess saw the sights in town.

Ned Grace happened to arrive in Sydney while they were there. He had been summoned to Governor Brisbane's office, and once he had completed that appointment, he had some days off, which he spent with his friends.

Ned introduced Marcus and Jess to his friends Sam and Annie Corbett and their son Danny. Dan was Ned's good friend, and they caught up on each trip Ned made to the town. They enjoyed a mug of strong sweet tea and some delicious home-cooked scones before continuing their town tour. Ned pointed out that Sam and Danny were responsible for much of the new buildings they saw going up in the town.

Saying a fond farewell, Marcus, Jess, and their three travelling companions were soon on the way to Camden.

Ned had given Marcus the name of a drover to use if required, as from Camden, the stock would first need to be brought to Sydney before being transported by ship to Newcastle and then up the Hunter River to Maitland. There were two northbound roads under construction, but neither would be ready in time to be used for a flock of sheep. Marcus would collect them and drove them to the farm with Tom Landy's assistance.

Marcus had no experience at droving.

Ned had laughed when Marcus said to Jess, "Surely it can't be that hard?"

Ned wished he could hear what Marcus thought after trying to herd a flock of wilful sheep down an unfenced track. Ned had seen it done by professional drovers, and they still had trouble.

The planned time away stretched to five weeks before they returned. Marcus purchased his sheep, and wisely a drover was hired.

Jess had been relaxed, and Marcus had been happy to see her bubbly joy of life return.

Their nocturnal activities did not abate, often occurring first thing in the morning as well as at night. Her need for him to sate her own desires had increased, and as Marcus had no hesitation in wishing for her happiness, he willingly obliged.

The day after their return home, Jess realised that she had not had her monthly flow while away. The revelation had hit her in the middle of the night, and she could not wait to impart her news to Marcus. When she awoke, she reached for him as she often did in the mornings lately. However, he was surprised when she sat up and looked at him, grinning. Wordlessly, she took his hand and placed it on her stomach.

The look of amazement that washed over his face made her chuckle. "Really?" he asked in awe.

Jess nodded. "It hit me in the middle of the night that I didn't have my flow this month. You kept me so distracted that I quite forgot about it." Jess was grinning at him.

"How far along are you, my sweet?" he asked as he gently took her into his arms to congratulate her with many kisses.

She returned his ardent caresses with renewed vigour. Eventually, she replied, "I think I must be about six weeks, or maybe a bit more." She gave him another quick kiss. "Sweetheart, we are going to be parents finally." With that, she burst into tears again.

Marcus looked at her, confused. However, he cradled her until the weeping ceased.

The confirmation of her condition hit a week later when she woke one morning and needed to be sick. As this was all new for Marcus, he was very concerned, but Jess laughed as she was throwing up.

Marcus was amazed. He had no idea what was occurring.

As Jess wiped her mouth, she said, "Marcus, this is normal. But it confirms that we are expecting. I had a similar illness for a few months with Judith. It only lasted for a short while then my body settled into its new condition. Lucien would bring me black tea in the mornings, which really helped."

Marcus took onboard that scrap of information. Over the following weeks, Marcus hovered like a worried mother bird. Each morning before she rose, a mug of sweet black tea awaited her. He assisted her with everything, and he fretted if she wasn't resting enough. He remained within call most days should she need anything.

Knowing what was in front of her, Jess insisted they walk a lot. Every day they seemed to walk for miles.

Marcus was incredulous at her renewed vigour as well as her joy.

Felicity knew the importance of walking and often joined them with her children. Soon, her post-baby weight had gone.

Jess's melancholy attitude had vanished on the day of her miraculous discovery.

By the time she was four months along, and before her bump was even showing on her very slim form, she could already feel the fluttering movements of the child growing in her. As much as he wanted to, Marcus couldn't distinguish the baby's activity.

With Jess once again happy, the farm occupied his thoughts, and he could see that they needed better fencing. The valley on the other side of them was still uncleared, and the stock would often wander off their land into the scrub.

Tom Landy requested some help to fence this off, and with the entire outer perimeter of their new holding, soon it was fully enclosed, and Marcus relaxed.

By six months along, Jess was quite obviously with child.

Marcus delighted in resting his hand on her stomach and feeling their babe move. Sometimes it pushed against his hand. He would chuckle with delight.

Marcus had been so busy with the sheep, Jess, and preparing for the baby that he had little time to keep in contact with George. Marcus had written to the Government to request to purchase the twenty-acre valley adjoining his land with a delightful river frontage. The reply back was curt. It had already been sold, and the new owner would soon make contact. Although a little disappointed, he didn't worry.

About a month later, Marcus and Jess were returning from their afternoon stroll when they noticed a ball of dust coming down their track. By the time they arrived home, a carriage was pulling into the driveway.

Marcus was the first to recognise it. "Jess, is that George's carriage?"

Jess was delighted. "I think it is. I wonder why they are here?" They hurriedly walked to welcome their unexpected guests.

Sarah almost fell into Jess's arms. "I insisted that we have come to congratulate you personally. Jess, I'm thrilled at your news." Sarah withdrew from her arms, and the two women walked inside the lovely homestead. Sarah was obviously with child again herself. Georgie was restraining his two younger siblings.

George and Marcus stood outside chatting.

Jess heard Marcus say with glee, "Really, George? That's fantastic!"

Jess looked at Sarah. "What's fantastic, Sarah?"

Sarah smiled, then clutched Jess's arm. "We are your new

neighbours, Jess. George's request for a farm has finally come through. He has purchased the twenty-acre valley next door. Hopefully, we will build a house there and spend some time ministering to the new farmers in this area. I know Marcus has been taking services on your verandah, but you need a proper church." They looked at the hill overlooking their farm. "That's where we would like to build. We can wave to each other."

To their delight, George had been the mystery purchaser of the valley Marcus had wanted.

While he had waited to hear from the new owner of the valley, Marcus had instead purchased a one-thousand-acre property that had come up for sale on the other side of his farm. He had also been eyeing-off other areas in the valley; one was adjoining his back paddock. However, none of the other properties had a river frontage. With George now owning it, Marcus knew that they could access the river, which made the shipment of his wool clip much easier. Jess knew he would discuss building a short wharf.

The Middletons stayed with them for a week.

George had arranged that the weekend services in Newcastle were to be taken by one of the lieutenants. He needed a break and knew that if he didn't organise it himself, he would not get it. George had been frantically busy before they left, and as well as things to arrange, it was all done before he could send Marcus a note, so they had just arrived unannounced.

Jess was delighted that they would stay with them occasionally while the new house was being built. Over the time they had been in the Hunter Valley, they had made the offer of accommodation so often that they had presumed they would never come as the family had never accepted it. Now, finally, they were here and would stay regularly.

Before they returned to Newcastle, George had arranged for the construction of a homestead. They had come to meet with a builder who would start as soon as possible.

By the time Jess was due, the foundations of the Middleton homestead were in place. Only eight weeks after the departure of their friends, Elizabeth Jessica Ryan made her entrance into the world in April 1826. It was just shy of their second wedding anniversary.

Marcus had wanted to wait outside the birthing room, but Jess insisted that he stay with her. In the end, he had little choice as

Felicity and Mary Landy needed his assistance.

Rex and Tom, and the other men were on childminding duty as the women attended to Jess.

After six hours of gruelling labour, Marcus was called in by Felicity to give Jess both strength and moral support.

Jess was exhausted. All she wanted to do was sleep, but wave after wave of contractions hit, and she was so tired that she could no longer cope. "I can't do this, Marcus; I'm so tired," she wept in his arms. Her nails dug into his hand or arm with each contraction, and she groaned with pain.

After Marcus came and was cradling her to him, he prayed with her and reminded her that this was the child she had craved.

Marcus encouraged her and said, "Sweetheart, you have to dig deep and push it out."

Jess was teary but nodded. "I can't do it lying down, Marcus, but I'm too tired to sit up or deliver it squatting unless you hold me."

Marcus was horrified but knew that he had promised she'd not be alone, and she needed him to do this. He sat Jess up, and they moved from the bed to a chair. In the time it took for her to sort herself out, she knew she was ready to deliver. He sat, and she stood between his legs. She needed to use a basin and then said, "I'm ready to push."

Felicity and Mary prepared the floor with towels.

Jess hoisted up her nightgown and squatted between Marcus's legs.

He wrapped his arms around her so she could brace on his thighs. Marcus watched in silence, his stomach roiling with anxiety.

Their daughter arrived on the second push.

With his arms still supporting her, Marcus kept whispering encouraging and loving things to her and kissing her perspiring neck. He heard a whimper and saw the wiggling bloody baby in Felicity's arms. He was once more in awe at what Jess was going through to have a child.

"You have a daughter, and she's perfect." Felicity held the squirming bundle. The baby was slightly blue, but she took a gasp when Felicity smacked her.

The babe let out a healthy bellow.

Marcus saw a long pulsating ligature hanging from his daughter's stomach, and he realised this was the umbilical cord.

With the pains now stopped, Jess seemed to revive. "Marcus,

watch this; watch her turn pink. Look, the cord is pumping. It will go flat, and then Felicity can cut it."

The four people watched as the cord emptied and the baby turned pink.

Felicity tied the cord off; then she wiped the child's face and handed her to Jess.

Jess had stood up as the cord was emptying.

Marcus did too. He could see over her shoulder. It suddenly occurred to him, "Jess, we are a family. We have a daughter."

"We do, my love." She leaned back against Marcus as his arms once more slid around her lovingly.

Mary Landy was hovering expectantly nearby, and he wondered why.

Marcus soon found out why.

"Now, Mary, quick!" Jess handed her the babe and told Marcus to sit again.

Once back in the squatting position with Marcus holding her. Her fingernails dug deeply into his legs. She pressed her head back onto his shoulder and let out a bloodcurdling scream.

His pain was nothing to what she was experiencing. The awful sound she emitted made Marcus ask what was happening. She had not cried out like that even when delivering the child.

Felicity explained the anguish of Jess's cry. "It's the afterbirth, sir; this is the bit where the babe is joined to its mama. It too must be delivered, and it hurts far more as it is attached to her insides." Felicity would have said more but saw Marcus blanch.

Marcus wished he had not looked down as just at that moment, as Felicity was holding an oozing, bloody mass. She placed it in a basin and told him that it would be buried outside. "You can put her into bed now, sir."

Mary had already laid the babe in the crib. She placed a folded towel where Jess was to lie. She was covered in blood and would need a wash.

Marcus took a tired and wobbly Jess in his arms and gently placed her on the prepared bed.

The three women suggested that he sit on the far side of her while they cleaned up, and then she could feed the baby.

Marcus was well out of his comfort zone but did as requested. He watched as Jess undid the front of her nightgown and exposed her whole breast. Marcus wished to cover her but saw the other women were not watching or were they even worried.

Jess knew her milk had yet to come in. Even though sleepy, she explained to Marcus that letting the babe suck would help the milk flow and assist the bleeding in stopping. She had previously explained that the bleeding would take about six weeks to dry up.

Marcus watched the tiny child and was astonished that his daughter knew what to do. The tiny hands clasped her mother's breast, and she sucked. "Jess, she knows what to do; look, she's even holding on to you." He watched his daughter feed and saw that Jess had not stopped smiling. He watched as she lovingly stroked the downy cheek to keep the baby awake and feeding.

While still gazing adoringly at their daughter, Jess said, "She is our gift from God, Marcus. Our blessed miracle. I know we thought about Louisa for her, but Jessica means a *gift from God*, and Elizabeth means *God is my abundance*. So, what about Elizabeth Jessica? Elizabeth after my mama and Jessie after me?"

Marcus could hardly tear his eyes from the feeding infant still at his wife's breast. The sight was one he had never expected to see. "I think that's a perfect name for her love. Just perfect! Sweetheart, Elizabeth is also my mother's name."

After the birth, Felicity had finished cleaning up the mess and was now waiting to place the sleeping child in the crib. Elizabeth had been born on their daughter Victoria's first birthday. Mary said she would stay, and they sent Felicity back to her children.

Chapter 15 Unexpected Mail

$\mathcal{B}$essie was a delightful baby. Vicky always wanted to hold her and learnt very quickly that if she plonked herself on the ground, she would be allowed a cuddle of the babe. Damien had given her the nickname of Bessie when he heard her name. Once again, Marcus heard Jess's joyous laugh echoing around the house. Marcus discovered an entirely new level of contentment. He adored his dark-haired, dimpled daughter. Her face would light up when he entered the room, and he would bend down and pick her up. Her joyous giggles would often set them all laughing.

By four months old, she could sit up without tumbling backwards, and she was soon able to roll over and move across the timber floor unaided.

Jess chastised Marcus for spoiling their daughter rotten. However, as she did this with a laugh, he knew she was not that worried. Bessie was crawling at just over seven months old, and Marcus was often down on his hands and knees playing with her. He would lie on his back on the floor and hold her up on his feet. Lucien had done much the same with Judith.

~

Life was good for them all. By the time Bessie was nearly three, Jess and Marcus were resigned to just having one child.

Rex and Felicity were happy with their two adorable children. Tom and Mary had moved out of the servant's room into a new cabin Marcus had built for them. They now had a small dairy herd, and the farm was producing abundantly.

Months before, Marcus had written for permission for Jess to accompany him on a trip to Cape Town and then return. It took until late September before he heard back. Ned had written, including the reply from the Governor. The mail also included a letter from Cyril Hargenhour in London. Marcus had read it and now stood looking out the window. His heart sank; both letters had brought unwanted news. Marcus knew he could no longer delay the trip to Cape Town as now their business was hanging on the contract that Marcus needed to negotiate personally. He knew he had to go.

The other letter was from Ned, and it contained the refusal to allow Jess to go with him. He knew that this trip had been inevitable but hoped to have her accompany him. He now had to tell her that he had to leave her for a few months; Marcus was shattered. He heard the door of his office open and felt her hand slide around his waist. Jess knew in an instant that he had received bad news. "Marcus, what's wrong? I saw your face when you got that letter. Is it from Ned?"

Marcus was close to tears as he felt he was breaking his promise to her. He drew her close and kissed the top of her head. He had a lump in his throat, and it was some time before he answered her. "One was from Ned, and one from Cyril." He couldn't say more. He had told her he had written, and she knew what it was about. Now he had to let her know permission had been refused. He didn't want to say the words that he had to leave her alone. He held her tightly.

"Permission had been refused, hasn't it?" Jess knew by his silence and the strength of his grasp that something was wrong. She knew that the news wasn't good.

His reply was a strangled "Yes." He tightened his grip on her. "And Cyril's letter was to say I now have only three months to sort out the contract. I can't postpone the trip any longer, Jess; I have to go or lose the entire business. If it were just for me, I'd say hang it, but there are so many employed by our firm now that I'm responsible for their wellbeing." Again, he felt his eyes water. He was breathing deeply so as not to sob as he wished to do. "I have to go, and that means I have to break my promise to you. I said I would never leave you, my Jess, and that you would never be alone again, but now I have no choice."

She had never seen him weep before, and she felt his tears seep into her hair. "Marcus, I'm here and safe with Felicity and Rex and the others. I have Bessie, not to mention George and Sarah possibly coming here soon, and we have so many friends nearby that I shall be fine." She looked up at him and saw the sadness written on his brow. "Come back to me, my beloved; I shall be waiting." She cupped his face and stretched up to kiss him.

"I promise, Jess, I promise I will return to you." He kissed her like a man possessed.

Two weeks later, Marcus and Colin had packed for the trip. Jess accompanied them to Newcastle with Giles and Jaques to keep her safe. The town had grown substantially in the years since they had moved to the farm. Giles and Jaques would stay with her, and both had promised to be her bodyguards. They vouchsafed to fight off the devil if need be. At twenty-one and twenty-eight years old, they were keen to fight off anyone if required.

Marcus smiled at their possessiveness of his Jess. They treated her like an elder sister rather than their mistress. The night before he sailed, they stayed in their old room in the rectory. They slept little, knowing that it would be the last night together for many weeks. Bessie was asleep in the bed in the boy's room, and thankfully she was now sleeping through the night. They wept, talked, and frequently loved through the dark hours. The dawn brought more tears but words of love and adoration too.

Sarah was expecting their fourth child, and the two little boys and a tiny girl were protected by their older half-brother Georgie. Charles and Osman were mini images of their mother, and Sarah Ann was an adorable imp. By the time their next child arrived, their mother, Sarah, would be only twenty. She had taken to both the rectory life and motherhood with glee. She knew she had much to thank Jess for and told her so often.

George was happy and contented, but Marcus discovered that things were a little unsettled below the surface, not between them but with the parish. George had even mentioned that if the so-called undertones in the parish didn't settle, he may resign and move to the farm full-time. Thankfully their house was completed, and they had acquired more land, which was now well-stocked. The farm could now support them if required. George promised he would keep his eyes on Jess and for Marcus not to worry about them. If needed, they could even return to the rectory. It was only this promise that gave Marcus any comfort. He knew Jess would be safe.

Jess knew he loved her and would return as soon as he could;

of that, she was sure. Nothing that he could control would keep him away.

There were quite a few queueing to board, but Marcus and Jess only had eyes for each other. They stood off to the side, waiting for him to embark. He enfolded her in his arms. Bessie had stayed at the house as Marcus said that bidding both farewell would be more than his heart could take. He had kissed his daughter as she had been put down to sleep, and he had crept out.

Ignoring the shocked faces, he gave Jess a final passionate kiss; disregarding the public scrutiny, he looked like he was almost eating her. Then just before the gangplank was raised, he cupped her face in his hands and gave her a last, loving kiss; he said farewell and added, "When I return, I shall never leave you again. As I said before, no more, my love, ever again, and that is a promise!" He turned and boarded the ship. His ticket was booked for the first vessel leaving for Cape Town. He didn't care what sort it was, just that it would bring him home again as soon as possible. He watched the shore until the cutter rounded the headland, and Jess's waving arm faded from view. His heart sank.

Jess turned to Sarah for comfort. As the ship vanished, Jess melted. She was sobbing so hard that George was worried about her. Finally, she told them why. "I had a dream last week…" Her unfinished words explained little, but the sobs told them much. Between the sobs, Sarah caught a few words, pirates, kidnapping and London, but it didn't make sense. Sarah looked at George, and he shrugged in reply. Neither Jess nor Marcus had voiced any concern at all to him. Why had she not said anything?

Henry had once again been hoping for a fare. He had become a cab service for the families and always scored a few pennies, at least for minimal effort. In the intervening years, he had upgraded his wagon and now had a padded bench seat that fitted four adults. The passengers were content to sit on a rug on the back. Henry had also promised Marcus that he would keep his eyes on Jess on his delivery trips westward. She had been the key to the success of his business. As a matter of fact, she had suggested it. The town had no cab service, and it needed one. Henry had a carting business with little to cart. Nowadays, he met every craft arriving at the dock and soon had a government contract for small loads.

~

Onboard the small cutter, the wind was behind them, and

soon the boat was powering down the coast with every sail billowing in the stiff breeze. Marcus was oblivious to it all, only knowing that he was being taken from Jess with every wave they crested. He had an ominous feeling about this trip and had delayed going for as long as possible.

Colin watched him and could see his sadness. He also knew that this trip was unavoidable. He had certainly not wished to leave as they had just employed a new dairymaid, and she had been trying to decide which of the three men she liked best. His departure whittled down her choice to two, Jaques or Giles. Both were closer to her age, but he was more mature. He sighed; she had been pretty too. He found that his desire to marry and a lack of suitable women were difficult.

~

Jess finally made it into her room before she gave in to the tears that had nearly overwhelmed her. She had not had what her mother termed a *fit of the vapours* since the first night in prison. Jess had succumbed to her tears that night. Then she had turned to God and begged for His help, and now she realised that she needed to do that again. She had done so often over the years that she released her husband into God's care. She dried her tears, rolled onto her elbows, and prayed for Marcus's safety. A feeling of peace soon flowed over her. The serenity that enveloped her soon saw her asleep. She awoke thirty minutes later, refreshed and ready to face the lonely months. Bessie was ready for dinner, and she needed a walk. Jess had just sat up when Sarah appeared with Bessie in her arms.

Sarah saw that Jess had a smile on her face and looked content. "I kept her occupied as long as I could, but she wants her mama." Sarah was holding the little girl in her arms. "I'm hoping this one is a girl too." Sarah handed Bessie to her mother.

Jess prepared herself to give her daughter a comfort feed before her proper dinner. Bessie would still put her hand on her mother's full breast and stroke her. Their eyes would connect, and Bessie would smile at her while feeding. Jess loved that connection. As Bessy was now three, Jess knew she should wean her, but she adored that bond, especially now that she was all but alone again.

Vincent had married Milly in the intervening years, and they had one little boy with another on the way. The household was changing; even the cook had married and had left with her husband. Other cooks had stayed some months, then gone. They currently had another bonded girl, and she was fast becoming one of the extended family. She was only twenty-three and quite skilled with her menu.

Jess stayed for a week before returning with her two minders and Bessie. Felicity and Rex were waiting for her. She had promised Marcus she would keep the farm running. As she saw the top of the colossal bunya pine tree on the boundary of their property, she knew she was home. Home, or was it just an empty house with Marcus not there? She felt empty. If it weren't for Bessie and Felicity, she would have stayed in Newcastle with Sarah.

She leaned forward and watched through the window as the beautiful homestead came fully into view. Releasing a long sigh, she was glad the travelling was over. Jaques and Giles had done their first job well; they had once again brought her home safely. Bessie had slept much of the trip. She loved the movement of the carriage. Jess now had less than three years to serve before her time expired in May 1830. Hopefully, Marcus should return in about three months. She knew she had to go home and shake off her melancholy.

~

By the time Jess arrived home to the farm some six days later, Marcus had not only arrived in Sydney but had been delighted to find Jon Park had left the *Jupiter* and taken a position on a different merchant ship transporting freight. He had just loaded his next cargo and was due to sail to Cape Town in forty-eight hours. Marcus was ecstatic and booked passage for himself and Colin. He had time to see Ned and get him to keep his eyes on Jess, even if it was from a distance. Marcus also signed a form that permitted Ned to act as his proxy should the need arise. He left other instructions with Ned, just in case. Marcus had been having bad dreams for the past week and felt he should protect Jess at all costs. He knew Ned would look after her if anything should happen to him. He really wished he could cancel this trip.

As the ship weighed anchor two days later, Marcus was standing on the upper deck with Colin close by his side. Jon was busy doing his captain stuff, and Marcus knew they would get a chance to chat later in the voyage. Marcus dropped his head and said a prayer, "*God, please bring us home safely and look after Jess and Bessie. I love them so much.*" A man who had shown little emotion before meeting Jess, Marcus was astounded by how often he was moved to tears over his wife and their daughter. His beautiful girls, oh, how he adored them.

Chapter 16 The Journey

*J*ess received her first letter from Marcus to let her know what ship he would be on and that he was travelling with Captain Jon Park on his new vessel, the *Warlord*. She knew Marcus said that Jon was a brilliant captain and was sure to see them home safely. At least he had friends nearby. Jess gave a sigh of relief. She kept reading and saw that her assignment had been transferred too Ned to oversee while he was absent. She knew this had to happen, but she hated the sound of it. While she really liked Major Ned Grace and realised that he was an old friend of Marcus's, she just wished her husband had not had to leave in the first place.

Jess started to knit Marcus a jumper from his own fleece from yarn that she had spun herself. This was to keep occupied during Marcus's absence. She had dyed the wool and made it thick so that he would stay warm and dry when he needed to attend to his flock in the middle of winter. She had started making it as soon as she had arrived home from seeing him off on his trip.

She made herself busy with chores around the homestead, and she delighted in looking after their daughter. Bessie's joyous giggles made Jess happy but also sad too. She could see Marcus in her mind's eye, sitting on the floor, playing with Bessie. She knew that he was unhappy that he'd had to leave them. He would not have gone if his factory, full of staff in England, didn't rely on him.

After three months, she hoped to hear from him anytime soon, and she wanted to get the jumper finished before he returned. She had missed him dreadfully at Christmas.

Then New Year came and went with no sign of him or any further word from him.

January faded into February…

Jess finished the jumper and a scarf and was now making socks. It had taken ten days to complete the first sock, and she was about to turn the heel on the second one. Hopefully, he would be back by the time it was done. Jess was still knitting when she stopped mid-stitch. Her eyes flew open, she had not had her flow since Marcus left, and she had been so preoccupied that she had not even noticed. She realised she was carrying another child, probably conceived the last night Marcus was with her, and he didn't even know. The knitting fell to the floor, her hands cradled her stomach, and the tears flowed. She realised that this was why she was so tired and also weepy and why she'd thrown up a few times last month. She smiled; she now had wonderful news for his return.

The month passed with no news about Marcus.

March and April came and went with no more news.

Finally, a word about Marcus arrived with Ned. He arrived unexpectedly in early May 1827. He had sent no word about visiting. He knocked on the front door of the lovely single-story homestead. The wide verandah kept the house cool in summer.

Rex welcomed him.

As Jess was officially in Ned's charge, he had to check on her occasionally. Mainly, Ned usually contacted her by mail. However, this time he had come himself.

The red-coated soldier standing at the door made Rex forget to welcome him. Ned's unexpected arrival meant bad news.

Before Jess saw him, Ned said to Rex, "Get Felicity, and both stay close to her."

Jess heard Ned's voice as he spoke. She walked to the door, and as soon as she saw him, she knew something was wrong.

As Jess moved to greet him, he noted she was about six months gone with child and knowing the information he carried; he knew she would be distressed. Ned was now even more concerned about how she would take the news. Marcus had said nothing about expecting another child.

Jess did not need to hear his words to know that Ned carried terrible news.

Without Ned saying a word to her, Jess fainted.

Ned caught her as she collapsed and carried her into the

sitting room, where he lay her on the settee. Kneeling beside her, he stroked her cheek, "Jessie, wake up; Marc is not dead, just missing. Jess, wake up." Ned kept stroking her cheek, trying to rouse her.

Rex hurried in with Felicity on his heels. Surveying the situation, both joined Ned to assist Jess.

It took some minutes before Jess roused, and then her eyes focused on Ned.

His worried face spoke volumes. "Jessica, he's not dead, but I have a story to tell. Can you sit up?"

Jess nodded and was soon nestled beside Felicity and prepared to listen to Ned's saga.

Before he started speaking, he sent Rex for Jaques and Giles. He said, "Both needed to hear what has happened to Marcus." Once they appeared, Ned waited until all had settled themselves before starting the story.

Rex had brought in a tea tray while they were waiting.

Ned watched Jess's face, concerned about how she would take the news. He wondered how she would cope with what he had to tell her. He had never liked delivering news like this, and this time it was worse, for Marc was one of his good friends. Marc had watched over him for over twenty years, in fact, since he was just six.

With all now seated and hanging on his words, Ned started. "Jess, as you know, Marc caught the *Warlord* with Jon Park as skipper. Things went well until they left Cape Town for their return journey; they were headed out into the Indian Ocean and became caught in a huge storm. It blew them far to the north, ending up on the northwest coast of Madagascar. There they had to put ashore for repairs, and with virtually nothing on hand to make these same repairs, it took a lot of time. He was on his way back, Jess." Ned heard her gasp and saw her put her hand on her stomach, but she motioned for him to continue.

Ned did and said, "From there, they eventually got the ship seaworthy and set off to round the north of the island. They were heading to Cape Town again to repair the ship properly. We only know all this as they met a ship off the top of Madagascar and exchanged mail. I have a letter for you from Marcus, Jess." Ned passed it over but suggested that she read it later in private. He had also received one with the full and unadulterated details of what had happened until they swapped mail. Marcus assured him that he had not put the details in Jess's letter. Ned knew that there had been little food and many insects, which they had eaten. Marcus had written the long screeds to both of them while awaiting the repairs. At least they were both otherwise unharmed. He was pleased Colin was with him.

Ned leaned over and took Jess's hand before continuing, "They were under sail and heading south, having just left the other ship. The *Sophie Marie* was now headed out to sea as it was heading to Ceylon, hence the delay in receiving the letters and news. Now back to the *Warlord*. The crew of the *Sophie Marie* saw a third ship approach the *Warlord*. The new ship had black sails, and Jess, it was a pirate ship."

This time everyone gasped.

Giles was now on the edge of his seat. He gasped and uttered, "Pirates took Mr Marcus?" Giles was almost reeling. He knew he would be living on the street, but for Marcus, his boss was a father figure, and he adored him as such. He had been almost angry when he was not permitted to go with him, but Marcus had asked him to stay and look after Jess and Bessie. Now he may not see him again. Apologising, Giles said, "Sorry, please continue, Major Ned."

Ned nodded. "Yes, but friends, this group of pirates are known as kidnappers for ransom rather than plunderers and murderers. Jess, this is why I have come. Somehow, sometime, you should receive a ransom letter from them, and you will be asked to pay for their release. The letter will not be a hoax. When you receive it, contact me as soon as you can. The Governor and I will arrange the transfer of funds. I imagine that £100 would be the asking price for each unless they learn of Marcus's true worth."

Felicity was now sitting with her arm around her friend.

Jess dropped Ned's hand, turned it into Felicity's shoulder, and wept again.

Ned saw her distress and let her mourn. It was a lot to accept, especially in her condition. "I have more, but I will give you a few minutes to yourself." Ned was feeling the tension himself. He subtly motioned for Jaques, Giles, and Rex to accompany him as he left the room.

The four men left the room.

Ned asked to use the facilities. Due to nerves, the tea had gone straight through him and left to do so.

The other three men had their heads together, discussing what to do, and wondered if there was actually anything they could do.

Ned returned and said to the anxious men, "Marcus is in big trouble, men. I won't tell Jess everything, but we will have to protect her as much as possible. I'm hoping that, somehow, we can assist Marcus from here. But there have been a few cases where the kidnapped persons are never heard from again. Thankfully, Marcus had been too Cape Town already, so his business is safe. I know that, or he would not have been on the ship coming back here." Ned turned to Marcus's tiger. "Giles, it might mean that you have to take the ransom for him when required. I'm prepared to help Jess as much as I can, but it's not going to be easy. I have spoken to Governor Darling, and he's told me that he would sign an Absolute Pardon for her when her term is up. But, if we can't get Marcus back, it might be better that she stays here." Ned had seen Giles blanch when he suggested that he be the courier. However, he knew that he would assist if it should be required. "Let's return to Jess." Ned walked back into the sitting room.

Jess was waiting. She had obviously been thinking. "Ned, I need to know the worst. Please don't hold back. I need to know what the likelihood is of his return. Marcus didn't give up on me when I was arrested, and I won't give up on him. He chased me halfway around the world; I'll do the same for him if I have to. I will sell everything if it means I, no, we can get him back. He belongs to us all." She swiped angrily at the tears that fell.

Ned could see that Jess had realised the situation was dire. He shrugged, looked at the other men and thought he would let her know more of the situation but would not let on Marcus's danger. "All right, Jess, I'll tell you more. The next part of the story is from various other historical incidents related to me by the Governor himself. Governor Darling worked in Mauritius, which in the scheme of things, is not that far from Madagascar. He is the one who told me what to expect the pirates to demand." Ned saw Jess's eyes were fixed on his lips. She was absorbing his every word.

Jess listened. "Ned, please, what is the probability of him being released? Do they always let them go? And what about Colin and Jon? Have you heard anything about them?"

Ned leaned close and retook her hand. "Jess, we have not heard anything about them. What is worse, we may not for some time, possibly even years. We know these pirates usually keep the prisoners alive as they are all worth money. Although forced to work on their farms, they are usually not even mistreated. They won't try to escape as lions as the like would eat them." Ned had little more he was prepared to tell her. Governor Darling's description of the living conditions was detailed and not fit for a lady's ears. He had interviewed survivors before and therefore knew what they would endure. The prisoners would be sent into various villages and be forced to hand dig the farm plots as they had no tools but sharpened sticks. They would live on a fermented dough-like meal made into flatbread and then stuffed with a highly spiced rice mixture called *bariis iskukaris,* followed by bananas in one form or another. Their accommodation would be in a grass-thatched roof hut called an *aqal,* and they would sleep on the floor. Knowing that Marcus would probably be kept alive to work the fields, Ned sighed with relief when the Governor told him all this. Now they all just had to wait. There was no way of contacting the pirates. The only active thing they could do was to pray.

Ned was astounded that Jess was holding together so well.

Jess, however, was smiling. "Ned, I had a dream that this would happen, but I didn't tell Marcus, as I knew he had to go. Ned, he doesn't even know about this little one." She rubbed her stomach. "I need to get him back, Ned. I need my children's father at home. I want my husband, no matter what it costs. If required, I will pay whatever they ask, even the same for each of the entire crew. Marcus will not mind the expense. If, as you say, he finalised the business arrangement in Cape Town, then his finances will be quite healthy."

Ned was shocked at her words. "Marc doesn't know that you are expecting?"

She shook her head. "I only realised three months ago."

Ned watched her face soften as she looked down at her distended stomach. He smiled at the beauty of the young mother before him. "Then Jess, we have another reason to make sure he returns, don't we?"

Ned stayed for three days before making tracks to return to Parramatta. During that time, he walked daily with Jess. He told her about his school days with Marcus and the antics of him and his friends. Talking to her about Marcus made it a little easier to pray for him. As he rode off, Jess felt the baby kick.

~

Almost a year to the day from Marcus's departure and six months after Ned left, a carriage arrived.

Jess had been waiting for this visit for some time. She greeted them with her three-month-old son, Stephen Marcus, in her arms and Bessie clutching her gown tightly.

Sarah and George alighted. Sarah almost fell into Jess's arms. "Jess, we're not going back; George has resigned because they wanted to send him to Port Macquarie. So, we're moving here to *Glenrose*. Everything finally has come to a head with Major Morriset, amongst others in Sydney, and we are now to be full-time farmers. This also means that we can be here for you. Have you heard anything yet from Marcus?"

Jess shook her head. She was delighted at Sarah's news as it slightly lightened her overwhelming sadness. Their friends would now be very close. They didn't stay long with Jess on that first visit as they had to unpack and settle in. The two homesteads were visible to each other. The Middletons would now be able to come over regularly and comfort Jess.

Since Ned left so many months ago, each day had grown more challenging and harder to get through. Initially, it was only because her daughter needed her that Jess managed to rise from her bed at all. She felt crushed. However, since Stevie's arrival, the babe had given her a new spark. Marcus had a son and an heir.

Jess still spent many hours when in bed in tears. She now slept cuddled up to an old worn shirt belonging to Marcus. She found it stuffed at the bottom of a bag that he had placed on the top of their wardrobe. The scent was not strong and was now slightly musty, but it was his smell. Her arms so craved to be filled with him, for him to cradle her lovingly as only he could. She wished to hear his loving endearments. The thoughts of those many moments brought tears afresh.

Jess believed the verse in Mark 10 v 29 was meant to comfort her. It went, *"And Jesus answered and said, Verily I say unto you, There is no man that hath left house, or brethren, or sisters, or father, or mother, or wife, or children, or lands, for my sake, and the gospel's, but he shall receive a hundredfold now in this time, houses, and brethren, and sisters, and mothers, and children, and lands, with persecutions; and in the world to come eternal life."*

Admittedly, Marcus had gone for work, but wherever he went, he could not help but share the gospel of Christ. From what he said of Captain Jon Park, he was the same. She knew Colin also had a strong faith, but she didn't know about any of the others with them, but she prayed for them anyway. Her prayer times she now did twice a day, and Marcus's safety was always the main point, along with their children's health.

Jess spent at least an hour praying before everyone else was up in the mornings. She now relished the dawn as the silence of the waking day refreshed her soul. She had checked the globe that Marcus had in his study. She looked up where Madagascar and Somalia were and worked out where Marcus had been kidnapped, and she traced her fingers over his route and where the storm had taken them. She followed where he had travelled and how he should have returned. She worked out that with the distance around the globe, Marcus would still be sleeping as she was waking, or she hoped he would be asleep. All she could do was pray for his safety.

Giles had told her of a painting that Marcus's mother, Elizabeth, had in her room. Jess smiled at the memory of that picture. He had forgotten she knew of it. He said little Stevie looked remarkably like the baby in that portrait. Jess knew it well, but she had forgotten about the picture in Elizabeth Ryan's bedroom where she had spent those two fateful days.

Jess also prayed while she fed Stevie. It was true; their little boy was so like Marcus as a small boy that she could hardly release him after he had taken his fill from her breast. She spoilt him with kisses and cuddles. Bessie was often sitting next to her and would get cuddled while she watch her baby brother feed. Jess just wanted them both close. The sweet little boy even had his father's chin.

~

Still, Jess had waited to hear from the kidnappers. Every time the mail arrived, Jess hoped the pirates would have written. The time passed with gruelling slowness.

Nothing, absolute silence!

Jess was desolated. She still prayed morning and evening for her husband, and he was never far from her thoughts. She ached to be held and to tell him of her love. Lucien's leather Bible would be caressed lovingly each time she picked it up. Marcus had insisted this was the book they used daily for their daily devotions, just as she and Lucien had. It was because of her mention of maps that he had purchased the world globe when he had found a book of Biblical maps for her. It now represented both of her beloved husbands.

She flicked open the cover of the precious Bible to the much-loved words. The much-fingered book fell open at Genesis 31; her eyes fell to the words that Marcus had explained only shortly before he departed. It was about God's promise between two parties.

He had said, *"At the time, we are absent from one another,* in verse forty-three, read the story of Jacob and Laban and the promise." Marcus had explained the Hebrew word *Mizpah,* which meant the unbreakable bond between two people. Jess had that faith in Marcus; she had it by the bucketful. She prayed that God would watch over her beloved and bring him home. She just knew Marcus was still alive. She would never let him go.

Marcus had read the other words to her from Psalm 121,
"I will lift up mine eyes unto the hills, from whence cometh my help.
My help cometh from the Lord, which made heaven and earth.
He will not suffer thy foot to be moved: he that keepeth thee will not
slumber. Behold, he that keepeth Israel shall neither slumber nor sleep.
The Lord is thy keeper: the Lord is thy shade upon thy right hand.
The sun shall not smite thee by day, nor the moon by night.
The Lord shall preserve thee from all evil: he shall preserve thy soul.
The Lord shall preserve thy going out and thy coming in from this time
forth, and even forevermore."

Jess had read this Psalm so often that she could recite it. She walked out onto the verandah, lifted her eyes to the quiet hills, and prayed. Often tears would follow, but as time passed, the words would be followed with only a sigh of resignation. But she never gave up hope. Every mail delivery, Jess checked through the letters for the long-awaited ransom note from an unknown hand.

It never came.

Stevie was now running everywhere, and Bessie was learning to read. Marcus had missed it all; not only that, but he also didn't even know he had a son. Stevie had been born in July, three months after Ned's visit and nine months to the day from when Marcus left.

No one had heard anything of Marcus, not even the Governor.

Ned's weekly letter kept her updated with news from Sydney. Ned wrote that JT and Harmon sent their regards as they were back in town. JT promised that the next time he was in the African waters, he would ask around and see if he could find out anything. Jon was a friend of theirs, and they would word up all the other skippers and crews at all the ports. Surely someone somewhere should know something.

~

Two years after his last visit, Ned came again. The news he brought this time was, on the whole, good, although not about

Marcus.

Jess greeted him with a welcome kiss on his cheek and asked if he had brought news of her husband.

Ned shook his head. "No, I'm sorry, Jess, but I have brought other good news." He handed her a sealed letter. He walked from her side as she flicked open the seal. He stood looking out the window at the beautiful garden as she read the contents.

Jess walked to another window and unfolded the large sheet of paper holding enclosures. There was a letter, and enclosed in it were her freedom papers. She took the Certificate of Freedom in one hand and the Absolute Pardon and a letter in the other. She had no words. Marcus had begged for her to have this sheet of paper or even just permission to travel. If she had gone, their children would now be in prison or working as slaves in the village gardens. Reluctantly, she admitted that again, she could see God's hand at work even back then, protecting her and keeping them safe. Stevie might not be here if she had gone. She was sure she would have lost the baby. Now the adorable little boy was Marcus's heir.

A thought suddenly occurred to her. She swung around to Ned. "I have to take him home, Ned. I need to make arrangements for Stevie to inherit his father's business."

Ned knew this. After more than two years of silence, he no longer held much hope for Marcus's return. Maybe he, along with the others, had been killed when first kidnapped. His own acceptance of the inevitable had been gradual.

Even Jess realised that they should have heard well before this. Over the years, she often said, "Ned, I still feel he's alive, though, somewhere."

The unending silence was so hard for either of them to accept.

Now, Jess needed her thoughts voiced. She saw Ned's face and said, "He's not coming home, is he, Ned?"

Ned had a massive lump in his throat. He shook his head. "I don't think so, Jess. Not now; it has been too long."

Marcus had always been there for him throughout all but six years of his own life. Now there was absolutely nothing he could do for his mentor and friend. He felt useless. Obtaining the paperwork for Jess had been almost like a final act on his friend's behalf. He had watched over her from afar, knowing she was safe with her friends in the Hunter Valley. Ned had used his friendship with Amelia,

Governor Darling's nanny, to obtain the Pardon. It had meant revealing Jess's identity to the Governor. However, as Amelia's brother was one of Ned's best friends, he didn't have to explain much. They were still able to keep his own identity secret from the Darlings; however, they could reveal Jess's real identity to the Governor. When Ned had told Eliza Darling about Jess and what had occurred, the Full Pardon was a foregone conclusion.

Jess's world collapsed. The thought of her return to England without Marcus hit hard. She walked into Ned's arms and wept as her heart had finally broken. The valuable sheets of paper fluttered unnoticed to the floor.

Amelia had wept into Ned's shoulder often enough. She, too, had been innocent and convicted. According to her brother, it was to save the face of her family. He had not told her he knew some of her family's story. He found he was getting used to comforting beautiful weeping women. Yet none stirred his heart; that thought made him smile. One day God may have someone for him, but it was neither Amelia nor Jess.

After some time, her sobbing eased. She sniffed in a very unladylike manner, and Jess said bravely, "He's gone, and we have to go home."

Ned heaved a sigh of relief, he hadn't wanted to tell her, but he knew this was the right course of action for Stevie's sake. "Jess, I will do everything I can to assist. And yes, I think you should take Stevie and Bessie home. If fact, after Steve was born, I wrote to Marcus's mother to let her know she has both a granddaughter and grandson, and I informed her that I know that they are Marcus's children. I know this dear lady well, Jess, having spent many a holiday at their place. This information will ease the path of your arrival. However, you will need to personally take your paperwork and present it to Marcus's solicitor, including your marriage certificate. I shall also write you both a reference and a letter of introduction." He had not released her while he spoke. "Jess, did Marcus tell you how I know him?"

She nodded against his chest.

Ned continued, "Then he told you what my real name is and who my parents are?"

She nodded again.

Ned smiled. He knew why Marcus adored her. Not many women would not keep silent with that knowledge or use it against him somehow. Her beautiful nature shone through her, even in her sadness. Before he spoke, he checked the door. It was open, but no one was nearby. "Jess, then you know my father is Duke of Gracemere, I will sign my letter with my real name, and I must confess, even though I am a mere Lord, that has a lot of sway. Even if you lose the rest of the paperwork, my letter alone would be enough to make them all acknowledge the children and who you are. If you have problems, take it to my mother in Kent, for I will reveal all to her too in the letter you will carry."

Jess quickly pulled back in his arms. "Ned, you can't do that. They will discover where you are and the name you are under."

Ned was flabbergasted. "Jessie, are you truly worried about me? With all you are going through, you are worried about me? My parents know I am in this country, just not the name I am using, so it will reveal nothing to them. One day I will possibly go home; it depends if I am needed. If Marcus told you everything, you would know what I mean. Knowing whom my brother married, I don't feel David will have any children of his own, so being the second son, I may be needed at home at some stage; I just pray that I'm not. Other people know my contact details; Amelia's brother Jimmy is one of them." Ned had told Jess about aiding Jimmy's sister, Amelia, on his last visit.

Marcus had filled her in about the group of boys from Christ's Hospital. Jimmy was one of four friends that Marcus had mentored. The other boys were Robbie and Gerry, and of course, Ned had made up the four. Marcus had bailed the four junior boys out of numerous scrapes. Two years ago, Ned had delighted Jess when telling her of their pranks when children. Because Marcus had always been the senior boy, Jess thought of Ned as a little brother, and that was how she treated him. He was ten months younger than her; however, he was a blonde giant, standing well over six-foot, and he towered over her and had the strength of two men. She trusted him absolutely, and so did Marcus.

Jess drew out from his arms and pointed to the settee, then moved to sit down. They were seated, chatting, when Rex brought in the tea tray a few minutes later.

After being thrust together and caring for Jess, Rex and Ned became friends. On Ned's last visit, they had spent a lot of time in the kitchen drinking the hot sweet tea. There were no dainty teacups in this house but big mugs of sweet black tea for the gentle blonde giant.

When Jess had visitors, Rex once again took up the role of the butler, although, these days, he found he almost preferred to be out with the sheep. Felicity still kept the house tidy, but they now had two young maids to assist with the children and the cleaning, and they also had a full-time cook.

Felicity was kept occupied looking after the four adorable imps.

Rex knew that Ned was more than an ordinary friend; he was Marcus's protégé. He also knew that Jess had been left in his care. For Rex, that spoke volumes of how Marcus trusted him

Shortly before Marcus had left, he had handed Rex an envelope with a document in it. It was the title for a fifty-acre farm at the end of the valley. It was now his own farm.

Rex thought back to his last private conversation with Marcus, "Rex, you are a free man, yet you dedicated your life to watching over Lucien and Jess and now me. I can never thank you enough for all you and Felicity have done for her; this is my way of saying thank you. You have earned so much more than just your pay or even this, but it will give you some security. You are now freehold landowners. Use it as you wish." The envelope also contained £100 in various notes. Rex had been speechless. Only three days later, Marcus had caught the ship to Sydney.

In the intervening years, Rex had started building a farmhouse for Felicity and their children. It would mean he had a home to leave to Damien when he died. That was something he had never thought possible. In England, they would always be servants; here, they were now landowners. He would do anything he could to help this family. If Marcus were dead, then Jess would need them even more. He would do whatever Jess now asked of him. Being only next door, he could oversee things from their new home. But, no matter what happened, they would not leave her alone in the house.

During the two weeks that Ned was with them, Rex was reeling from the unfolding developments. Rather than travel with them, Jess was to return home with Giles and Jaques; he and Felicity would stay in the valley and oversee the farm.

Both young men had recently married, and their wives, who were sisters, were reasonably new arrivals as free settlers and had come with their sizeable families.

Rex and Felicity had been asked to stay on and run the farm. This situation was not to Rex's wishes, but he acquiesced as he had frequently said that he would do as requested. He realised that someone had to oversee the wool production on the new farm. He had worked closely with Marcus for the years they had worked together on the farm. He knew each sheep by name.

Felicity was not happy either, but for the sake of her family knew it was the right thing to do. She knew there was no future for either of them in England. Here they had an independent future without the confines of class, as did their children. Here they could make something of themselves.

Tom and Mary Landy would stay, too; they were happy and settled. Now they had a small dairy to care for; they were content. Tom was promoted to overseer under Rex as manager.

George and Sarah Middleton had settled into their homestead. Jess had loved the weekly service now held at George's home. All the local farmers and their families came as often as they could. George had never had permission for the organ to be placed in Christ Church, and Marcus had never donated it to the church, so George had brought it with him when they moved. It now sat in the lounge room near the tall French doors and was used for their services. They were already talking about building a small timber church in the growing town one day. They had already held services in the schoolroom, but more could fit on the verandah.

George had filled a massive gap in the community and was soon as busy, if not more than he had been in Newcastle. The ministry of the word was only part of his work. He cared for his flock, and for him, that was not sheep. He planned for a permanent brick church to one day be built to house Marcus's pedal organ.

Chapter 17 Introducing the Heir

With the decision to leave now made, the household was thrown into turmoil. Packing cases, crates, and boxes were all over the house. Jess packed the children's clothing and other items. Jaques took over Jess's clothing and then insisted on packing all of Marcus's clothing and personal items as Colin was not there. Jess refused to leave any of his belongings behind. Jaques knew that she slept with one of Marcus's shirts, and it dearly needed a wash; however, he dared not do that. He would place it in her cabin bag along with her Bible and other personal items.

Sarah and George came and helped where they could. It was more often to take the four children to play with their growing brood. Jess found it hard to accept that her time in the colony was over. Mid-conversation, she would get up and leave the room. She would generally go into Marcus's office gazing out of the window.

Ned could not assist with much of the personal packing, but he did offer to sort the office. Jess wanted Marcus's personal paperwork and correspondence packed, but the farm books and farm correspondence were left in situ. This was something that Ned could do. He had been trained to work in the office of the family estate at home. So he knew what was needed or not. He soon had Marcus's items sorted and packed, ready for transport. Ned stayed and would escort Jess, her children and the four adults accompanying her as they returned to Sydney.

Jess made her very sad farewells to Felicity and Rex. So much and happened since she first met these two wonderful people years before. They were all on new paths in their lives. Rex and Felicity stayed on the farm when Ned took Jess away to Newcastle. None could face a public farewell.

Jess found saying farewell to Sarah challenging but not as hard as parting from Felicity. She had been far more than a servant. Felicity was Jess's best friend for many years. Neither of their lives had followed an easy path, but both women now believed they were where God wanted them, and both shed many tears.

Jess and her entourage left with Ned on the coastal cutter. Not only was Jess taking all her possessions, but she insisted that all Marcus's things were packed and taken too. Marcus's brass-topped cane, his old work shirt and his new jumper, scarf and socks lay inside the top of her main suitcase.

Giles and Jaques's wives, Helen and Lydia, were both expecting babies and were ill on the sea voyage south. Once onboard, Jess knew that they would only have one night on board, but she was stunned by the speed at which everything had occurred. Jess was still in a daze.

Everything had happened so fast that she had had little time to think. Jess had her hands full with her children, and Stevie was at the age when saying no to him meant very little. Bessie's world had been the farm. At five, she was still clingy and rarely did she release Jess's gown. Both children would be in harnesses for their safety for their entire time onboard.

Ned was wonderful with Stevie. He explained to Jess that his friend Charles Lockley had six children, and he had nursed them from the day the eldest boy, Charlie, was born. Jess knew the Lockley's second son, Eddie, was named after Ned, as he was born on Ned's twenty-second birthday.

When Ned arrived at the farm, fifteen-month-old Stevie stood in awe of the blonde giant. Stevie looked up at Ned, and he asked him the question he asked every new man he met. The words were unchanged, be it the postman, someone delivering firewood from the back paddock, or the men collecting the wool clip. Stevie's question was, "Are you my papa?"

Jess cringed each time she heard it. If only Marcus would return. Ned smiled as he picked up the dark-headed lad. He had a sorrowful frown on his brow. "No, lad, I'm not, but I hope you will meet him one day, for he is a wonderful person. You, though, are going on a long boat trip, and you will meet your papa's family and your Grandmama. You must be good for your Mama and stay close to her. Will you do that?"

The dimpled dark-headed boy in his arms grinned and nodded vigorously. Ned continued, "You must also look after your sister for me. I promised your Papa that I would always care for you all; however, I will not be around, so you will have to do it for me." Ned flicked a dark curl from the child's forehead. He had no expectations that the small boy would have any understanding of his words, but he felt he needed to voice his thoughts. The toddler was still in a smock. Ned knew that he would be breeched when aged about six, and he would grow beyond recognition in no time at all. He and Marcus would miss it all. Ned had watched his friend Charles's four sons shoot up, and at ten, nine, four and two, he could see that the years would fly away all too fast. Ned, at thirty-one, knew that it was unlikely he would ever marry. He had his soldiering work, and it kept his mind occupied and off the messy situation that had caused his flight to the Antipodes over ten years before. He was content with the rank of Major and the one hundred and twenty men assigned to him from the 48th Foot. He could have purchased a promotion to Lieutenant Colonel, but that would defeat the purpose of staying incognito. He had received no word from home nor expected any, as few knew where he was. He adored his mother and had wished he could somehow send her a letter. His eyebrows flicked up; with Jess returning, he knew that he could trust her to deliver a screed to his parents and tell them he was well and happy. He could also trust her not to reveal his new name. On the trip south, he set to writing the various letters she would carry home. Using the ship's stationery meant it would not give away his location as it was un-monogrammed.

After two peaceful days onboard the coastal cutter, their arrival in Sydney was hectic. Ned calmed their panic and soon had them settled in The King's Arms Hotel before he returned to Parramatta. The hotel was a decent establishment that had no taproom. The quality of rooms at this building was good, and they were also clean and roomy. As it had a quality dining room, they had little need to leave the building.

Ned had to depart for duty the next day but would return in four days to make arrangements for their travel to London. Ned had checked with Mr Stewart, the manager, on arrival that no ships were departing in the next four days. He managed to introduce Jess to his friends, Sam and Annie Corbett, only to find that Marcus had already done so some five years before. Their son Danny, his wife Vanessa, and their three daughters were presently in England.

Jess liked the older lady as soon as they met. She reminded her of an older version of Felicity. Annie Corbett rarely left the quaint front cottage and rear stone house built near the church glebe. She had once run a bakery from her tiny cottage; since then, Sam had become a skilled draughtsman. Annie no longer slaved for hours to make ends meet. She was currently recovering from a winter illness.

Sam made Jess welcome and then left her to the ministrations of his wife while he returned to work. Annie cuddled one or the other of the two small children while they chatted. She missed her granddaughters.

After a delightful hour with Annie Corbett, who had recently discovered that their last name was Garney, Jess and the children returned to the hotel. The children had been allowed to pick and eat strawberries straight from their garden. She promised to return for another visit if they had time before they sailed.

On Ned's return, he booked them on the *Dunvegan Castle,* which was due to sail in a few weeks in early July. However, it was mid-August before it finally weighed anchor.

Jess visited Annie a few more times in the eight weeks before they departed. The three-masted convict ship awaiting them reminded Jess of the first view of the passage to Sydney Cove. The Lord had protected her then; now, she was making the return trip in a similar ship just over seven years later. Thankfully, she had been kept safe on the upper decks on her first voyage. Now she was returning to a life similar to the one she had left, only she would no longer have a title.

As the ship was scrubbed and the back-load cargo was safely stowed in the hold, the captain and doctor came to the hotel with Ned and met their passengers, most of whom were staying at the hotel. Captain William Warmsley and surgeon Robert Dunn were greeted warmly. The doctor particularly wished to meet his two prospective passengers, who were both due to deliver en route. He wasn't too keen about having young children on board, but they should be safe enough if they were well-controlled. He spoke to all the passengers about his insistence on regular consumption of lemon juice to ward scurvy away.

Jess had heard about this fact years before and had lemon trees growing at home in the Hunter Valley. She made lemon cordial, which they regularly served in their home. Her children both loved the bitter-sweet drink.

There was not much a single lady could do in Sydney Town. So, her four travelling companions and Jess took the children for long walks along the foreshore and would often sit on the grassy hillsides near Mrs Macquarie's chair, watching the activity on the harbour. Newcastle harbour had been almost deserted compared to the numerous comings and goings of the bay in front of them. They watched vessels arrive and be tugged to the new wharf to unload. They saw others having to anchor until they could get a berth. Some were just waiting for cargo to arrive before they could load up. Others were ships in quarantine due to illness on board. The *Dunvegan Castle* had sat riding at anchor for weeks before she was brought to the wharf in late July and had the remainder of her extensive cargo of wool loaded.

When Jess heard what the cargo was, she wondered if it was a shipment Marcus had arranged with his agent. The captain had asked her to dinner with the doctor and her companions. They were to eat onboard and view their accommodations. Knowing she had funds available, she enquired about spare cabins. On finding that there were few other passengers, she booked three excess cabins for their use. The ship had maids and even a butler of sorts, whom the captain referred to as a steward.

Jaques insisted that he still be her dresser and care for her clothing. It was something he loved to do. Giles volunteered to oversee the children's safety.

The time for departure had come. Sam and Annie stood next to Ned as the ropes were finally thrown off and drawn aboard the ship. It was towed backward from the jetty and turned before heading out to sea.

Once out of the bay, the westerly wind caught the unfurled sails, and Jess felt the ship lift and pick up speed. Soon the vessel was sliding gracefully through the towering Sydney Heads. Jess still had not left the railing. Jess stayed waving until Ned's red coat was finally too far away to see.

Helen and Lydia had the children in their care and took them below to settle into their cabin. Jaques was already in Jess's cabin unpacking for the family for the months ahead; Giles stayed close to

Jess to see if she needed anything. Both men would see to their wives later.

Jess knew that either one or the other men would shadow her at all times. She knew Giles was close, but she thought miserably that the only person she wanted was Marcus, and no one could bring him back.

Ned had brought both children a toy, which awaited them on their bunks. Bessie was given a rag doll in a pretty dress, and Stevie had a farmer doll with some knitted sheep.

She knew she would not see this sight again and didn't wish to miss anything. One hour, then two, she hardly moved. Only when the land was gone from sight, she finally went below deck. Giles followed at a discreet distance. He, too, missed Marcus, but he would not let his mistress suffer if he could help her.

The passage to Wellington in New Zealand was considerably smooth. Both young mothers-to-be were seasick and took to their bunks. Their husbands and the ship's maids took turns nursing them, and by the time they were two weeks out of New Zealand, both had recovered enough to enjoy sitting outside in the weak sunshine and getting some salt spray on their faces.

Jess and the doctor insisted that both children were only allowed on deck if harnessed and attached to an adult. Neither minded as it meant more cuddles. Both were secured safely on every venture above deck.

One of the empty cabins had been turned into a playroom and schoolroom for the group to relax. A second empty cabin was between the two couples and would double as a nursery when the new babies arrived. It already had a big cot and lots of baby clothes waiting for the two new babies. The girls were due only weeks apart. The third empty cabin Jess claimed for herself. In this, she sat and read her Bible and mourned the absence of her beloved.

While in Sydney, one of the meetings Jess had been with the Governor and Eliza Darling. Ned had introduced them on his return and Eliza greeted Jess with a hug.

Jess had wanted to find out more about the pirates. She pumped the Governor for every skerrick of information he had. Sadly, there was so little information that she felt none the wiser. She would never know what happened to Marcus. She was now resigned that after nearly three years, he was truly gone. She could mourn him if she knew he was dead, but in her heart, there still remained a spark of hope. She clung to that. The words from the end of Psalm 121 kept coming back to her. *"The Lord shall preserve thee from all evil: he shall preserve thy soul. The Lord shall preserve thy going out and thy coming in from this time forth, and even forevermore."*

In the meantime, she had to pave the way for Stevie for his heritage. Bessie also needed to get to know her aunt and grandmother. Jess had never met either of them, but they had written often over the years. Since Marcus's disappearance, their letters had nearly stopped. Jess still wrote, but only an occasional letter came in reply. She knew Marcus had explained her conviction, but she was now free. With their hurried departure, there had been no time to let them know she was returning. True, Ned had written, but she had not. They would have five months or so on board, and their welcome in London and Brighton would be uncertain, to say the least. Jess was thankful she had the support of both Giles and Jaques; one was her friend and the other Marcus's protégé. Giles at least could vouch for who she was and that Marcus was the father of her children.

~

After two months at sea, the young wives were finding the movement underfoot was more difficult as their condition progressed. Their husbands were beside them every time they moved above deck. Neither was allowed to care for the children as they found it hard enough to keep balance themselves. Jess and the ship's maids would have the children in hand. Even the doctor would assist Jess with young Stevie. He had taken to the small boy and was often at hand to help Mrs Ryan with her family. Doctor Dunn adored the well-behaved children and offered to escort Jess when she wished. Before the captain sailed, he had finally put one and one together. Mrs M. Ryan, the passenger, was the wife of Marcus Ryan, Esquire, owner of the precious cargo of wool in his hold.

From the moment she stepped on board, Jess was treated like royalty. When he revealed the cargo over dinner on the first night onboard, Jess smiled and nodded, seemingly disinterested.

Far from being disinterested, Jess knew that discussing Marcus in public would assuredly lead to more tears. She stayed mum until he offered to walk her back to her cabin. They had diverted to the deck, and while outdoors, she poured out the story and that Marcus was still missing.

The captain had promised to keep his ears open for snippets

of gossip about Marcus in the various ports. Captain Warmsley said, "Mrs Ryan, there were often ships in port that have sailed down through that area, and now I have a reason to ask more questions. I shall spread the word amongst my friends until I eventually hear something. Not knowing is the hardest thing."

Again, Jess thanked God for allowing her to be under the care of a sympathetic captain and one who knew of Marcus. They passed through storms and starry nights saw dolphins, meteor showers and even the bioluminescence in the water. All these things did little to ease the pain she was suffering. Her heart hurt too much. When the stars above seemed to fall from the sky, she watched them with unseeing eyes. Everything seemed to be occurring around her, but she didn't feel part of the world anymore. She had almost disconnected from the world. Only when she was in bed and hugging Marcus's shirt did she weep. During the daytime, she stayed strong for the children and her friends. She spoke when spoken to, but none heard her laugh. Even her smile needed to be forced. The further she travelled from their farm, the quieter she became.

November arrived with the birth of the first child. Jaques and Lydia welcomed a daughter into the world. Little Genevieve Lydia, named after her grandmother and mother, had a pair of very healthy lungs, and Jess was pleased that she had placed the nursery cabin on the other side of the passageway and far away from her room. She had forgotten how the night-time crying of a tiny child was so loud in the dark hours.

Genie's cousin, Marcus Giles, was born weeks later as they rounded Cape Horn and headed up the coast of South America. Surprisingly the child had a shock of dark red hair. But both Lydia and Helen said that they had two red-headed grandmothers and that the red hair typically skipped a generation. Little Marc had inherited this lovely deep auburn hair. As both girls were very fair, it had never occurred to Giles that his son would not be either blonde or dark like himself. He would be found gazing in wonderment at the tiny babe. Jaques was never far from his wife and daughter. Both now understood the awe that Marcus had voiced when Bessie was born. Neither had fully grasped the importance of the role and the weight that fatherhood now pressed on them. Each had a new respect for their wives. Doctor Dunn had needed both men in for the births. Jess had attended both, too, as had one of the maids, but the girl had been useless as she nearly got sick. Jess had sent her from the room.

With regular periods of being becalmed and intermittent storms, they passed Christmas and New Year in the middle of the Atlantic Ocean, nearly sitting still in the glassy water. This period did allow the children to have more time on deck, and even a game or two of tag was allowed. To run and squeal was a delight, and Stevie was also taken up to the enormous ship's wheel and allowed to steer. Keeping a two-year-old occupied was now a full-time occupation. Once, he had woken early and managed to escape his cabin. Thankfully one of the crew saw him and grabbed him before any harm came to him. Jess picked him up and gave him a swift spanking, then hugged him whilst weeping. She could so easily have lost him. He was so shocked that he promised that he would not leave the cabin by himself again.

After over five months onboard, a seagull landed in the rigging. Stevie watched a sailor scurry up the rope ladder into the crow's nest on the top of the mast. Stevie said, "Mummy, look, he's going to fly." He had seen the man put out an arm.

Soon a cry of "Land Ho" was heard, and sails were adjusted to change their course. The days stretched on with only light winds, but soon land was visible from on deck. By early February, they were about to enter the Thames estuary. From there, the ship would have to travel with the tide. Captain Warmsley had used the term *go with the flow*, but Jess had no idea what that meant until she saw how the myriad of sailing ships traversed the Thames River. As the mass of watercraft all but blocked the wind, all vessels were restricted to travelling up and down the river by the ebb and flow of the tide. Depending on their direction, they had to anchor off to either port or starboard side of the river, then wait for six hours or so until the tide changed again and carried them further up or down the river. Depending on the winds and volume of water traffic, this could take up to a week.

The first thing Jess noticed about being back in London was the smell. It was not just salt in the air that she was used to, but the air stank. It wasn't even the salty estuary mud; it was just the stench of garbage and decay. London in early 1831 was dirty. Jess had forgotten that the smell of the filth in the city had turned her stomach eight years ago. Lucien had only stayed in town as long as he had to before returning to Crawley. The years in the pristine valley in Australia had made her forget that London was not a pretty place to live in comparison to the extreme cleanliness of their farm in the small Patterson Valley.

She had already penned a long letter to Felicity and Rex to let them know they had arrived safely. She had sealed it as they spent the last night on board. They had been allocated a berth at the main passenger wharf and were just waiting for the tug to manoeuvre them to their allocated berth. Giles would then go ashore to the London house and bring carriages and other personnel to assist with luggage. Hopefully, Elizabeth would welcome Jess and the children. She wondered how to contact this lady as she didn't know where she'd be. Jess had made special clothing for the children and hoped that Stevie would at least stay clean. She usually didn't worry about Bessie as she didn't like dirt. Even when eating, if some food stuck to her lips, she would wait until someone wiped them before taking another mouthful. Stevie was the opposite. If there was dirt anywhere, he would find it and usually would be sitting in it and smearing whatever it was all over his face. Rather than scold him, Jess would smile, clean him up and watch him harder. Somehow, he always found some way of becoming covered in a mess.

Two hours after Giles left, he returned with a bevy of staff and an older lady. Jess presumed this was her mother-in-law as she saw Giles fussing over her. Jess may well have slept in her bed and even seen the portrait in her room, but they had never met. The woman in the painting was so much younger. Back then, she had not realised that the baby was Marcus. She wondered if the lady would come on board. She didn't. Giles seated her on the dock, waiting for them to disembark. He would return to bring his wife and son ashore after Jess, and the children had met Marcus's mother. That had to be his first job. Jaques was arranging everything below deck. Jess knew that the girls had packed their cabins already.

Jess had hoped that she could meet Elizabeth in private for the first time. To meet on a public wharf that was bustling with activity was awkward. Jess would already be watching her children and knew that both were afraid of what was ahead of them. They could obviously feel her fear.

Giles led the way down the gangplank.

Jess had Bessie's hand, and Giles had Stevie in his arms. Both were in their harness straps, and until they were in the carriage, the harnesses were to stay on. If Stevie took off, Bessie would follow to catch him. Considering Jess had met Marcus through a carriage accident, she didn't want history repeating itself. Jess was watching the children, not the lady on the dock, and did not notice that she had risen and come to the bottom of the ramp.

Jess gave a sigh of relief that the children had made it onshore clean, dry, and safe. She lifted her eyes to where the lady had been sitting, only to see the bench seat now empty.

"I'm here, dear," she heard from beside her.

Jess turned and saw the lady waiting to greet her. "Welcome home, Jessica." She had outstretched arms, and Jess realised her welcome was to be a warm one. Elizabeth quickly enfolded Jessica in her loving arms. Now that she was up close, Marcus's mother was easily recognisable from the portrait.

Jess didn't know what to say. Elizabeth Ryan held Jess at arm's length and looked deep into her face. "Oh, my dear girl!" With those few kind words, Jess could no longer hold her tears. Elizabeth once again drew her weeping daughter-in-law into her arms. Jess had much to tell her, but that could wait. Elizabeth let Jess weep for a few minutes. Both were missing the same dear man. Bessie stood watching and eventually wrapped her small arms around her mother's legs and said, "Don't cry, Mama." Her young voice broke through Jess's sadness. She needed to present her children to their grandmother. Jess pulled gently from Elizabeth's arms and introduced the two children to their grandmother. Bessie stood looking at the older lady before remembering to curtsy to her.

Elizabeth knew not the press the children for a hug. That would come. For now, she was a stranger. Yet when Elizabeth turned to meet Stevie, she gasped. Up until now, the little boy had his face on Giles's shoulder. He now looked up, and Elizabeth looked stunned. He was the image of Marcus at that age.

Stevie turned to look around him and saw the lady holding his mother. "Who's you?" he asked her in a slightly angry voice.

Giles offered to pass the child to the outstretched arms of his grandmother.

Elizabeth didn't push him to come to her but stood with her arms outstretched to him. Jess said, "Stevie, this is your Papa's mama."

Stevie leaned toward her with his arms outstretched, and she gathered him closely. "You is my Grandmama?" He stroked her downy cheek. Then gave her a slobbery kiss.

Elizabeth had her first cuddle with her grandson. "Yes, my young man, and you are the image of your father."

Stevie put his arms around her neck and took a deep sniff of her neck. "You smell like Aunty Sarah. She likes violets too." He snuggled down into her arms and laid his head against her neck, just as he had been with Giles.

Elizabeth was delighted. "Jess, he is so like Marcus; I would have picked him out in a crowd." Jess knew that she would not have to produce Ned's letter. The two ladies and the children walked back to their seats to await the arrival of the rest of their travelling companions. Giles left to assist his wife and son and arrange for the luggage to be transported to their home. Jess had mopped her eyes and regained control. All the fear and trepidation of her welcome had been for nothing. Elizabeth had accepted her and their children. From there, they could discuss the rest privately.

They spent two weeks in London before leaving for Billingshurst. At Elizabeth's request, the lawyer was summoned to their house, and Jess presented all her paperwork, including Ned's letter. Elizabeth had also insisted on purchasing an entirely new wardrobe of clothes for the entourage. Elizabeth even ordered new outfits for her travelling companions; however, Jess insisted that she be allowed to pay for those. Jaques was added to the Ryan household payroll, and the girls were welcomed into the extended family. Elizabeth told them they would both be allocated apartments in the house at Billingshurst. The lawyer had informed Jess that she would have a monthly allowance that was an enormous amount. It was more than she spent in a year on the entire household budget at home. Home, she had to work out where that was now. She might have stayed in the Hunter Valley if it had just been Bessie. However, Stevie needed to one day take over the business and to do that; she first had to learn it herself. She had decided to return to England for her son's sake. She knew that it was his heritage, and she wanted Marcus to be proud of his son. Not that he had even known he existed. Jess revealed the entire story soon after they had arrived at the house. Ned had given permission for her to reveal his presence to Elizabeth but asked that it not be spread further. On arrival, Lydia and Helen took the children to the nursery upstairs. Jess was now alone with Elizabeth and filled her in on the saga and the long years of waiting with only silence as the reply. She told Elizabeth that Captain Warmsley and Marcus's friend JT were still looking for him. Jess would never give up. She still held a glimmer of hope. She clung hard to that.

Chapter 18 Billingshurst

Elizabeth made the decision that they would return to the house in Billingshurst. Jess had heard much about this late Elizabethan Manor House and its impressive next-door neighbour, *Meldon Hall*, from Marcus over the years. She had been stunned to find that it was here that Danny Corbett Garney had been and that Sam was now its owner. Again, it was another of God's strings He pulled. She had no idea that Marcus and Sam had been so well-known to each other so well.

Marcus's home, *Padmorre Park*, had been refurbished. The Tudor section she knew had been stuccoed over, and it had since been added to and redesigned after Marcus purchased it. She had confessed to him soon after his arrival in the colony that, while supposedly unconscious, she had loved listening to him tell her about his home. He had described it well. The tall, twin turrets at the main door and shorter ones along the front of the building, the various rooflines and an eclectic array of windows were most different from each other. Even the chimney stacks were of varying styles, yet the overall edifice was one of warmth and comfort. Immense though it was, it was a home, not just a grand house.

She knew Marcus had purchased it as a deserted semi-ruin. He had spent many an hour describing the state of the building when he first saw it and what he had done to it. On arrival, Jess stood and gazed at the facade in front of her. Marcus's words returned to her. Some of it was large stone blocks, some were of brick, and on other sections of the building, she could see where he had stuccoed and whitewashed the exterior. Rather than look odd, it somehow worked. Marcus's description of the house was good, but his words did not do justice to the pleasing appearance of the entire aspect.

On arrival, Elizabeth lifted Stevie into her arms and walked up the few steps into the open door. Bessie clung to Jess and tugged at her hand, "Mummy, Grandma is leaving without us. Quick, or we'll get lost." Bessie tugged at Jess's skirt and dragged her towards their new life.

Again, the foyer of this incredible house was a mix of styles. The staircase was wide at the bottom and split into two narrower ones, curling around the room and creating an incredible circular effect. It was magnificent, yet it was not that that had caught her eye.

The life-size portrait on the staircase's first landing was of Marcus when Jess had first met him. He was painted standing beside a white horse and was dressed in his riding attire. He was looking directly at the artist, and it was as though he was watching her as she slowly walked up the stairs toward him.

Jess had dropped Bessie's hand and now stood in front of the painting. She reached out to touch his face. "Oh, my love, where are you?" She stood gazing at his beloved face. She so wished he would take her in his arms once more, but his face remained unchanged, and his hands did not move. Jess wiped away her sad tears, realising the painting was not her cherished husband, only a pale reflection of him.

Elizabeth moved to her side. "I'm sorry, dear, I should have warned you about this. Marcus had this commissioned shortly before he left to find you. He has not seen it. He had been posing for it on the day the accident occurred; Doctor Wayne filled me in on the situation." Elizabeth placed a caring hand on her shoulder. "Come upstairs, dear, and see your rooms. I have put you in the master suite, of course. I never slept there as Marcus purchased this house after my husband died."

Jess looked over her shoulder at the portrait as she climbed the staircase. The portrait's eyes followed her with each step she took.

Elizabeth kept chatting as they climbed higher. "Marcus had our tea import business, which he sold to your first husband when my Stephen died. It was then that Marcus focused his efforts on the woollen trade. He told me about it all in one of the many letters he wrote. I now have lovely rooms overlooking the formal gardens.

They catch the sun…" Her talking continued, but Jess didn't hear the words. The shock of seeing Marcus left her reeling. Each time she thought she had her tumultuous emotions under control, something would trigger a memory. Her tears fell unnoticed; the grief was nearly overwhelming her all over again.

Elizabeth led her into a magnificent mahogany-lined room with a huge four-post bed. It was in perfect taste, with everything just where she would have placed things. Elizabeth opened closets, drawers, doors and all the windows. "The staff have not had much time to air them, dear. Open everything wide and blow away the cobwebs." Elizabeth noticed Jess's tears and that she'd not said a word. Elizabeth, too, missed her son, but she had accepted that he was gone and unlikely to return.

Jess wanted to know if Marcus had slept in this room. "Did Marcus used to sleep here, Mrs Ryan?"

Elizabeth rounded on Jess and said while smiling, "Dear, I have already asked you to call me Elizabeth, or Mama or even Grandmama, but Mrs Ryan was my mama-in-law, and she was a trojan. I know it's not customary, but neither am I."

Jess nodded. "Thank you, Grandmama; I will try."

Elizabeth responded, "As to your question, yes, he did. He furnished the room himself. You may sleep in here or next door; the choice will be yours."

"I shall stay in here, please. It will make me feel close to him." Jess sat on the big bed and stroked the cover. It would not have his scent nor the imprint of his head on the pillow, but it was his bed. Jess knew it was customary for couples to sleep separately, but they never had. Her tears were again not far away. Here she was close to him, as close as she could be.

Elizabeth noticed her glassy eyes and decided to leave her to settle in.

Jess didn't even notice Elizabeth had gone. Here she would cry herself to sleep as she had done at home. She succumbed to tears for a while, then pulled herself together. She knew that with her return, she now had to make a niche for herself in another new life; however, it would not be in society. So many times, she needed to start from scratch. She would do so again.

~

Over the following weeks, Elizabeth tried to encourage her to socialise; however, Jess refused all her efforts; she and Lucien had never socialised much as neither liked their shallowness. She was content to occupy herself with the children and learn about Marcus's business. Jess was determined to know how to run his concerns as she had done in Patterson. She had kept the books with Marcus at home, and she knew the gist of his overall business here.

Jeffrey Anthony, Marcus's secretary, had quietly sought Elizabeth's approval before embarking on Jess's tuition. He was surprised that his new boss knew as much as she did. Jeffrey had spent months trying to understand what the various terms of the fleece were called. He didn't understand what the crimp was in a staple of wool.

Jess, however, knew all about it. She actually drew him pictures to describe the terminology. She explained the difference between course rug wool, needing larger crimp or crinkle in the wool and fine crimp clothing wool. The staple was merely the length of the fleece. Their sheep in Patterson were fine crimp merino, and Marcus had selectively bred their flock to produce the best clothing wool he could. She also explained why their wool clip was now clean and, therefore, much more valuable, as not long before Marcus left on his fateful trip, they had built a washing trench where the sheep were washed as they were being herded into the pens. They would have the majority of the dirt washed from the wool before shearing. This meant that the final product was lighter and much cleaner. They had experimented with washing the cut fleece, but the washing of the sheep was far more effective. As the animal exited the trench, the soapy water was shaken off. Then the animals swam through a rinsing trench, and the wet animal again shook off the majority of the water. In the sun's heat, the beasts dried quickly, and by the time they were shorn, the wool was clean and dry.

Marcus knew that there was money in the delicate clothing fabrics they could produce in his woollen mills. He had never thought that the fleece being clean to start with was vital and saved much money. As Jess was carding a fleece once, she cried out when a nasty burr pricked her finger. He realised that burrs were challenging to remove, so he set about removing these from his paddocks rather than the fleece. Soon his farm was virtually clear of the pesky prickly weeds. His fleeces were top-grade and clean. Jess had chuckled when Marcus saw the results of the first soaped-up sheep. All had laughed heartily at the bubble-covered beast when it had emerged. Jaques and Tom had rigorously soaped it up and then sent it into the wet run.

They had chosen a particularly dirty and cantankerous ram to be the first candidate to wash. It had missed shearing the year before, its wool was extraordinarily long, and it was covered in burrs. De-burring it had been the first challenge as it wasn't keen on having the lumps cut out.

Marcus had hand-washed this beast and soaped it up, looking like an enormous walking soap bubble. He then pushed it into a new timber-lined run he had recently built. They discovered that the soap and the rinse trough had done their job.

The ram emerged, admittedly angry but almost snowy white. After another rinse, it shook itself and was left to dry in the stockyards for several days before shearing. Once dry, the clean-shorn ram was happy to return to the flock. The fleece from this one animal was a 'triple A' grade fine crimp wool with an eight-inch staple. This ram had been one of Macarthur's Spanish merinos that Marcus had first purchased.

Marcus and Jess had also discussed plans to expand the business and build new mills in England with the best and latest equipment available. So this was something else that Jess knew about; however, she wanted to see the existing mills for herself. She new that the new mill Marcus had built was fully operational. However they had plans of extending its scope.

In Patterson, Marcus had discussed the problems with machines replacing the cottage hand spinning and weaving with factories. Jess had suggested building new, fully equipped workrooms for the actual production of clothing from the fabric they made. The sewn garments could be hand-finished and embroidered at home. It was a branch of manufacturing he had not thought of entering.

Yes, this was a different skill, but Jess was sure they could learn, especially if they were paid a little more. Jess knew that two of these new buildings should now be completed and would soon be ready to start production.

Jeffrey was astounded that Jess had suggested this new branch of the company. Marcus's instruction had been delivered by letter and Jeffrey had followed them implicitly.

Jess knew that with Marcus gone, she had to keep growing the firm so Stevie would inherit a successful company. So, she threw herself into the work.

Elizabeth took care of the children while Jeffrey took Jess on a tour of the mills and the new manufacturing plant. They would be away for nearly a week.

Jess knew much about the production and wool clip and even how it was shipped. She had even shorn a sheep herself. That activity had given her a new appreciation of the shearers who spent hours slaving over a heavy, often wriggling, animal. After that, she never complained that the shearers were taking too long. They were paid for the flock, not the time. Therefore, it had never really been a problem. The longer they took, the less they would make in a season. After just one sheep, her hand was sore from using the sharp clippers, and the poor beast had various nicks that the tar-boy had to dab with the black gloop to stop the bleeding. Marcus had shown her how the shorn fleece was thrown, graded, and then packed.

Jeffrey first took her to the warehouse, where hundreds and hundreds of bags of raw wool were stored. After leaving there, he escorted her to the first of the mill buildings. There they were met by the manager. Mr Gordon was a giant of a man and was the overseer for the entire process, though each section also had individual managers who were experts in that field. He escorted them through the mill and factory, explaining each procedure. The first floor he took them to was the dying house.

Jess saw where the raw fleece was unpacked and then individually dyed. Each colour and shade needed specific techniques of pressure and temperature to achieve a uniform colour. From there, the coloured wool was sent for blending. Here, she learned that seven dyed fleeces would generally be mixed to give an even yarn before spinning. After this process, the dyed mass would be sent for carding. The air in this room was thick with dust from the brushed fleeces. Jess used a hand comb made from fencing wire at home, and then she spun the raw wool and dyed the finished yarn. She really only ever de-burred the fleece before spinning, rarely even taking time to make proper rolags of the soft fibres; consequently, her yarn was not nearly as smooth as it could or should have been.

Jess had always felt a little guilty about this, but she never worried too much, but her knitting didn't do justice to the fine ply yarn. The carding technique she saw was similar to using carding brushes but in such vast quantities that she stood watching the various processes in awe. The clean scent of lanolin invaded her nostrils.

Once the dyed wool had been carded, it was sent for spinning. This involved massive machines that in no way resembled her spinning wheel. Hundreds of spools were being spun at once. There were many giant spools of single-ply thread that sat stored around the room. Mr Gordon moved the group on to the next part of the floor.

Jess saw three newly spun single-ply spools placed on spikes, then threaded onto an empty cone. The machine started with a growl, and soon the three fine threads were reversed and spun into the finished three-ply yarn she was familiar with.

Mr Gordon explained they usually made a three-ply yarn, but two-ply was also common for knitting. Often for fabric weaving, only single-ply was used. This process involved oversized machines and, therefore, a lot of noise.

Jeffrey thanked Mr Gordon and then the three left and went to a different building in a nearby part of town. Jess could hear a cacophony of sound as they opened the door.

Jess thought those working the looms certainly needed sound protection of some sort. Voices were singing, machines whirring and mechanical bangs and crashes that were almost deafening. She found it hard not to put her hands over her ears. She would insist that everyone who worked in the factory in any area would be offered some form of ear protection. The carding area would also require masks, as the dust from the fleece was visible in the afternoon air. Jess knew that the dust had made her cough. She wouldn't insist that the staff use masks; however, she would recommend that they did.

Next, Mr Gordon showed them the weaving looms. She saw some of the finished yarn threaded onto enormous weaving looms as the warp thread. On the next machine along, she saw a red-based tartan being woven. The lovely deep rich colours of the Stuart Clan tartan magically appeared with the weaver's skill. A foot pedal lifted or dropped the level of warp thread before a different colour shuttle shot back through the elevated yarn. The shuttle slipped back and forward with astonishing speed.

The manager and Jeffrey watched as she checked the roll of fabric that was steadily growing. She turned to Jeffrey and asked if this was the final product.

He had no idea and turned to the weaving manager, Mr Creighton, who had joined them as they entered this section. "Mrs Ryan, you will have to ask Mr Creighton. It's no use asking me; I know the process, but he runs the factory." He turned to the man, silently pleading with him to assist him.

Mr Creighton smiled at his new boss, impressed at her understanding of the process. "Mrs Ryan, you are correct. Once the fabric is woven, it still needs treatment. This occurs in stages: scouring, milling, steaming, pressing, measuring, and finally rolling again. The fabric is then ready for use. Up until recently, the bolts have been sewn in bags and sent to a warehouse until sold."

Jess smiled; hopefully, they would now see her idea as the final step.

Mr Creighton watched her as she gazed around the floor; she motioned for them to go somewhere quieter as she had more questions for him. He led them to his office overlooking the factory floor, and there they had tea over various discussions.

Jess sat sipping the minute dainty cup of tepid milky tea, cringing with each sip. She had become used to the thick sweet black brew served in mugs in Patterson. If she hadn't been so thirsty, she would put it down. "Mr Creighton, I suggested to my husband that a new manufacturing stage be added, and I believe that the first of the new buildings is now complete. Has the design and manufacturing of clothing been started yet?"

Mr Creighton was flabbergasted. "Ma'am, that was your idea? I…" He was stunned and lost for words; he attempted to say again, "I… well, I'm astounded that you are so forward-thinking," he stuttered.

Jess frowned. "Mr Creighton, even in the Antipodes, we hear about what's happening here. However, I have only lived there for a few years. I know about the Luddites and the causes of why they are rioting. To stop that we have to supply other work for them. We have the finances to make sure all are employed well. Hence it will benefit us all. I gather that their main concern is the lack of employment, not the actual work they do. If that is so, then I will promise not to sack any of them except for shoddy workmanship. My plan is that we take the next step to manufacture clothing and retrain and employ the excess workers, which should help with the problem. I do not want a situation similar to Mr Horsfall's demise, sir. If we can waylay the situation before it reaches the point of rioting, then everyone should be happy." Without waiting for his reply, Jess walked to the interior window in the office and looked over the machine floor. As she stood and watched the workers, she saw children appear from areas she had not seen. She was horrified; she did not like them working in such conditions.

Jess watched three little girls who would not be much older than Bessie. She turned and beckoned the men to her side. Pointing to the children, she said, "This, though, must stop. Why are they not in school? They should be learning to read and write, not working in a factory."

Mr Creighton was quite upset she had seen them. When he heard that the new boss was a female, he told the floor workers to keep the children out of sight while she was there. The staff had, but, not realising that Jess was still watching them, the children had gone back to work.

Jess stood watching when an idea struck her. "Mr Creighton, I presume they work here for mere pennies? That's why you employ them, isn't it?"

Abashed, he nodded.

Surprisingly, Jess smiled, "Then I have an idea. Mr Anthony, I will need you to check wages and get this idea costed, but I propose that the children be still paid, but only *if* they go to school, which we will also supply. This will also help with our personnel problem. The children are taking positions an adult should be holding. The jobs they do will be filled by unemployed adults or at least children over twelve."

The two managers were reeling. This decision could well set the proverbial cat amongst the pigeons for other factories. Jeffrey stood behind them, grinning and silently cheering.

All three men knew this would set a precedent for other factories, but it would certainly take the pressure off their own. Neither of the managers had wanted to discuss the employment situation with her. However, she had pulled the carpet from under them and may have even solved their major problem of not having enough jobs to go around.

Jess then turned and asked Jeffrey if there was a free medical clinic available for her staff, as this was another thing she wished to see done. Jeffrey was speechless; a free clinic was not something any of them had heard of before. He shook his head.

Jess just said, "See to it. They need it. I'm sure there is some room on the ground floor that we could use."

The day after the tour, while Jess sat in the hotel room with her journal, Jeffrey had returned to see if there was an area where the children could be educated. Surely there would be a spare area in one of the buildings.

There was, and it was suitable. Mr Gordon showed an empty space to Jeffrey. Jeffrey called in Mr Creighton, who admitted that the top floor of the dying factory was vacant as that floor was not reinforced for heavy machinery. It had not been used for years. The floor foundation was structurally sound and warm in winter due to the heat rising from the drying room. However, as it also had roof ventilation, it could also be cooled in summer.

By the time Jess and Jeffrey left two days later, the rooms had been inspected; finances sorted, parents informed, and orders placed for slates, desks and other requirements for the new school. They had even found two literate, maimed soldiers prepared to teach the children.

Jeffrey had also found a ground-floor office and storeroom just off the weaving floor suitable for a clinic. They just had to find a doctor and equip it for him.

Jess handed Mr Gordon a fifty-pound note. "I wish to know exactly what you use this for, and I will be back to check the school and clinic later in the year." She turned to Jeffrey and said, "Mr Anthony, the next trip will be unannounced."

Jeffrey jumped slightly when she said his name. This woman certainly had her finger on where the problems were, and he had not said anything to her. She had obviously come prepared, as not many people usually carried a fifty-pound note. Behind her back, he shrugged in resignation at the two managers, but secretly he was thrilled. He, too, hated seeing the condition of the partially dressed, malnourished, filthy children. Their poverty tore at his heart. At least now, they would get much the same chance he was given. Jeffrey had also set to work on arranging the rooms set up for the new clinic. It had been the old manager's office, but the factory floor was not visible, so it had been turned into a storeroom. Until they found a doctor who could come, one of the village women, who was known as a healer, would come for a daily clinic for an hour each day.

This clinic would also be a boon for the Ryan Mills. Many minor injuries were left untreated and festered into unsightly wounds that would sometimes permanently maim the person. He considered this a *stitch in time,* thus preventing significant injuries and illnesses. Once fully staffed, all members of mill families would get free care, whether they were actually employed by it or not. Other non-employed families would pay a small fee to use the service. Again, Jess insisted that no needy person be turned away. They could afford the pittance required to start and run this service, which would benefit the town considerably.

On the trip back south to Billingshurst, Jeffrey preferred to sit up with the driver for the first leg. He knew that if he sat inside with Jess, he would be pumped for more information that he didn't have. Marcus had left him in charge of things, and he had done the best he could, but she already knew far more about the entire process than he had learnt in years at Marcus's side. He had much to think about and a new respect for his mistress.

Their arrival back in West Sussex was met with glee from both the children. Elizabeth had taken them to meet their cousins. Gemma and Miles now had three children who were quite close. After a short visit to their place, the family had come to stay while Jess was away, and they had had a wonderful time with their cousins.

Jess and Jeffrey put their heads together, and after two days closeted in the office, they notified Cyril Hargenhour to tell him what Jess had arranged.

Jeffrey knew that by then, Mr Creighton would, by now, have reported to him.

Cyril arrived from London the next day. Rather than be angry as they expected, he was delighted. Apparently, he, too, had been concerned about the children. The idea of a school was added to the budget, and new teachers were to be added as the need grew. Jess ordered many boxes of children's books and Bible stories from Hatchards Books in London and had them sent to the new classrooms.

Mr Gordon had told him of the excess of children who had turned up to learn. If they turned up to lessons regularly, they settled on a ha'penny a week per child aged between five and twelve, and a meal of hot food would be provided at lunchtime each weekday. They were to have weekends off and be expected to help at home. If the children could learn to read and write, better employment prospects would open for them.

Three months later, the Ryan Mills' chairman, Cyril, joined Jess and Jeffrey for a spot inspection of the factories.

All three were interested in what would await them; their arrival was met with the sound of laughing children. It was lunchtime, and they had just finished their hot stew; amazingly, they were all orderly and clean. The snap inspection also showed that the managers now took her seriously. Both gentlemen greeted her with awed respect and admiration. They had instigated her suggestions, and even the employees thanked her. Many now wore masks while at work, and few showed signs of the malnourishment she had seen before. When she left the floor of the weaver's factory, they showed their appreciation with applause.

Seriously embarrassed, Jess left hurriedly. She was sure Marcus would have approved her changes.

Now content that things were as she wished, she and Jeffrey returned south again. Cyril returned to London with much to thank her for. With adults now at the machines, productivity had increased by a third. The business was picking up, and the minimal cost of setting up the new projects had already paid for itself with the more proficient workers at the machines.

Promising more snap visits, they departed. Jess knew her children awaited.

Life settled into a routine at Billingshurst.

Chapter 19 Just Desserts

$\mathcal{I}$n summer, the family travelled down to their Brighton house.

Jess did not call in to see Egbert but heard from her staff that everyone in society shunned them. Egbert had no title to open doors for them, so they were not invited anywhere. St Nicholas's Church was one of the few places where they were welcomed; unfortunately, they had not bothered to rent a pew, so they had to sit at the back with the servants.

Egbert saw Jess and Elizabeth sitting near the front in the Ryan pew. After the service, Jess saw the mincing popinjay making his way towards them. She groaned and drew a deep breath waiting for the showdown that was obviously about to occur. He was drawing close when Jess saw Jeffrey and Jaques step in front of Egbert, forcing him to stop in his tracks.

Soon after their return to London, Giles and Jaques had been discussing something Lucien had said to Jaques some years before he died. After Judith was born, Lucien told Jaques that he was transferring ownership of the new tea importation business into Jess's name as a gift. The business would never become part of the inheritance should he die without a son. Lucien had planned that Jess would not be left without income. As she had been arrested and they had left hard on her heels, Jaques had never thought about it again.

When Jess arrived back from the factories after the last trip, it had taken a couple of weeks before he spoke to Jeffrey. Jeffrey had sent to London for information, and word had just been received at the office in Brighton. A copy of the letter had been sent to Jess's old residence. However, Jeffrey had been handed the original document when he arrived at church. He grabbed Jaques as soon as he could, and they finally had the proof they needed. Jeffrey tucked the paper into his coat pocket and, with Jaques in tow, went to find Jess. Jaques nudged him as they saw the mincing steps of the lavender and yellow clad person making his way towards Jess. Sidestepping a few notable persons, they managed to get in front of him only feet from Jess. Giles wasn't going to miss out, so knowing something was up, he was hard on their heels. The men were nervous, but they all had reason to protect Jess from this nasty person.

Egbert attempted to step around them, and Jeffrey spoke in a voice that drew the attention of all around them. "Sir, I have reason to believe that you are a thief as you have stolen property that does not belong to you."

Jaques was watching the fop's face; it blanched. He nodded for Jeffrey to continue.

Jess froze. Elizabeth, and the minister to whom they had been talking, heard the words and paused to listen.

After a few moments, Jeffrey said, "I have a document here that proves that you have been helping yourself to funds that you are not entitled to. The said property belongs to Jessica, Lady Elkin, as she was, but now is known as Mrs Marcus Ryan."

Jess gasped. She had no idea about this. Why had they not spoken to her first?

Egbert muttered something unintelligible.

Jeffrey was beginning to enjoy this. He then noticed Giles standing behind Egbert, grinning widely and nodding for him to continue. Conversations were silenced, and more people were now taking notice. Jeffrey continued. "When you laid charges against Lady Elkin about her stealing her own jewellery box and her husband's Bible, you omitted to say that you had already discovered that the jewellery was her personal property. The judge, of course, threw out those charges and handed back her family jewels." There was an audible gasp from all those listening.

A man stepped to stand beside Jess, but she did not even look at who it was. Her eyes were glued to the situation developing in front of her.

Jeffrey saw that the eyes of the entire congregation were now watching the tableau unfolding before them. "Mr Elkin, you threw her out of her home without even permitting her to get her clothing. You offered her no quarter at all, let alone accommodation. Where was she supposed to go? To the workhouse? You had no care for her well-being. She had just lost her husband and daughter. You cruelly deposed her and made no provision for her as the previous owner's widow. Not even offering her the use of the Dower House at Crawley, as was your duty as heir."

Jess watched a few ladies turn their backs to Egbert's shrewish wife, Cynthia. The overdressed woman stood watching, unsure of both what to do or say. However, Jeffrey was obviously not finished. Elizabeth subtly took Jess's hand and gave it a gentle squeeze of comfort. Jess clung to her. Gemma and Miles were also watching from the side of the crowd. Thankfully they had all the children with them.

Jeffrey took a step closer to Egbert; this made Egbert step backwards. Jeffrey put his hand inside his coat and withdrew a document. "Do you recognise this? I'm sure it looks familiar! A copy of it was delivered to your house by accident, but this, sir, is the original document." Jeffrey waved the parchment in the man's face.

Egbert again mumbled. He was now shaking.

Jeffrey looked around at his audience. "This document states that Mr Elkin inherited Sir Lucien Elkin's houses but not the business. As Elkin Importing was the source of most of the income for the estate, Mr Elkin has been using stolen funds as his own for over eight years." He looked at those around him and said, "This man spent much of Lady Elkin's money, as she was titled until she remarried Marcus Ryan, Esquire in 1824, in Newcastle in New South Wales. The money in the past years adds up to the value of Elkin's Crawley Estate and the Brighton House. However, the London abode is yours to keep, but the courts have upheld a request that you forfeit the other two properties to Mrs Ryan in lieu of her pressing embezzlement charges."

Out of the corner of Jess's eye, she saw Cynthia collapse and then watched as only her maid attended to her. No one else went to her aid. Jess's attention turned back to Jeffrey.

The man beside Jess laid a comforting hand on her shoulder. She still didn't turn to look at who it was. She noticed Jaques grinning and heard Elizabeth gasp. Jaques knew Jess had always hated the London apartment, so she presumed that was the reason for his smile.

Jeffrey held the legal document up and read for a few seconds. "Oh, and by the way, all the livestock and carriages belong to Elkin Importing, not to the personal estate of Sir Lucien Elkin." Jeffrey looked up and again took a step closer to the overdressed popinjay in front of him. "In essence, sir, you are washed up and bankrupt. If Mrs Ryan decides to press charges, as she is entitled to do, then I would not blame her. The law is on her side, regardless of her conviction for stealing her husband's Bible, which I believe is the charge you bribed the judge to press upon her."

An audible gasp spread like a wave through the listening crowd.

It was at this moment that the man beside Jess stepped forward. He was followed by three other very well-dressed gentlemen.

Jess gasped; King William had been the one to offer his empathy with his caring hand on her shoulder. That is why Jaques was grinning and why Elizabeth had gasped. Jess was a commoner and an ex-convict at that, and he had offered her moral support.

The King was now standing beside Jeffrey and in front of the accused fop. He took the document from Jeffrey and briefly perused it before handing it back.

The congregation stood waiting for his edict. It came in one word.

The King looked over at the now prostrated, overdressed lady on the ground just behind her husband; with his normally impassive face now seething with anger, the King looked at Egbert. In a voice of authority, he uttered one word. "Go!" With that, he turned his back on him and folded his arms.

Every other person there, except Jess, proceeded to do the same. She watched Egbert storm through the crowd; he bent down, grabbed his wife's arm, and dragged her towards the carriage. This overpainted vehicle was the one he had owned before Lucien died. Egbert had thought it was the epitome of good taste, but others knew it as a thing of mirth. This vehicle was nearly all he now owned. The two clipped poodles that sat next to the puce liveried driver set off the hilarious spectacle. They drove off as soon as the door shut, and the satin-clad footman jumped onto the back of the carriage. His ostrich feathered hat nearly fell off.

Jess hoped they would pack and leave as soon as they arrived at her old house. With them now gone, she realised she should be in a full curtsey before the King. She looked up at his smiling face as she dropped to one knee.

His Majesty put out his hand to her. "I believe, my dear, that there was more to your story. I hear that he also accused you of stealing your husband's Bible. Did you know he bribed the judge to have you sentenced and banished to the Antipodes?" He raised one eyebrow questioningly. His words floated across the silence of the gossip-hungry listeners. He had heard about this case but had not known who the accused person had been.

Jess nodded. "Yes, Sire, the reason for my conviction is true. But how…?"

The monarch smiled as lifted her from her deep curtsey. He also made Elizabeth rise to support Jess. In a voice those around them could hear, he said, "I am the Monarch, my dear. When my advisors heard of this gross injustice, they informed me. This case puzzled me as there was no gossip or taint associated with your name, so I wondered if it were merely hearsay. As a matter of fact, all I could find out was to your benefit. You have started school, improved conditions for your workers and even fed the poor in your factories. I only heard of all this last week when Mr Anthony started making inquiries; then, the various scraps of information fell into place. Firstly, your crime of theft has now been wiped away, and I will ensure your property will be restored to you."

Jess was stunned; he knew everything. "I was never worried about the things, sire; they are mere possessions. I just want my husband to return to me."

The King smiled at her. With empathy in his voice, he said, "Sadly, I cannot do anything about your missing husband."

The pageant that had just played out before her eyes had been retribution for Egbert and Cynthia. Egbert had been dealt a severe blow to his esteem and stripped of the wealth he had been using. She was way beyond holding any animosity toward him. Her things were only material items; Marcus had already reclaimed her clothing and personal items. She still knew that no one could return her husband to her. The monarch ushered Jess and Elizabeth away from society's inquisitive eyes and ears. Jeffrey followed them to safety as His Majesty personally escorted them to their carriage and saw them off. Gemma and Miles followed in the other carriage with all the children, including the staff's infants. Once they departed, the congregation mobbed their remaining friends and asked for Mrs Ryan's direction. It took time, but eventually, Jaques, Giles and their wives managed to walk the few blocks home.

It took three weeks for the visitors to the *at-homes* in Brighton to return to a pre-announcement state. Prior to the Sunday events, their weekly *at-homes* had been poorly attended; recently, it had been standing room only. Jess and Elizabeth were now mobbed on every outing, and they were also invited everywhere. For the King to know Jess was convicted, served time as a convict, and still supported her absolved her in the eyes of society. Jess understood that his Majesty publicly absolving her of her crime was beyond expectation. She had never sought success, fame, or a position in society; it had now been thrust upon her. However, she still shunned it where possible. Jess wanted to politely decline the invitation to be presented until Elizabeth mentioned that Bessie could not have that honour unless her mother submitted to the ordeal. She groaned and said she would do it, but not until next year.

Both ladies were invited to dine with the King while he was in Brighton. He wished to hear the full story of Marcus and his kidnapping. However, he reinforced to Jess that he could do little to assist with her search.

~

The ladies decided to return to Billingshurst until things died down and life slowly returned to normal. Jess had not realised how the knowledge of her conviction had weighed on her. With it removed, she found new contentment with her life. In the weeks since the return of the tea importation business to Jess, Jeffrey had investigated Lucien's company. He found that Jess was extremely flush with funds despite what Egbert and Cynthia had spent. Lucien's manager was a capable fellow, and it was still running well. Jeffrey had previously assisted Marcus with the tea import business before splitting the companies and selling them to then concentrate on the family wool processing factory. Jeffrey still found it unbelievable that Marcus had sold this arm of his business to Lucien Elkin, of all people, and that Jess was the link. Jess had known but had never mentioned it to him. Again, she went another step up in his estimations.

Chapter 20 Developments

*J*effrey led Jess into Marcus's office to hand over the keys to his desk. He was nearly at the desk when he heard her gasp. When Marcus turned twenty-one, Elizabeth had a sketch portrait commissioned. Marcus had hung it on his office wall.

Ignoring the reason for going in there, Jess stood and gazed at a much younger version of her beloved Marcus. She wept as he gazed down at her; tears cascaded unchecked down her cheeks.

Jeffrey smiled, presuming that this would probably occur. He left them alone. He would give her some time and return later. He had avoided taking her into Marcus's private den as he knew this portrait captured him at a deep moment. Up until now, they had met in his own office at the back of the house. Jess had never asked to see Marcus's private workroom. Elizabeth was the only other person to frequent this room.

Elizabeth was delighted to have her grandchildren close, and she spent as much time as possible with all five of them.

Gemma and Miles were frequent visitors from their home in the next village of Itchingfield. The five children adored each other. Rupert and Bessie were six months apart at seven, and Gemma's youngest, Quentin, was a year older than Stevie. At nine, Frederica, or Freddie as she preferred to be called, was the oldest of the children. She had been born the week Marcus had met Jess.

Stevie had recently turned five and had wanted a pony for his birthday, as his cousins both had been given miniature ponies. Bessie was now the proud owner of a pony trap given to celebrate her special birthday. Jess also knew that soon she would need to seek a tutor for Stevie. One day he would go to boarding school as his father had. As an old boy's son, he would gain a place there. Sadly both Eton and Christ's Hospital schools only took boys aged eleven and up. So until then, Stevie would need a tutor. Although Jess gave the children the best of everything, that was not always best for them; sometimes, earning money was more appreciated. With her own money now at her disposal, she encouraged the children to earn their pocket money. Each had to keep their rooms tidy, and they had to learn to dress themselves and do little things for others.

Elizabeth, Miles, Gemma, and she had debated the pros and cons of her next project; it was three against one. Jeffrey refused to give his opinion as he had already decided to always side with Jess. With a staff of nearly one hundred at *Padmorre Park*, Jess horrified Elizabeth by encouraging her children to play with the staff's children.

Jess knew how important it was for children to be allowed to see both sides of life, rich and poor, master and servant. She discovered how quickly life could change one's position in life. Jess intended to start a small school in one of the back rooms of the Hall. She wished Felicity and Rex were here as she was sure they would have backed up her idea. They corresponded often and she knew their lives on the farm were far better than they would ever have had here. Jess still wrote regularly and was delighted when she received mail in return. Sarah wrote periodically. Sarah's letters brought news of another child each year. Jess was sad she could not be there with them, but she needed to be in England for Marcus and her children.

Eventually, Elizabeth could see her point to educating the children, but bringing the staff children into the house was not ideal. Jess explained that they were already living in the house anyway. She had no intention of bringing in the village children. She smiled benignly as she already had plans for their education but decided to keep that between just Jeffrey and herself for the time being. A largely abandoned stone skeleton of a house was being rebuilt for a village school. It was near the church and would double as a church hall. Elizabeth had not yet discovered this project.

Jeffrey was supportive of this plan, and if discussing it with the family, they would refer to it as the new hall.

Gemma and Miles were aghast and were vocally against the project of a school for staff. Elizabeth eventually threw up her hands and said, "Jessica, it's your money; I suppose you can use it as you wish." Elizabeth's reaction wasn't the support Jess had wished for, but at least the family didn't try to stop her.

Jess set about getting the antiquated retiring room set up as a classroom. It was next to the Long Hall and located towards the back of the house. She scoured the library and nursery, finding books suitable for children, and finally, Jess placed another order for delivery from Hatchards Bookstore in London. She asked for the top-selling fifty-two children's stories to be delivered as soon as possible. This would mean a new book each week. They were placed on new bookshelves, and Jess had an oversized armchair set in front of a French window. Here she planned to sit and read stories to the children.

Jess also had a large blackboard made, and she purchased a pile of new slates with boxes of chalk placed ready for use. Even if only her children came and learned their letters, it was a start. She hoped that others would permit their children to attend. Once they had a few regularly in class, she would find a teacher to take over. She knew about twelve children of school age lived in the house other than her children, but she would not force them to attend.

On the first morning, she took her children down to the classroom at nine o'clock. She was stunned to find that all twelve staff children were waiting with a parent. Three mothers asked if they could stay and help as they wished to learn too. Jess willingly accepted their assistance. Their husbands were the employees, but they didn't work there, Jess had no reason to make them leave.

Within weeks, Jess had asked Jeffrey to seek a new teacher. Although she loved the work with various ages of the students, it made teaching difficult. Another teacher could take over the younger children, and she would continue with the older ones and mothers.

Elizabeth watched on in awe. It was a raging success rather than a dismal failure, as she was sure it would be. One classroom soon grew to two, then three. With the staff wishing to learn to read and write, Jess brought more teachers into the school. The adult night lessons were soon full.

Gemma secretly had been jealous, and it didn't take long for word to spread amongst her staff. Her coachman had taken word home at what Jess was doing, and soon Miles asked Gemma if they should try an in-house school. It would also stop the children from running wild on the estate, this annoyed Miles as they would not stay out of the front garden.

Some months later, Jess took another surprise trip to the mills with Jeffrey. It was now just after winter, and as the snow had melted, Jeffrey had suggested it would be a good time for a visit. He realised that they should now have implemented all of Jess's ideas. He hoped that any dissent from the managers had evaporated. Jess's promise of bonuses for the implementation of her ideas certainly helped. Jeffrey already noted a change in their attitude on their second visit. Production had certainly increased substantially, and the new clothing manufacturing arm was now supplying items for immediate sale. The new seamstresses had also started teaching the older girls from the school how to draft patterns and sew clothing using the damaged ends of the bolts. These less-than-perfect clothing items were distributed to the surrounding Parishes for the poor. The new manufacturing arm brought in more business for the town. Rather than lose jobs, the company's extension created twice as many by replacing the old machines. The working conditions had improved, and with this increase in production, their pay also increased. However, Jeffrey knew there was more to do.

Jess gave instructions for the managers to share their ideas and even details of the increase in profit figures with other mill owners and encourage them to do likewise. Jess's factory only produced wool, so the cotton mills, linen mills, and other woollen mills could duplicate her ideas. Her new mills were clean and light; the productivity increased fourfold. Other mills saw that, and they were amazed that she permitted them to view her changes. There was room enough for them all in the growing market. Jess just wanted everyone fed and employed. She was even considering a lunchtime meal to be made available for all staff. Jess also increased the pay for the staff, including the children attending school.

Jeffrey, however, knew of one glaring hole that needed attention for the people. After a stray comment from Mr Gordon last visit caused him to ask a few probing questions. He had discovered that the village accommodation was abysmal. He had not seen it for himself but had heard that the open sewers were the least of their worries. The water was contaminated, and the roofs were decaying. The staff were living in horrendous hovels with little warmth and almost derelict cottages.

Jeffrey had seen the changes Jess had effected in the few years she had been home and knew she would understand what he was about to show her. He asked to take her for a drive. "Ma'am, we have come this far, and the factories are doing well; however, I have heard there is one area where there is a dire need for improvement." He was wondering how to explain the dire need when they turned into the first street. "Ma'am, the accommodations of these poor souls are in desperate need of repair." They passed the first cottages of the squalid village where the workers lived.

Jess saw the conditions of the streets; the stench of open sewers, the filth, and horse dung assailed her nose. The mangey dogs and rag-clad, starving toddlers that watched the carriage as they passed made Jess turn in her seat and gasp. "Jeffrey, why did you not tell me they lived like this before?" she said. "I had no idea! I am horrified. How can anyone live in this squalor? Is there anything we can do? Would they be prepared to move?"

Jeffrey had hoped this would be her attitude. "Ma'am, this village is part of the factory land. They have tried to improve things, but it's the position of the place. The entire village needs to be replaced rather than repaired." Jeffrey was shocked; it was much worse than he had imagined or been led to believe. Marcus would be disgusted that Jeffrey had ignored this.

They had stopped in the middle of the so-called town square by now. This was supposed to be a water pump by a horse trough. Both were dysfunctional.

Jess wanted to do something then and there but didn't know where to start. She dropped her head and prayed as she had done with her other ideas. As she was doing so, an idea popped into her mind. She expected an argument from Jeffrey but said, "Jeffrey, see if you can find the village midwife for me, will you? I'll wait here."

Jeffrey hopped out quickly and asked a child nearby if he knew where the midwife would be.

The filthy child in threadbare clothing nodded and pointed to a house three doors away. "My mama is birthing now, mister." The child led Jeffrey to the house and was about to knock when a buxom woman emerged.

Jess was watching through the opened door of the carriage, so she heard Jeffrey explain his quest. She saw the two of them walking towards her, so she alighted and waited.

The cumbersome gait of the lady slowed their pace, but eventually, they arrived beside Jess. The woman was about to drop a curtsey when Jess stopped her. "There is no need to bow to me; I am a commoner like you. I wish to ask you something."

The midwife stood gazing at the elegantly dressed woman in front of her. She nodded. "Yes, ma'am, I'se all ears."

Jess dived in headfirst with her idea. "I know the mill owns this village, but I own the mills. I wish to know if new housing was to be provided for the people, would they be prepared to leave this area?"

Both Jeffrey and the woman were stunned, but Jeffrey was delighted.

The midwife was open-mouthed. "Leave here, madam? Where would we go?"

Jess chuckled. "How about into brand new houses with running water, sewers, and every possible modern convenience that could be included in a new home? Do you think they could keep them clean and maintained? Would they be willing to learn?"

The midwife's jaw dropped open again. "New homes? Running water? No sewer in the streets? Oh, ma'am, that would be a dream." She wiped a tear from her wrinkled cheek.

Jess saw Jeffrey nodding his approval, so she continued, "I thought if we built one row of five semi-detached cottages in a new area, the families most in need would get the larger end ones, and those who kept their places tidiest could get the middle ones. I'm sure you could assist in choosing who they would be. You would, of course, be included. Once more cottages are built, we could work out a ballot system unless you could think of a better way of allocating the accommodation until everyone is housed in the new town. We would include a village green and a village produce garden and farmyards for the stock. There would be a village school and a big hall, think about what else you would like. Do you think it would work?"

The woman nodded as Jess talked, "Yes, ma'am! Oh yes, that would be so wonderful." She wiped her teary face with the back of a wrinkled hand. "I know just who needs things most. And, ma'am, I also know where the best spot to build it would be. It used to be the old village before fire destroyed it fifty or so years ago, this village was only ever supposed to be temporary, but they never replaced it." She sniffed back tears of joy. "I could show you now, ma'am."

Jeffrey and Jess took the lady up into the carriage and saw where they would build the new village.

That afternoon they met with the mill managers and arranged the plans to be finalised. Mr Gordon knew all about the fire and presented Jess with plans that Marcus's grandfather had already draughted. These only had to be modified and updated. Jess and Jeffrey had spent two days longer in the town than planned. By the time they departed, the new village was already pegged out; they had ordered the construction materials for the first row of cottages, and the old streets were already under repair. The new village of Marcusdale would become a reality.

Jeffrey sat in the carriage, watching Jess as she dozed. Yet despite the speed at which she had achieved this, it was the naming of the new town that astounded Jeffrey. He knew she loved Marcus, but to honour him thus made him smile. Jeffrey knew now that he would do everything he could for his school friend's wife. It was no wonder Marcus had gone traipsing halfway around the world to find her. She was not only magnificently regal, beautiful and rich, but she was so darned nice that he, too, was prepared to fight tooth and nail to protect her.

Jeffrey so wished he could do something to solve the question of what happened to Marcus. He had no idea at all how to find his friend. When at home, Jeffrey would catch Jess standing gazing at the portrait on the staircase with her hand on Marcus's face. He knew she still felt Marcus was still alive, but after so many years, how could he be? Yet, she never gave up on him, always speaking of him in the present rather than the past tense. He knew she would never give up on him. She never referred to Marcus as in the past, only that he was just absent. One part of her would always hope. He knew that she prayed for Marcus daily and that he would be kept safe and well until he could return to her. Jeffrey hoped that one day he would come home.

After her return from the colony, Jeffrey discovered that every decision she made had to follow two criteria. One was, what would Jesus want her to do? And the second was, what would Marcus do? The new town followed both; Marcus would hate to see the employees living in such squalor, and she had stepped in to fix that as soon as she heard about it. Jeffrey knew he would have done something about it himself if he'd known. He felt somewhat guilty it had reached this state of neglect, but his efforts would not have included a new town. Jess had not just taken the idea on board to mull over. No, she had ideas ticking over in her mind by the end of the conversation with the midwife. He was still gazing at her with his arms folded when he realised she was awake and watching him. He was unaware that micro frowns crossed his brow.

Jess smiled as she watched his face. He realised he had been caught staring at her. "Jeffrey, what's up? You have a worried frown on your face."

Jeffrey smiled, his face lightening perceptibly, "Why the midwife, ma'am?"

Jess gave a chuckle. "It's simple, Jeffrey; if you wish to know what's going on in every household in a village, the midwife will know. The upper-crust toffs, or in my case, free-settlers in Newcastle, didn't watch what they said around the staff or convicts; however, many will confide in midwives. The midwife would normally be the one person they could trust. I needed to meet her to see what sort of woman she was. I could see this lady was immaculately clean and not a drunk. A midwife has entry into every house in any community. She knows more about what makes each village tick even more that the vicar. She usually has more sway with the women too. If she says to the poor families they have to clean up, they will normally listen to her."

Jess relaxed against the squab seats. If that was all that was worrying him, she was content. They would be home tomorrow. She would once again see her children and caress the picture of her beloved Marcus. She had no idea what her mother-in-law would say to a town being named after her son, but it was not her call. She had run the name of Ryansville or Marcusville quickly over her tongue, but Marcusdale just seemed right.

The trip home was once again uneventful.

She found it hard to believe that she had lived here for over two years and that Marcus had been gone for nearly six. Her children welcomed her; she enfolded them in her arms and kissed them all over their faces. Both youngsters giggled so hard that it made her welcome home even nicer.

Once back at *Padmorre Park*, Jess and Jeffrey made adjustments to her investments to allow the allocations of funds to construct the new town. It was to be funded from her own money, not the mill finances; this meant she did not need to ask for anyone's permission for anything. With the funds she had access to, she placed orders for many items, like internal cookers, water heaters and plumbing, and even indoor hygiene facilities. She wanted the best for her people.

Jess insisted on being consulted regarding the designs and what was to be included in the cottages. A community village garden was also necessary, and it was already being cleared and dug while the new town was constructed. She had employed all the disabled and injured people she could who were unfit to work in the mills, each given roles according to their ability.

Every man, woman, and child of working age were given jobs in the building and preparation for their new village. Older or disabled adults cared for the children while younger ones worked. Soon the walls of the first row of cottages were up. They had first cleared the cobbled roads from the old village to access the new building sites; the well made ancient cobbled surfaces needed minor work to be made serviceable again. Some villagers took to clearing the old village green and discovered a disused well in the middle of the area. They tested the water and found that once cleared of debris and sooty logs that had fallen in over the past five decades, the water was sweet and clean. A roof and new winder were quickly built over the well, and freshwater was available without visiting the creek.

Jess was sent monthly reports and was thrilled that the new village was well underway; all were keen to get behind the project. They also realised that new construction meant more work. Jess insisted that all local people be given the option of employment as labourers. Only those positions that needed specialist skills were to be brought from outside.

~

Six months after her last visit, the first row of cottages was ready. Jess gave instructions that the centre cottage was to be for the midwife, and then she was to choose who would be her neighbours. Jess would not return for the opening, as she was content that the plans were progressing far faster than she had hoped. If only Marcus could see it. She said that when he returned, the village would be officially named, and then they could have a celebration then.

Jeffrey wondered if that would ever occur.

More and more often, one or other of the staff or family would catch Jess as she stood looking at the portrait on the landing. However, they did not see how often she stood in front of the picture in his office. The traditional setting was of him seated and looking at the artist. His eyes seemed misty and sad, but she could run her fingers over his lips in the privacy of his office.

How Jess wished she could kiss them again. She had taken to doing her morning prayer in his office so she could share them with him. Sometimes she would steal away from the activity of the house and gaze at his face.

Jess had caught Elizabeth doing much the same more than once. She would walk up to the older lady and slide her hand into her mother-in-law's one. More often than not, they wept together. Jess would turn to Elizabeth and tell her that she was sure he was still alive somewhere.

Elizabeth didn't believe her. She mourned him as only a mother could, but she did not confess her thoughts to Jess.

Chapter 21 Promises

Years before, Elizabeth had learned of Jess's faith's strength from her son's letters. She had received the letter Ned had sent on after Marcus had run aground in Madagascar. Then silence.

Nothing had been heard since his last fateful journey. Since Jess's return, Elizabeth had watched her daughter-in-law's decision-making and her actions to assist so many people. Only now could Elizabeth understand Marcus's decision to follow Jess to Sydney. She was initially furious when she found that her son had abandoned everything and followed a woman he barely knew. She thought that Jess had ensnared him and persuaded him to follow her. It was only when he wrote and explained he had found her did she understand Jess had no knowledge of his actions. Only when Elizabeth read that they were to marry as soon as they had permission did she realise her error. She realised that Jess had not even known Marcus had wished to follow. Jeffrey filled in more of the background. Rather than trap Marcus, Jess had barely spoken to him. Her son had done all the chasing. Now that she knew Jess better, she could understand Marcus's actions.

When Marcus had poured out details of his pursuit, Jess had been totally unaware he was all but stalking her. Rather than ensnare him, Jess barely knew he existed. She had thought of him kindly, and she had even trusted him, but that was all. Jess was in mourning for all the things she had lost, her husband, her child, and her previous life. She had not sought to attract him at all, and mayhap that had been part of the attraction. Jess had been oblivious to his adoration. It was Marcus who had done the chasing and finally found his quarry in the tiny coal settlement of Newcastle in New South Wales. Rather than return, Marcus had settled there and supported both her and her new friends. Elizabeth was impressed that the minister and his very young wife supported and encouraged them both.

Elizabeth then read everything she could about Reverend Middleton. He had also been a man that Elizabeth sounded unsure about; that he, a man in his thirties, should marry a girl half his age and just out of the schoolroom horrified her until she realised Jess had only been seventeen when she had married Sir Lucien. She also realised that in London's high society, girls as young as fifteen were betrothed and married, often only weeks later. She sighed.

Jess had since spoken often about the friendship of Sarah and George. She admitted that when they heard how young the bride was, they, too, had been shocked. Sarah had reluctantly come north with her new husband; however, with Jess's assistance, she soon settled into the role of stepmother to a small boy and minister's wife.

By the time Marcus and Jess moved to the farm, Sarah had grown into her role. She supported George in all his decisions, and soon after Marcus's departure, they moved next door to them in Patterson. Jess had all been delighted they were once again close to each other. Elizabeth had been informed of all this by Ned. She knew him to be a Duke's son, and if he said Jess and her friends were above-board, then that was enough for her. Elizabeth had been determined to accept Jess, but when she arrived, Elizabeth realised Jess was everything Marcus and Ned had claimed her to be. Jess adored Marcus, and that alone had been enough to make a place for her in the grieving mother's heart.

In the years they had been in England, Stevie had not grown out of asking every new male he met if he was his father. He even had initially challenged his Uncle Miles. Jeffrey had been shocked when first quizzed, as had the visiting minister. Cyril Hargenhour had not been phased when questioned but took the small boy's hand and showed him the portrait on the staircase landing.

Stevie often stood looking at his father's picture as he caught his mother doing.

Jeffrey, too, had picked up the smock-clad child and pointed to the man's painting next to the big horse. "This is your father, lad, and he is my good friend. We all miss him and are praying that one day he will come home. We were at school with each other from when we were little. We were not much older than you are, and you are very like him."

Jess still insisted that any mention of Marcus by any person was to be in the present tense. She was sure he was still alive, and one day he would return to her as he promised. She clung to that.

Jess just knew it. She could feel it deep within her.

~

Jess had been preparing for Stevie's sixth birthday the following day. He was just breeched and was in his new shorts. He now looked like that active little boy he was. Stevie was the image of his father from one of the many pictures in Elizabeth's bedroom.

It was July 1833, and Jess had been back in England for nearly four years. Her heart had been heavy, and she had woken teary and somewhat melancholy. Marcus had been gone for so long. One day less than six years and nine months, to be exact. She knew that one day she must release him, but not yet. Jess was on the way to the office for a few quiet minutes before the children were released from class. She heard a carriage on the driveway, but as she wasn't expecting anyone, she presumed it was another delivery. She hoped it wasn't a visitor as she didn't feel up to entertaining.

Jess felt that she needed to take some time out and pray alone. Walking past the portrait on the landing, she did as she always did; she stopped and ran her fingers over Marcus's lips. She stroked his face and said softly, "My darling love, you promised never to leave me, you promised that I would never be alone, but you left me, and I want you back. Your last words to me were..." She did not finish her sentence as a voice came behind her.

"No more, my love! They were my last words to you, and I will repeat them again. No more will you be alone, not ever! If I go anywhere, you will be beside me."

Jess spun around at his first word. Her heart pounded with joy and excitement.

Marcus walked up the steps towards her as he spoke.

She was gathered to him as he reached her side. He had aged and was much thinner. He had grey at his temples, but Marcus was home.

Tears mingled in united joy, and they were enfolded tightly in each other's arms. Neither prepared to let the other go.

How long they stood like that, neither cared.

Marcus devoured her face and lips like a man starved of water.

Jess was overwhelmed; her tears continued to fall as he kissed them away. Marcus had returned. He had kept his promise as she knew he would.

He kissed her cheeks and her forehead and then claimed her lips again and again. He lifted his lips from hers only to kiss away more tears.

They became aware of encroaching voices and the sounds of running feet.

A small hand soon tugged at Marcus's jacket. "Why are you kissing my Mama? Papa is watching, and he won't like that."

Marcus slowly relaxed his tight hold of Jess, though he still kept one arm around his beloved. He refused to release her even to deal with this small interruption. The child looked familiar, but Marcus was sure that he had not met him before. He looked down at the small boy and saw an angry frown on the child's face. He didn't know who this child was and asked, "Pardon, lad, what did you ask?"

With hands now on his hips, Stevie repeated his question. "Why is you cuddling my Mama?"

Marcus had no words for a reply. This was not Bessie, and he had no son. Who was he? Had Jess remarried? He turned to Jess and said her name questioningly, "Jess?"

Jess bent down and picked up Stevie. "Marcus, stand there beside the picture," She pushed him gently next to his portrait. "Stevie, look hard at the picture and then at the man. Now ask your favourite question." Jess had a mischievous smile on her beautiful lips.

Marcus watched, intrigued.

The boy in her arms looked at the painting behind him, then at his face. It lit up with excitement. The child's eyes were alight with delight. With his head now tilted sideways, he asked Marcus the only question he wanted to hear a positive answer. "Are you, my Papa?"

Jess nodded to Marcus and said, "He certainly is, son." She kissed her son's cheek. "Marcus, this is Stevie. Stephen Marcus, named after both you and your father. He was born nine months to the day from when you left Newcastle. He was breeched only yesterday and turns six tomorrow."

Marcus tore his gaze from her face to the boy in her arms.

He put his arms out to take her precious load. "I am your father, and I'm very pleased to meet you, son. Is your sister around?"

Stevie nodded, but he slipped his chubby arms around his father's neck and held tight.

Marcus was stunned at this development.

Bessie came running in with some of the other children. She froze when she saw a man holding her brother. She, too, compared him to the portrait behind him and quickly realised who he was. She was soon gathered into his arms, crying against his neck, "Papa, Mama always said you would come home. We prayed for you every night. She never gave up."

The staff children all heard and soon scattered and carried the word of Marcus's return faster than any town crier could have done. Shouts of "He's home!" echoed down nearly every hallway.

Elizabeth soon appeared, then Jeffrey, Giles and Jaques were not far behind.

The reunion was all that Marcus wished for. He hugged or shook hands with them all. Jess was never far from his side. Almost every staff member welcomed him home. After the initial greetings, he led his friends and family to the more private sitting room.

Once he put his children down, Marcus retook Jess's hand and didn't let her go again except to hug his mother for a second time.

Jess had a grin on her face from ear to ear. She wished to know the entire story, but that would come.

Marcus shook his head and said, "Now you are all here; I have a letter for you to read first, Jess. It was handed to me with the explicit instruction that I was not to open it until I was with you. All I know is that it was sent by the man who arranged our return. I was given it as soon as I landed. I have no idea how he knew about me." He smiled and kissed Jess again. "Although I had cleaned up on board, I needed to return to our London home for some clothes. On arrival there, Mrs Busselton told me you were here at the country house and not in New South Wales. I only took enough time to change; then I came directly here." Marcus dug into his coat pocket with his spare hand, pulled out a large wax-sealed letter, and handed it to Jess. "Apparently, you have made some fascinating and influential friends in my absence if the crest on this is any hint of the contents. You will need to explain the hows of that later, but first, you apparently need to read this."

Elizabeth wondered who had sent it until she saw Jess's eyes light up as she took the sealed letter. When she saw the monogrammed initials, Elizabeth gasped.

One glance and they could all see the royal monogram on the front. *WR* was emblazoned boldly with a crown pressed into the wax seal.

Jess flicked the seal and carefully opened the letter. She read words that made her shake. With everything that had occurred in the past half hour, she could not make any sound at all. She wordlessly handed Marcus the letter, and he read aloud the words from the King.

It started with the usual preamble, and then he read on aloud. He was surprised by the title His Majesty had used to address his wife, as it was obviously for her. He glanced at her, then read the remainder aloud.

"Lady Billingshurst, I have not forgotten that amongst the turmoil of that fateful day when you had all your worldly possessions returned to you, they were not what concerned you. You had, but one wish, and it was not wealth or position; it was that your beloved husband be restored to you. To have such devotion for one another is a wondrous thing, to the point that I was somewhat envious of you. I told you then that, unfortunately, I could not help in your quest.

However, I later heard that there may have been a glimmer of hope that your husband may still be alive and set forth to see if such rumours were true.

They were!

When hearsay surfaced from a Naval captain about the conversion of an entire village on the Somali coast, the news caught my interest. The only way this could have occurred was through the ministry of Christian witnesses. With what I had learned about your husband, I realised that there was a chance he, and possibly some others, may still be alive, yet unable to leave. I sent a merchant ship with a ransom in goods. There were cases of clothing, and many of the standard trading items, including Bibles, as I figured that they might be in short supply. There were also crates of tools, for these I knew were sought after by such people.

The ship I sent discovered a thriving Christian community. As part of the villager's conversion, they scuttled their pirate ships and changed their way of life. Hence you never had a ransom note. My Naval ship has just returned with over one hundred of the kidnapped men. I believe, however, that some men chose to stay. Ask your husband for details of this, as I think one was his valet.

Lady Billingshurst, please find accompanying this screed not only your husband, but I now have the joyous delight of informing you that I am bestowing the title of Baron upon him for the work he did with the pirates while a prisoner.

This commendation is my way of attempting recompense for your unjust treatment at the hands of a judge of my country, under my authority, who should have dispensed justice, not the miscarriage of the same.

William R

Marcus lifted his eyes from the illuminated screed with a slight frown on his brow. He turned to Jess again, and his eyes rested on her beloved face. "Jess, what does this mean?"

Jess could not reply. She stood mute and stunned at the news but grinning with happiness.

Elizabeth saw her dumbfounded state, and she answered for Jess. "Marcus, his gracious Majesty, supported Jess at a time of her need; we shall tell you of that later.' She paused before asking, "Darling, where is Colin?"

His eyes had not lifted from Jess's face while his mother spoke. Marcus smiled, finally acknowledging that his mother had asked him something. "Ah yes, well Colin stayed behind, as he took a wife and now has three children over there. Captain Jon Park returned home with me. However, he has now given up sailing and is in need of an occupation. He was thinking of turning his hand to teaching." Marcus's eyes fell on Jess again, devouring the sight of her as she still stood in the crook of his arm. "How did you get to know the King, sweetie? Lady Billingshurst, eh? What's this all about?"

Jess didn't care who was watching; she turned to Marcus and entwining her arms around his neck, she said, "It means, my beloved Marcus, that you are now The Right Honourable, Lord Billingshurst, and that you are back, and the King has granted the only wish I ever had, and that was for you to come home to me." She lifted her glowing face to his and drew his lips to meet hers.

Her welcome home to him was going to take a long, long time. Her beloved was back, and that was all she cared about. No more would she be alone. The rest of the story could wait.

He lifted his head and once more drank in her beautiful face. Before he kissed her again, he caressed her cheek and murmured, "No more, my love. As I promised, I am yours always from this day and forever more!" His lips once more claimed hers.

Bessie clung to her grandmother's leg, and Elizabeth picked up her grinning grandson.

The staff realised that it was time for them to leave.

As the door shut behind them, Marcus heard his son say words that delighted him.

Stevie said, "Grandma, my papa is home. Now we are a complete fambily, and I have a papa, and a mama and a sister and you too. I just knewed he would come home 'cos he promised Mama." Stevie's grin spoke volumes.

The invitation from the palace, along with the letter, fluttered unnoticed to the floor. The document from the King about the confirmation of his bestowment, making him Baron of Billingshurst, could wait.

Marcus had kept his promise to his only love, Jess. He had returned home and would never leave her alone again. All else was forgotten.

Did you know there is a 6 book series that follows Ned Grace's life?
The Lockleys of Parramatta
https://www.amazon.com/gp/product/B08T6WHD7Z?
ref_=dbs_p_pwh_rwt_anx_a_lnk&storeType=ebooks

Author Bio

Sheila Hunter and Sara Powter were a passionate mother-and-daughter team of amateur genealogists. While working together on their family tree, Sheila and Sara made many captivating discoveries. The greatest of these was finding four convicts, and these four had very different perspectives. They were sent to Australia from 1792 to 1814 during the height of Convict transportation. Before her passing in 2002, Sheila adapted some of these histories into enchanting stories, her Australian Colonial Trilogy. Sara later had these published. A fourth she left unfinished, and this inspired her to finish it. However, before she did, **The Lockleys of Parramatta** were created. The first two in the series were completed before she finished Dancing to Her Own Tune.

Vividly living through the Colonial Era, these books delve further into the theme of overcoming adversity in Colonial Australia and how it developed, the demise of the Convict system and the discovery of mineral wealth.

Sara intricately weaves real archival data and a charming narrative to create a series of tales of faith, love, loss, and redemption.

And so, two hundred years after her family's arrival in Australia, Sara continues the Australian Colonial stories started in *Lockleys of Parramatta,* followed by the **Unlikely Convict Ladies** Trilogy and now with her first dedicated romance.

More Historical Fiction books are to follow… as six more are already in the editor's queue.

See her web page to keep up to date with more stories.
With an online store available for a signed copy of Sara's books.
www.sarapowter.com.au
(Australian Postage only)

Amazon Aus QR

Feel free to email me at
saragpowter@gmail.com

BOOK BUB
https://partners.bookbub.com/authors/6273615/edit

FACEBOOK
https://www.facebook.com/profile.php?id=100063887262514

Thank you for reading my story. I hope you enjoyed it, and on the
following pages are more that are from the same era.
Sara

If you loved this book, these are similar.

Unlikely Convict Ladies - Trilogy

Dancing to her Own Tune

Co-authored by Sheila Hunter and Sara Powter

Sydney 1790s to England 1830s

Annie White is released after serving seven years as a convict in Sydney. She gets a visitor who, with his help, she can start a baking business. She is then asked to assist another sick man, **Sam** Corbett. Annie nurses him back to health, and a relationship develops. They settle into a life together, barely making ends meet; she realises she's expecting a child. Sam has his past laid bare and must adjust to the revelations. They both must face their accusers and find that the answers to their questions are not what they thought. Their life experiences seem to cling to them, and unable to shake it they finally, they end up back in England, facing their ghosts and discovering they are not who they think they are. How can they turn their anger and spite into love and forgiveness? The Dance of Life goes on.

ISBN 9780645110715   ISBN9780645110722

Long-listed in the Historical Fiction Company Competition 2022

October2021

https://amazon.com/dp/064511071X   https://amazon.com/dp/B09JC378YV

Amelia's Tears

Parramatta 1828 – England 1840s

In the Parramatta Female Prison, **Amelia** awaits her assignment. Forced to leave the relative safety of gaol, she is assigned and now faces her worst nightmare. A foul man claims her and makes her life a living hell. Then her world goes black. A glimmer of hope arises when she hears from her brother, Jim, who has enlisted a friend to help her. She writes to Jim, pouring out her heart and telling him of the horrors of her new life. He encourages her to stay firm in her faith. All she can do is pray. When Major **Ned** Grace, her brother's friend, enters her life in Parramatta, he starts to ease her path. Things have changed, as now she has a child in tow. How can Amelia forge a new life for herself? What man could want her with her background and a child at her side? Who is the gentleman who turns her tears of sadness into tears of great joy?

ISBN: 9780645110739   eISBN: 978-0-6451107-4-6 Hard Cover ISBN 979-842061-7953

April 2022

https://amazon.com/dp/0645110736   https://amazon.com/dp/B09SS855BR

A Lady in Irons

England 1800s - Parramatta 1808+

Katy is mourning the death of her husband after he dies in a shooting accident. Barely coping, she awaits the birth of their child. If it's a girl, she must hand the family home to her husband's brother. The day after giving birth to a daughter, she and her daughter are left on the side of a road. She collapses and is found by someone she thought had died in a fire ten years before. **Perry**, badly scarred himself, nurses her back to health. They marry and move in with her widowed friend, Mary.

After some years, she discovers her husband and friend in each other's arms. Now living in a love triangle, she flees. Grasping the only straw available, she intentionally gets arrested and is sent to a colony far away. By doing this, her marriage can be annulled.

What happens in the Colony is different from what she expects. Governor Macquarie comes to her rescue.

But what of Perry and her children?

ISBN: 9780645110784   eISBN:9780645441505

November 2022

https://amazon.com/dp/0645110787   https://amazon.com/dp/B0BCWSXB9Z

The Convict Stain Collection
NO MORE, MY *Love*
Hunter Valley, NSW 1820s

Jess Elkin is distraught when tragedy ravages her family. She becomes the victim of a carriage accident and is nursed back to health by the driver, **Marcus Ryan**. Marcus was not expecting to fall in love. Yet, when Jess's fortunes suddenly turn for the worse, Marcus must decide how far he will go to pursue her. As time passes in Newcastle, Australia, Marcus must take a business trip and is taken by pirates. Jess is left wondering if her will keep his promise to return to her... Will she ever see him alive again?

ISBN: 9780645441536   eISBN 9780645441581
April 2023
https://amazon.com/dp/0645441538   https://amazon.com/dp/B0BSBH143Q

The Vine Weaver
Hawkesbury River area 1820s+
New Beginnings and Old Threats

In the 1820s, Australia, **Joel and Hetty Walker** live on a secluded farm on the Hawkesbury River which becomes a healing haven for the protection of young convict women.

A series of events brings **Fran Rea** to the attention of Hetty, and she is taken to the farm. Fran and Hetty develop a cottage industry under the compassionate eye of farmhand **Hector Macdougal;** Hector's loving words change lives. It is to him that Fran turns when threatened.

The vines now must draw them close to survive the future revelations, and of those, there are many.

ISBN: 9780645441512   eISBN: 9780645441529
June 2023
https://amazon.com/dp/0645441511   https://amazon.com/dp/B0C6Z552Y2

The story continues in Scotch at The Rocks...

Waiting at the Sliprails
The Bathurst Road 1830s
A Convict's Tale

Bea Dawes's term of conviction nears an end, and she has few options other than marriage to a stranger or going on the street.

Jack Barnes, the hired drover, wants a wife. Bea accepts his offer; then she discovers that he could be gone for months, leaving her alone with **Billy and Netty**, part of the tribe of aborigines who live on his secluded farm. Bea learns to love her husband and also this wonderful aboriginal couple.

Drought ravages the farm, and Jack must hit the long paddock with the flock. In his absence, a visitor arrives, threatening to destroy everything she has worked so hard for. Can Bea touch her heart? Can she cope? Will the drought ever end? And when will Jack return?

ISBN: 9780645441543   eISBN: 9781923097032
August 2023

SCOTCH AT THE ROCKS
Glasgow, Scotland, early 1800s to The Rocks, Sydney 1830s

Orphaned children Brodie Stewart and Heather Anderson live on Glasgow's streets. Although hungry, somehow they survive and keep out of trouble. Heather finds a job and looks to be settled; things go pear-shaped for them both. Eventually, they marry by declaration, yet even that gets messed up, and they are both arrested soon after they make their vow. In 1838, they got transported to Sydney as convicts. Heather arrives within weeks of Brodie, and they are assigned close to each other. They are now living on the docklands in Sydney, called The Rocks. They now have to forge a new life halfway across the world from their homeland.

Adventures abound, and Brodie gets press-ganged. While he's away, Heather's life changes and soon, she's officially selling Scotch Whisky at a shop in The Rocks. You can take a Scot out of Scotland, but where did the Scotch come from?

ISBN 9780645441550 ISBN ebook 9781923097001

November 2023

Convict Shadows of the Past
Two Jennifers, two hundred years apart

When aged eight, **Jenny** Kellow learns of her convict family history and discovers that she was named after a convict from nearly two hundred years ago. Her grandfather's stories inspire her to dig deeper into her ancestors' convict past. From her grandfather, she hears stories of bushrangers, convicts, and life in the infant colony of Parramatta. She sets about retracing the footsteps of her convict great-great-great-grandmother to honour her. Jenny's search starts with microfiche back in the 60s, and she learns about the small tin mining town in Cornwall and the production of a cheese that sets London afire. Then she discovers her ancestor has brought these cheese-making skills to Parramatta, where she taught others her craft. Echoes of the past can still be heard if you know where to listen. But who was the first **Jennifer**? Why is she so elusive?

ISBN: 9780645783315 ISBN ebook 9780645783322

A NaNoWriMo 2022 book winner

January 2024

In Defence of Her Honour
London 1800s to Parramatta 1819

Bill Miller had been raised and educated with the sons of the family. The youngest, Bert, had been his best friend. However, jealousy intervenes when Bill's excellent schoolwork curtails their friendship. He wins a scholarship and enters Oxford University. When Bill's father, the old butler, dies unexpectedly, Bert insists that Bill take over the position, but it's more to oppress him. Bert's jealousy grows and festers. Now looking for a way to rid themselves of their new butler, a ruckus ensues, and Bill is arrested for assaulting Bert. The housekeeper and her daughter **Molly** vouch for him, but it's too late; Bill has been arrested and sentenced to be transported. With Bill gone, Molly now needs to defend herself from Bert. After hitting him with a pan, she is arrested and sent to Sydney. Bill and Molly arrive with letters of introduction and compensation from Bert's father. Soon they are running the best Inn in Parramatta with an endorsement from the Governor.

ISBN 9780645441567 ISBN ebook 9781923097049

April 2024

Gentle Annie Soames

A 1788 First Fleet Convict Story

Her dreams lead to unexpected outcomes. An Australian First Fleet story.

Annie Soames is shattered by the cancellation of her debut into society, so when she hears of a position as a carer for the nearby Marchioness, she grabs it.

Oliver Quilpie, the recently married Marquess, discovers his arranged union is not to his taste; he is drawn to his wife's companion. Unfortunately, he is unable to keep his hands off her. For revenge, Annie mimics his every move while riding but is dressed as a highwayman. However, she has now fallen in love with him. This action finally leads to her arrest and transportation to a faraway land.

After some years, Oliver's wife dies, and his thoughts turn to Annie. He seeks to find her, but she has vanished. He is horrified to discover she was transported to New South Wales as a convict on the Lady Penrhyn. He follows with a shipload of supplies.

Will Annie want to see him?

ISBN 9780645441574 ISBN ebook 9781923097063

July 2024

I can't stop Tomorrow

Irish Famine 1840s to Avoca Beach, Australia

Escaping bigotry and prejudice in Ireland, the **O'Shane** family live on a secluded farm on the west coast of Ireland. The potato blight soon decimates their farm. It's always darkest before dawn, and the two remaining girls cling to the hope of a new life. With the kindness of strangers, the oldest girls, **Clare** and **Kerry**, head to their cousin, Sal Lockley, in Parramatta, Australia. A new wonderful life awaits them both.

Shéamus Connor is the annoying teenage boy who reluctantly draws Clare's affection. However, living in a convict town means ruffians abound.

John Moore is an angry and troubled Irishman, content to live alone on another secluded farm until he discovers Clare and two other lads need rescuing.

Can John protect her from the pain inflicted by an evil world?

Can Shéamus find his lost love who had fled?

ISBN: 9780645441598   ISBN ebook 9781923097056

October 2024

Madeline's Boy

England 1830s to New South Wales 1840

All is not straightforward when money and a title are involved.

Madeline is asked to care for her best friend's son when his life is in danger.

Christopher is the pawn between a greedy, unscrupulous uncle and his inheritance. Maddie must do everything she can to keep him safe, including moving halfway around the globe to take Chip to his guardian, Major Humphrey Downes, in the Australian Corps in Sydney. Humphrey's best friend, another soldier, Major Tim Hinds, meets Maddie, and with the support of these two men, a chase around the colony ensues.

Will Maddie and Tim be able to find happiness together?

Can the three adults keep Chip safe until he's old enough to claim his inheritance?

ISBN: 9780645783308   ISBN ebook 9781923097094

January 2025

Tuppence to Pass

London 1800s to Parramatta 1820s - Governor Lachlan Macquarie

Josh Callan is a London lad who makes the best of the life that has been dealt to him. Stealing from the man who killed his father gives the family a change of direction. Josh is arrested, but the judge belittles him and says he's not worth tuppence. He is sent to the penal colony of Sydney as Governor Macquarie's term starts. He proves his worth and falls on his feet, becoming the Governor's groom. Life in the Colonial town opens opportunities they could never have dreamed about in England, but can Josh find his niche in life?

Where will this new life take Josh and his family?

ISBN : 9781923097070 eISBN: 9781923097087

Coming 2025

WHEN UPON LIFE'S BILLOWS

Sydney 1795-1800 - Governor John Hunter

Captain John Hunter is born to a life at sea. The wind blows where no man knows, and John is caught up in the gale. From the wrecking of his ship, the HMS Sirius, in 1790 to become the second Governor of the colony of NSW, John seems to always be in the wrong place at the wrong time.

Helena Rosedale is not a typical female convict. She fights tooth and nail to stop The men from abusing her. She gains the name of Helena Hellcat.

Crispin Milroy is one of the Governor's security detail. Can he win the fair lady's heart? Life in 1795 in Sydney Cover. I it raw at best. Food is scarce, and disease often raves the settlement. Life throws them everything possible except death. Somehow they survive. What trials will the young couple face to make a new life in this raw town? How can John ease their path?

ISBN: 9780645783339   ebook ISBN: 9780645783346

Coming 2025

214

A 100-year, six-part Australian Colonial series
Lockleys of Parramatta
Hands upon the Anvil
A blacksmith's life and love are more than work
Parramatta 1830s

Eddie Lockley's parents were transported for their crimes. Can a steadfast lad rise above his origins and guide others to succeed in a land of opportunity?
Ten-year-old Eddie longs to help his mum and dad. Living in a convict town with his family, the keen youngster has been working with the local blacksmith since his sixth birthday. But when a lieutenant doesn't stop abusing his older brother, the young boy yearns for the day when he can stand up and end the torment. Though he's thrilled when his mentor offers to send him off to learn his letters, Eddie fears he won't be around to watch his sibling's back. But as he takes on the biggest adventure of his life, the brave believer soon discovers God is looking out for everyone he loves. Does this young man in the making have what it takes to change everything for the better?

ISBN 9780994578235 Ebook ISBN 978-0-9945782-5-9 Hardcover 9798496177368
Released 2021
https://amazon.com/dp/0994578237 https://amazon.com/dp/B08TB51L19

Out Where The Brolgas Dance
Gold is found, and so is love
Parramatta 1840s
How can a question change so many people?

It's the 1840s, and discoveries across the Blue Mountains continue. Major Mitchell's new road is complete, and towns are planned and being built. Abundant land is available for those who want it.
William **"Wills"** Lockley, 18, has laid a solid foundation for a respectable career as a blacksmith, but the Lockley lust for adventure flows deeply within his veins. He dreads the monotony of work at the blacksmith's forge and yearns for adventure in a new frontier. Wills meets six Englishmen who have the means to make his dreams come true. What they discover changes the Colony and their lives forever. Gold fever ensues. Now on the road West, Wills has to deal with an uncertain romance. Does she even want him?

ISBN 9780994578242 Ebook ISBN 978-0-9945782-6-6 Hardcover ISBN 9798755445504
Released 2021
https://amazon.com/dp/0994578245 https://amazon.com/dp/B08T6NS3XX

Diamonds in the Dirt
Diamonds, love and money… but there is much more to life.
Parramatta 1850s

Luke, the youngest Lockley son, has completed University, and his life has no direction. No job, no money, and no love. Desperately alone, he prays for guidance. How can Luke trust that God has a plan for him if he can't even find a job? He does the only thing he can … he prays. Within a week, life has changed … oh, how it has changed as his brother Wills turns up with a suggestion. Would Luke be interested in joining the expedition with John Evans? Reverend William Clarke needs assistance on a Government Mineral Survey. The challenge, adventure and finds are life-changing for many. However, it gives Luke meaning, purpose and direction. The condition of his heart problems also takes a turn. Can he walk away?

ISBN:9780994578273 Ebook ISBN: 978-0-9945782-8-0 Hard cover ISBN 979-8788011141
Released 2022
https://amazon.com/dp/099457827X https://amazon.com/dp/B09NH1MLXZ

The Earl's Shadow
Who or what is the 'shadow'? How does it affect so many?
Parramatta 1860s

Charles is the Earl of Coxheath and spends his youth as a convict in Parramatta; he had no idea he was an Earl. He had minimal education and few social skills. His eldest son **Charlie** is no different.

Now faced with his own mortality, Charles has to work out how to live the remainder of his life after a near-death experience. He is called to step way out of his comfort zone in London. His action will change the world for many. The echoes from the past still haunt Charlie. London is calling the family, and they can't postpone the trip. How does **Jim**, the Cobb and Co coach driver, fit in? And precisely what is *'The Earl's Shadow'* that he speaks about? What happens if the 'Shadow' is gone?

ISBN: 9780645110708 Ebook ISBN 978-0-9945782-9-7
Released June 2022
https://amazon.com/dp/0645110701   https://amazon.com/dp/B0B158SKSK

Once a Jolly Swagman
An old black Billy Can contain the secrets of an incredible life
An Australian Historical Novel
Set in 1870s Parramatta and Kent UK

Rick Lockley, battling his family's expectations, runs away to become a swagman. Jack, a jolly swagman takes him under his care. Even after years together, Rick knows little about the old man.

On his death, Jack leaves Rick his precious Billy Can; the contents reveal Jack's identity. Stunned, Rick must travel to England to finalise Jack's wishes. There he uncovers Jack's life of love, betrayal and a link to his own family. Rick discovers there is much more to learn about this enigmatic man.

ISBN 9780645110753   Ebook ISBN 978-0-6451107-6-0
Released Sept 2022
https://amazon.com/dp/0645110752   https://amazon.com/dp/B0B5JN1WCV

Jonty's Journey
Gems, Love, Artists and a Golden Lion
Australia and South Africa 1880-1902

Sydney Jeweller, **Jonty** Evans' passion for gems takes him to Africa at a volatile time. He finds the diamonds he wants and gets given a lion cub. Jonty gets all but kidnapped. His experiences in the Transvaal plunge him into questioning everything he knows of life. Soon nightmares haunt him.

On return home, he nearly messes up his love life with **Lottie** before it even starts, and he struggles to settle. Lottie's father, **Luke** Lockley from Parramatta, takes him in hand and points him to someone who can help.

Jonty is then recalled to Africa as a liaison and reconnects with his lion, Chimbu, when he saves the life of his security detail. His life journey introduces him to the most amazing Heidelberg artists, politicians, poets, rebels, and the scapegoat soldier Harry Breaker Morant. Can Jonty bury the past and regain the peace he's lost?

ISBN 9780645110777   Ebook ISBN: 978-0-6451107-9-1
Released Feb 2023
https://amazon.com/dp/0645110779   https://amazon.com/dp/B0BLJ7ND1Q

Australian Colonial Trilogy
By Sheila Hunter
Co-Winner of 1999 NSW Senior Citizen of the Year, In the Year of the Senior Citizen

Mattie
Coming of Age in Convict Australia
Woodslane/Hand in Hand Publications ISBN 9780994578204

Twelve-year-old London street urchin **Mattie Paul** is convicted of petty theft and sentenced to seven years of transportation to the penal colony of Port Jackson, NSW. Peg, another female convict, takes Mattie under her wing and gives her a chance to make something of her life by teaching her to read. Mattie seizes every opportunity that comes her way. Though life is not particularly kind to her, she battles through earning her freedom, marrying and becoming a mother in her homeland. On this journey, she encounters bushrangers, is widowed, and becomes an entrepreneur in the Bathurst goldfields. She mixes with escaped convicts, but her spirit is indomitable, and she becomes a pillar and much-loved treasure of her adopted community. Mattie may be a fictional character, but her experiences are only too real and invest us in immersing ourselves in the lives of those remarkable women who helped to make Australia what it is today.

ISBN 9781503252370 & ebook AISN BOOTTEDBTO
(The Story continues in The Earl's Shadow)
Released 2015
https://amazon.com/dp/150325237X   https://amazon.com/dp/B00TTEDBT0

Ricky
A boy in Colonial Australia

Ricky English and his mother immigrate from England to join his father in the new Colony of Sydney. On arrival, there is no sign of his father. Ricky's mum uses the tiny amount of money they brought to get lodgings in a run-down building. Things go from bad to worse when his mother dies, he is thrown out of the rooms, and the caretakers confiscate all their possessions.

Ricky lives on the streets of Sydney Town as a street waif. Ricky finds safe places to sleep and befriends freed convicts who can help him survive. One day he encounters a lost child and helps reunite her with her family. These people try to help him, but because of his stubbornness, he insists on doing things his way, but he has found a mentor and confidante. The story follows him through his life. He survives and turns his life around, helping others along the way.

Paperback ISBN 9780994578211   Kindle ASIN: B00MLYN6IG
(The Story continues in Jonty's Journey)
Released 2014
https://amazon.com/dp/1500770574   https://amazon.com/dp/B00MLYN6IG

The Heather to The Hawkesbury
Four Scottish families brave a new life in a strange land.

Mary Macdonald and husband **Murd** and family; her brother **Fergus** MacKenzie; sister-in-law **Caro** MacLeod; cousin **Alex** Fraser and all their families who have had to emigrate from the Isle of Skye during the "Clearances."

The story follows the four families from Scotland on the ship out to the NSW colony in the 1850s. Mary does not cope with the changes and losses that occur in the first months in the colony. The other women in the family rely on her, and she nearly crumbles. The families struggle together through accidents, losses, trials, floods, and hard work and forge a strong bond with their new country. Trials, tribulations and triumphs see the four families make a firm mark in their new homeland. The immigrants from Scotland helped make Australia what it is today.

ISBN 978994578228   ebook AISN B01A21JYWQ   Large Print ISBN1533473641
Available on Amazon/Kindle & Large Print
Released 2016
https://amazon.com/dp/1503251438   https://amazon.com/dp/B01A21JYWQ

Bibliography

Mary III - convict ship (Sailed in July not June)
https://www.freesettlerorfelon.com/convict_ship_mary_1823.htm

Incl quotes from Elizabeth Fry and surgeon.
https://en.wikipedia.org/wiki/List_of_shipwrecks_in_June_1825
27th June 1825

Canon Paul Struan Robertson Proclaiming 'Unsearchable Riches.' Newcastle and the Minority Evangelical Anglicans, 1788-1900, CSAC & Gracewing, Sydney and Leominster, 1996.

Reverend Brian Roach
George Augustus Middleton BIO
https://www.researchgate.net/profile/Brian_Roach5/publication/335880807_Middleton_Thesis_2/links/5d81a45c458515fca1711fc9/Middleton-Thesis-2

George Middleton Dictionary of Biography
Niel Gunson, 'Middleton, George Augustus (1791–1848)', Australian Dictionary of Biography, National Centre of Biography, Australian National University, https://adb.anu.edu.au/biography/middleton-george-augustus-2450/text3271, published first in hardcopy 1967, accessed online 11 December 2022.

Major James Thomas Morrisett Bio
NB He left Newcastle at the end of 1823. (the year I have Jess arriving)
https://adb.anu.edu.au/biography/morisset-james-thomas-2482

Charles Wesley Hymns
https://www.invubu.com/music/show/song/Charles-Wesley/O-For-A-Thousand-Tongues-To-Sing.html

Thomas Lawrence 1827
portrait of **Rosamund Hester Elizabeth Croker, Chap 3**
https://commons.wikimedia.org/wiki/File:Lady_Barrow00.jpg

Some chapter heading by CM Hammond
https://en.wikipedia.org/wiki/Christiana_Mary_Demain_Hammond

Notes
The Jupiter actually sailed on June 2nd 1823, not July 2nd.

(NB *most of Reverend Middleton's documents were destroyed by floods, and very little is known of him. I have therefore used artistic licence with his personality*) my two main references have been form Thesis by **Rev Canon Paul Robertson & Rev Brian Roach.**
Sarah bore 14 children to George.

Christ Hospital School, Hertford and Horsham
Christ's Hospital School only moved to Horsham in 1902 and took students from aged eleven and upwards.

Characters

Sir **Lucien** Elkin (Waterloo soldier & Tea merchant)
b 1792 d 31 May 1823
m 1816 **Jessica Bates** (Lady Elkin) (m aged 19) 24 in 1823
b 1799 January
>> **Judith** b 1817 d 30 May 1823 aged 6
>>> *Both Lucien and Judith died of mushroom poisoning.*
>> *Jess was arrested on June 3rd, 1823*
>> *transported Mary III 10 June 1823/H Oct 5th/Syd 18 Oct*

m2 May 29, 1824, **Marcus Ryan** *owner of the Woollen mill sth of Sheffield and a wool trader*
b 1792 (son of Stephen & Elizabeth Ryan) *Padmorre Park* at Billingshurst
Children 2+
>> 1 **Elizabeth Jessie (Bessie) Ryan** b April 1826
>> 2 **Stephen** Marcus **Ryan** b July 1828
>> *Jess returns to England 17 Aug 1830 - Arr Feb 1831*
>> *Marcus returns July 1834*

Stephen Ryan (dead)- Marcus's father
Elizabeth Ryan Marcus's mother
sister **Gemma** & Miles live at Broadbridge Heath Road, Itchingfield)
>> 3 children,
>> **Frederica** b May 1823
>> **Rupert** 1825
>> **Quentin** 1827

Rex Harris - Lucien's butler
m June 1823 **Felicity** Matthews - housekeeper - London house
>> b January 1824 **Damien** Harris
>> b April 1825 **Victoria**
Jaques Le Beau - French Valet for Lucien b 1803
>> (Lucien found him after Waterloo aged 12 in 1815) b 1803
m 1829 **Lydia** Smithton
Colin Morrison - Valet for Marcus -
>> stayed in Somalia with his wife and three children
Giles Green b 1808 - Marcus's Tiger,
m 1829 **Helen** Smithton

Mrs **Edwina** Busselton - Marcus's housekeeper in London/Brighton
Jeffrey Anthony - Marcus's secretary & friend. Is the illegitimate son of an Earl
Phillip Clarke- Marcus's butler
Cyril Hargenhour, - Marcus's chairman
Egbert Elkin - Lucien's cousin & heir, married to **Cynthia**
Tom & Mary Landy - farm hands on Marcus's farm
Ned Grace is Lord Edward Lockley, 2nd son Duke of Gracemere
Charles & Sal Lockley - Ned Grace 3rd Cousin - Jolly Sailor Inn, Parramatta
Bill & Molly Miller - Rear Admiral Duncan Inn, Parramatta

Real People from history.
Surgeon **Harmon** Cochrane - *Mary III*
Captain **JT** Steel - *Mary III*
Captain Jonathan (**Jon**) Park - captain of the *Jupiter* (He was not kidnapped!)
*(NB Although the above three are **true** characters on their respective ships, I don't know if they did more than one trip to the colony. I made up the trip where they are kidnapped)*
Reverend George Middleton b 1791 d 1848
M1 1817 **Mary**   d 1819
         Child 1 **George** b May 1818
M2 Feb 1824 **Sarah** Rose d 1863 (married aged 16)
         14 children
    Charles Robert b 1825 d 1912
    Osman Edward b 1826 d 1882
    Sarah Ann b 1828 d 1867
    Isabella Lydia b 1830 d 1914
    William Powell b 1832 d 1892
    Juliana Agnes b 1834 d 1902
    Francis Gilbert b 1836 d 1918
    Augustus b 1838 d 1838
    Georgiana b 1839 d 1919
    Alexander Dudley b 1844 d 1908
    Albert Ernest b 1844 d 1914
    Evan Augustus b 1844 d 1910
    Cecil Arnold b 1846 d 1925
    Clarence Tyrrell b 1847 d 1848

Governor Ralph and Eliza **Darling**
Major Morriset

The first Christ Church building in Newcastle

www.ingramcontent.com/pod-product-compliance
Lightning Source LLC
Chambersburg PA
CBHW031956240626
47153CB00003B/1007